DISCOVER WHY CRITICS RAVE ABOUT
ROBERT RAY AND MURDOCK—

"THE WEST COAST TRAVIS McGEE."
—T. Jefferson Parker, author of *Laguna Heat*

"A PRIVATE EYE WHO IS SMART, TOUGH, AND
IRRESISTIBLE TO THE LADIES. . . . Give Ray
an A for some interesting characters, a sharply
etched background of Orange County glitz and a
plot that holds up all the way."
—*Dallas Morning News*

"ALMOST CONTINUOUS ACTION, an expertly detailed evocation of the turf, characters good and evil
who become real presences, and a tone of sympathetic understanding of both victims and villains that
also is refreshing." —*Los Angeles Times*

"MURDOCK IS A RARE FIND . . . SEXY . . .
HARD-BOILED . . . TOUGH, LONELY, AND IN-
CURABLY ROMANTIC. . . . IN THE BEST TRA-
DITION OF THE GENRE." —*Booklist*

MERRY CHRISTMAS, MURDOCK

Robert J. Ray

A DELL BOOK

Published by
Dell Publishing
a division of
Bantam Doubleday Dell Publishing Group, Inc.
666 Fifth Avenue
New York, New York 10103

ISBN: 0-440-20778-9

Reprinted by arrangement with Delacorte Press

Printed in the United States of America

Published simultaneously in Canada

December 1990

10 9 8 7 6 5 4 3 2 1

OPM

For Ben Kamsler,
Agent, Friend, Guide, Guru, and
Mentor of the Marketplace

In Xanadu did Kubla Khan
A stately pleasure dome decree:
Where Alph, the sacred river, ran
Through caverns measureless to man
  Down to a sunless sea.

Samuel Taylor Coleridge
"Kubla Khan"

Prologue:
You Better Watch Out,
You Better Not Cry

Bone-weary, Marvin Holly hung a hard right off Coast Highway and aimed the nose of the Chevy at the gatehouse to Jamaica Cove. The gatehouse was made of cute red brick, a Hansel and Gretel hutch with a fragile slate roof and spiffy French windows. The Chevy, a rental from John Wayne Airport, squished to a stop on the wet bricks and a guard stepped out, Grendel at the Gate, a hefty, wide-shouldered kid with movie-star teeth, a deep tan, and a surfcat's easy smile. His name tag read WOOLFORD.

"Something I can do for you, sir?"

"Marvin Holly," he said, holding his temper. "Here to see Miss Cynthia Duke."

Taking it slow, the surfcat flipped pages on his Plexiglas clipboard. "Do you have an appointment, sir?"

"She's my daughter," Marvin said. "She knows I'm coming."

"I don't find anything, sir. What was that name again?"

"Holly," he growled, his voice catching. "Marvin Holly."

"And you are . . . Miss Duke's, uh, father, you said?"

"That's right." He revved the engine, *rumm, rumm, rummmm.* Damn the delays. Damn this smart-lipped surf Nazi. Damn the candy-striped traffic bar, symbol of ritzy Laguna Beach, the eternal Candytown.

The surfcat angled his chin at the rumbling engine. "One moment, please, sir." He strode inside the gatehouse like a storm trooper, picked up the telephone, and punched in a number.

Marvin's hands made greasy sweat tracks on the steering wheel and sweat broke out on his forehead as he pushed his glasses back up his nose. A two-hour delay this morning, getting out of icebound O'Hare. Another two hours destroyed in Dallas by engine trouble. And now Mr. Smart Lip regarding him through pale yellow eyes while he nodded, Yes, ma'am, Right, ma'am, into the phone before hanging up.

Marvin was not getting through the Jamaica Cove gate. Not today. Maybe not ever. The surfcat's smile and swaggering shoulder roll told all. No entry for Marvin Holly. No reunion with Cindy.

He was here to save his kid.

"Merry Christmas, Clyde!" Marvin went into first and punched the accelerator to the floor. The engine, a wobbly GM6, gave its imitation of a roar. Tires slipped on the wetness. And then the Chevy plunged forward, snapping the striped bar like a toothpick. Up ahead, a sign said BEACH TUNNEL, TURN LEFT. In the rearview mirror, the surfcat shook his fist.

Zipping through the tunnel, Marvin made two wrong turns before he saw Carcassonne. Dumb

name for a house, he thought. The French Middle
Ages, knights in clumsy armor, the blood-drenched
Crusades, archers launching arrows from black stone
turrets. But when he saw it, a skeletal bone-white
wonder, glass and stone cascading down the rugged
sea cliffs at the far end of the horseshoe cove, he
thought of summer in Saint-Tropez, steamy sunshine, vodka on the rocks, and how his ex-wife Barbi
had all the luck.

Marvin Holly hated Christmas.

He skidded to a stop on the driveway pavers, his
bumper quivering a half inch from the curlicued giz-
mos framing the garage. He rang the bell. More waiting, the agony building like a bulging bladder after
too many beers. The door was opened by a Mexican
maid. White blouse, starched to perfection, and a
dark skirt.

"¿La muchacha?" he said.

"No está," the maid said, starting to close the door.

Marvin brushed by her. He'd come this far. Might
as well penetrate the interior. This was the top floor.
To his right, a stairwell twisted downstairs, connect-
ing the levels of the house. Beyond the stairwell, a
small chrome kitchen. To his left, a wide door led to a
monster living room, party space for three hundred
guests. Marvin checked that first. White walls, white
furniture, a thick white shag on white tiles, the only
color a splash of ugly surrealist paintings bloodying
the walls. In the king-size fireplace, a fire smoldered.
Behind him, the maid was calling for La Señora.

A great view here, but no sign of Cindy.

The maid plucked at his sleeve as he hurried past
her down the stairs to bedroom level, where a door
stood open. He saw it was Cindy's room and went in.
"Cindy? It's Daddy. I'm here, angel. I made it." The
bed was neatly made, magazines stacked in racks,

her beloved Mac computer on the desk in front of the view-window. On the desk next to the Mac, wonderful drawings of prancing horses, dancing unicorns. His heart pounded. What a great kid.

"Hello, Marvin."

He turned to see his ex, bare brown arms folded, standing in the door. Barbi wore silver Lurex workout pants and a skintight pink sleeveless top. She was barefoot and sexy. Her black hair, worn in the latest mini-spike style, showed not a whisper of gray. Her skin gleamed with sweat. He hated her for not looking older. She had money. He hated that. She wasn't a reader. He hated that. She'd cheated on him, banging her way from Vancouver to Acapulco to Paris. He hated that. She could still turn him on with a wiggle, a shake, a Medusa look. He hated that, most of all.

"Where's Cindy?"

"Not here." Barbi waved a brown hand at the empty room. "How in the world did you get this far?"

"Where is she, goddammit?"

"Security's been called, Marvin. Your next visitation's not until February. Learn to count, dear. Learn to cipher."

Legs quivering, Marvin started toward her. She did not move. What the hell did Barbi do to ace Father Time? Did she step into a magic pillar of fire like Ursula Andress in *She*? Did she swill secret potions handed down from her Iroquois great-grandmother? Whatever it was, Marvin wanted a piece. "Cindy phoned me last night. Said some sickening things about Jamie, your beef-brain brother."

A warning flicker in Barbi's silver-blue eyes. "Security's outside, Marvin. Listen for hoofbeats, the sound of cavalry. Time's up, dear."

He grabbed her arm, fingers touching again the

buttery skin. Barbi smelled of sweat, marijuana, pungent incense. "Cindy said he puts his hands on her. Makes her feel dirty. Says things."

"She's your daughter, dear. With your dazzling imagination."

Upstairs at road level, he heard voices, the maid's shrill, trilling Spanish, and a man's blunt tones.

"Jesus Christ, Barbi. What are you doing to my kid?"

His ex, her face close enough for a kiss, gave him her best Duke Family Smirk. "You're out of here, Marvin. Call tomorrow. Make it after ten, okay? Maybe you'll see Cyn. Maybe not."

Booted feet pounded down the stairs. Marvin pinched Barbi's arm. "Where is she?"

"The little Mall Rat," she said, trying to pull away, "is at the mall."

"Xanadu?"

Before she could answer, the blond surfcat bounded into the room, swinging his shiny riot baton. Marvin let go of her arm and stepped away. The surfcat asked if he should call the police. Rubbing her arm, teeth shining, his ex shook her head.

"I'll phone Cindy later," Marvin said. "She better be here."

"Tomorrow," Barbi said. "After ten."

Behind the wheel of his rented Chevy, Marvin Holly followed the white security vehicle back to the Hansel and Gretel gatehouse. Where was Cindy? In her letters, she'd mentioned hanging out at Xanadu Mall, but where was it exactly? Five years now since he'd visited California. Like Pizza Hut and Colonel Sanders, one mall mirrored all the rest.

With a snappy squeak of rubber, the white security vehicle wheeled into a slot beside a blue Bronco 4×4. The license on the 4×4 said WOOLFRD, like

"Woolford" on the guard's name tag. Marvin coughed.

The surfcat climbed out and motioned Marvin down the exit. Marvin nodded, flipped the guy a finger, and headed out.

At the bottom of the exit, Marvin braked for the wall of holiday traffic. RIGHT TURN ONLY, a sign said. In the rearview, he saw the surfcat open the door of the Bronco and lean in. Okay, pal. Your turn. Holding his breath, Marvin threw the Chevy into reverse and backed up the hill, tires slipping as he fought for traction, watching the rear end of the Bronco bloom ever larger in his rearview, howling "Yaaaah!" as the rear end of the Chevy plowed into the new Bronco, crushing blue metal.

He raked the Chevy into first and zoomed away from Jamaica Cove, heading north with the traffic flow. In Corona Del Mar, he parked on a side street to scout for police cars, but no one was in pursuit. He grabbed a cup of coffee, saw Corona Sports across the street. Inside the store, he paid $29.95 for a Reggie Jackson autograph bat, a smooth white slugger. As he handed over his Visa card, he watched the clerk eyeball the expiration date, December 31, end of another crummy year, sweating as the numbers flowed through to the data base in Milwaukee, where, if they had added in the cost of his airplane ticket to California, he would be $2,455 over his limit. Soon, alarms would ring and blue plastic doors would crush Marvin Holly.

Armed with the bat, Marvin drove to the Duke Building, a three-story bunker made of imported stone that, according to Duke Construction publicity, dated back to the building of Mont-Saint-Michel and Chartres. The Duke Building covered an acre in Newport Center. He circled the building four times

before taking the ticket to raise the traffic bar to let
him into the parking garage, and then he spent ten
minutes searching for Jamie's car.

It was a Mercedes coupe, burnished gold in color,
parked in a slot that said JAMES P. DUKE. The license
read DUKE III. Hot damn. Leaving the Chevy running, he stepped out of the car and approached the
Mercedes. In his hand was the Reggie Jackson.

Humming, Marvin hefted his weapon and
smashed out the windshield of the Mercedes. *Whap,
whap, whap,* solid manly thunks from his boyhood in
Minnesota, where he had developed an easy swing
using a lumberjack's twin-bladed ax. Six strokes to
demolish the windshield, the rhythm building, memory of power and young muscles, enjoying his own
sweat, *whap, whap, whap,* not hearing the whoop of
the car alarm until he finished the windshield and
moved to the driver's window. Air raid sounds filled
the subterranean cavern.

He jumped into the Chevy and headed out. Near
the exit, Marvin spotted his quarry, a big man, shoulders made wide and neck made thick by long hours
hefting weights. A dark face, too thickly fleshed in
the jowls, dark cheeks pitted with pockmarks. A
thick head of hair, Iroquois black, like Barbi's. The
man was Jamie Duke, Barbi's creep brother, strutting along in his three-piece suit and jazzbo Italian
shoes.

Marvin braked the car in front of Jamie, cutting
him off. He climbed out, hefting the bat. The car was
still running.

"Hello, Creep," Marvin said.

Jamie peered at him. "Who's that?"

"Cindy phoned me, Creep." Marvin moved forward, his legs shaking. "She said you were messing
with her."

"Marvin, buddy? That you? Where on earth did you—"

"Stay away, Creep." Marvin feinted with the bat, forcing Jamie back. "Stay away from my kid."

"Marvin, pally. Listen. I don't know what you're—"

Marvin heard footsteps, knew then Jamie was stalling. The hesitation. The big beefy hand movements. Someone was coming from behind. Marvin turned to see a man running at him, a lean man with a lean face and a lean and terrible stride. The man came like the wind, arms pumping, knifing along the gray concrete, feet barely touching the cement, a wraith in the ghostly garage twilight. Damn. With Jamie in front of him and the running man behind, Marvin was outnumbered. Another three seconds and the running man would cut him off from the car.

He scurried back to the Chevy, tossed the bat onto the seat, and was just slamming the door when the running man threw himself at the car.

Marvin peeled rubber, tires smoking, swerving out. The running man was suddenly at the door, something in his hand, Christ, a pistol. He shouted something, orders, it sounded like. Army days. Right shoulder! Port arms! Ten-shut! He shoved the accelerator to the floor and flung the man off. As the Chevy whined toward the tollbooth and his second traffic bar, Marvin hunched his shoulders and waited for the bullet that never came.

Whew.

He cruised up Jamboree, Basher Holly, Wrecker of Traffic Bars, but saw no cars in pursuit. At the San Diego Freeway he headed south. The dashboard clock said 5:30. Still time to hunt for Cindy.

He passed the turnoff for Laguna Canyon Road, drove along a long curve, and saw lights against the night sky. As he drew closer, the lights outlined a pyramid, a whopper, thirty stories tall, maybe taller, pushing up from the flat California landscape to ram the heavens. A couple more miles to a lighted green signboard: XANADU MALL, RIGHT LANE.

Sweat broke out on his forehead as he hit the right blinker and slid into the right lane. The top of the pyramid had been strung with green lights, forming the tallest Christmas tree in southern California. The radio played an oldie, "Winter Wonderland."

Off the freeway now, Marvin joined the lines of traffic snaking toward the pyramid. It towered above the street, thirty stories, and he remembered a letter from Cindy saying she'd been taken on a tour by Gramps, her name for the old man, Wheeler Duke. He found a parking place at the far edge of the lot, near a huge Gothic support strut that curved from the pyramid wall down to earth level. Before entering the mall, he groped in his luggage for backup pack number 37. Carrying it under his arm, he entered Xanadu through an automatic door. Above the door, a sculptor had chiseled five lines from Coleridge:

> *In Xanadu did Kubla Khan*
> *A stately pleasure dome decree:*
> *Where Alph, the sacred river, ran*
> *Through caverns, measureless to man,*
> *Down to a sunless sea.*

"Terrific," Marvin said. "Great taste."

Inside the mall he saw smiling faces, glazed eyes, shoppers glutted on consumerdom. He heard music for the Yule. White Christmas. Santa Claus is coming. Doggie in the window. He passed a merry-go-round for the kids, traversed a line waiting for a jolly Santa

Claus. He turned right, almost had heart failure when he spotted a slender teen, blond hair and acid-wash jeans and high-top sneakers. "Cindy?" he called. But when the teen turned, it wasn't his Cindy.

It took him forty minutes, heart jumping, to cover all three levels of the mall. Sleek blond teens, mirror-twins to Cindy, floated in front of his eyes. He phoned Cindy at Carcassonne. A gaggle of teens passed, tight-bottomed and giggling. Three of them looked like Cindy. The maid's voice said, "Ceendy, she no *está.*" Marvin hung up. A blond girl skipped by, holding hands with a short-haired kid wearing leather. Was Cindy old enough for boys? She had one friend, Phyl, short for Phyllis, but had not mentioned a beau.

He worked the floors again, knowing he'd find her. She had to be here. Had to be. Damn the other malls. He saw her in the Choc Shoppe, slurping a soda. Again in the Wherehouse, gazing at records. And in Hers, a jeans shop packed with smooth-cheeked, laughing teens.

It was almost eight o'clock when he felt dizzy and had to lean against a wall while his head cleared. Those three martinis on the plane had caught up to him. His stomach growled. Even anxious dads had to eat. He rode the escalator down to One. The first restaurant served no booze. A second one was filled to capacity. On his right, Xanadu Books, sanctuary for a weary wordsmith. He ducked into the book-store and felt better, stronger, standing in a kingdom of words. On the mystery rack sat three volumes of his Derek Melville series—*Lady in Blue, Blue Dreamer,* and *Crime le Bleu.* He made a flat three thousand per book. He wondered what it would be like to write under his own name again.

If he could finish the new one.

If.

A bearded guy stood at the information desk. He was mid-forties, like Marvin, and an earring dangled from his right ear. His heart thudding, ping, ping, Marvin asked for a copy of *Jungles Burning*.

"Yeah," the clerk said, not batting an eyelash. "Sure. I think so. Right back here."

He followed the clerk to the literature section, where there were two copies of *Jungles Burning*, subtitled *Tales from Vietnam*. This was a fourth edition of a paperback original, first published in 1974. The photo on the back cover was of a younger Marvin Holly, a bright-eyed, bearded vet wearing an army shirt. He felt the clerk watching him.

"You're him, right? You're Marvin Holly."

Marvin blushed. "Yes. I thought this was out of print."

"Remainder house, man. I keep this sucker in stock."

"Thanks." Marvin felt his eyes fill with tears.

"I read your book, man. It was great. I caught your speech in Oakland, back in seventy-four. You were something, man. You were great."

Marvin stuck out his hand and the two men shook. He paid for the book with his overdrawn Visa. When you were the forgotten man, admiration was a heady tonic. It had been years since anyone had—

Then he saw Cindy coming in the door, saw her out of the corner of his eye, a blond teen wearing jeans and high-tops and a rain-damp parka, rucksack slung over one shoulder. She moved like his Cindy, an easy glide, the horse rider's cat-footed walk. He forgot the book and ran to her, feeling crazy. "Cindy?" he cried. "Are you okay?" The girl turned to look him full in the face and he stopped ten feet away, face flushed, blasted again by failure. Wrong again, grasping at straws. She was not Cindy.

He muttered an excuse and hurried out, his face overheated, his mind sizzling. Behind him, he heard the clerk call out his name, but he kept going, toward the exit.

He was standing outside, face turned up to the cool California drizzle, when the door opened and he heard someone call his name. It was the girl with the rucksack. In her hand was a paper sack with the Xanadu Books logo. "The clerk gave it to me," she said. "He paid me fifty cents to deliver it." She had a slight accent, Texas, he thought, or Oklahoma.

"Thanks."

The girl did not move. "You thought I was, like, someone else?"

He nodded. "Yes."

"Who?"

"My daughter."

The girl shivered and he smelled wet hair. "Does she live around here?"

"Yes. In Laguna Beach. I tried to see her today. I think she's in some kind of trouble."

"Aren't we all," the girl said. "Do you live around here?"

"No. Wisconsin."

"Snow," she said. "Like, a white Christmas."

"Yes."

Silence between them now, the book delivered, Christmas looming emptily on the horizon. A family went past, two adults, two jazzed kids.

"My name's Marvin," he said.

"I know," the girl said. "You wrote the book."

"What's your name?"

"Heather," she said. "Heather Smith."

"You live around here?"

"No. I'm, like, hitching . . . to San Francisco."

"Hitching. Isn't that sort of dangerous?"

"I can take care of myself."

He liked the sudden jut of her chin, the brave squaring of narrow girl-shoulders. He invited her to the Choc Shoppe for a cup of cocoa. She said okay. Studying her, the small hands cupped around the mug of chocolate, Marvin knew she was a runaway. Heather made him think of Cindy, a kid adrift, alone with her problem, buffeted by adults. He wished he could tell her things would be okay, life will work out, kid, but he was not sure.

A second cup relaxed her, got her talking. Her mother had installed her in a girls' school in Scottsdale. Yesterday she'd been in the airport, waiting for a homeward-bound plane—she wouldn't tell Marvin where home was, not just yet—and she'd left the terminal in a rush and caught a bus headed for Tucson, where she decided to hitch to San Francisco, where her father lived. He was out of the country, Japan, she guessed, as he did lots of business in the Far East. She'd had trouble in Yuma, where two men had taken her airplane ticket. In San Diego, she'd lost twenty dollars. She'd hitched this far and now she had six dollars, not enough for a bus to San Francisco.

Marvin held out two twenties. "On me," he said.

She reached for the money, but stopped. "Marvin. Can you afford it?"

In his wallet was one more twenty, five worn singles, and a Visa card with an alarm bell about to go off. "Sure."

"I don't believe you."

He touched her hand. "Have a good trip, Heather Smith."

"It's Blasingame," she said. "Heather Blasingame.

I'm from Austin, Texas, and I'm hungry and I don't have anyplace to spend the night."

"I'm hungry too."

Her face broke into a smile. She wasn't as pretty as his Cindy, but she had a nice face, honest and open.

"How old are you?" he asked.

"Seventeen." She brushed a stray strand of hair out of her face. She picked up his book and read the cover quotes out loud. "Hey, Marvin. You're, like, famous."

He took the book from her, opened it to the half-title page, wrote an inscription. *For Heather, Blake's Traveller in the Vortex. Marv Holly, Xmas in Xanadu.*

Tears came to her eyes when she read the inscription. "Who's Blake?"

"William Blake, an English poet. He wandered a lot."

"Vortex," she said. "That's like a whirlpool, right?"

"Inside the mind," he said.

"Far out." Heather took command. "Look, Marvin. They're closing the mall. How about if we, like, found someplace to sleep? I'm pretty beat, myself. Last night I crashed, like, in a park, and I can tell you that's not my scene. A man woke me up early, going to the bathroom. It was *très* grungy."

"Okay," Marvin said. "There's probably something on the Coast Highway."

"What's that?" She pointed at the envelope he'd been carrying.

He'd almost forgotten. "It's my backup pack. Computer disks. Notes. A chunk of manuscript. Been meaning to mail it all day."

"Well, let's."

Heather led him to a U.S. Post Office branch on the ground floor of Xanadu Mall. He bought stamps at the machine. She licked stamps while he addressed a label to Sue Crandall, in Beloit. He dropped the envelope through the slot. Gone.

Heather squeezed his arm. "Who's Sue Crandall?"

"A student. Writes a terrific critical essay."

"I'll bet you're a great teacher, Marvin. Boffo, I'll bet."

"Thanks."

They went outside. It was almost nine o'clock and the parking area had emptied out. "The car's over there," he said.

The book dropped out from under her arm and Marvin picked it up and handed it to her. "Oh, it's wet."

"Books dry out," he said.

He heard a squeal of tires. Bright lights rose up behind them, silhouetting the two figures against the curved support beam, and at the same time he heard the high transmission whine and the guttural deep-throated roar of a big engine, coming fast. Heather was slow to react as, in slow motion, he turned, saw the vehicle bearing down on him, a small, squarish truck, oversize tires, a solid bank of big blinding spots mounted on a roll bar above the cab, and shoved Heather aside before leaping to safety himself.

For a long moment, Marvin Holly was sure that he'd made it. For a long shining moment he hung in the air, propelled by his jump, Marvin the kid, Marvin the Minnesota woodcutter, his mind searching out a motivation for the driver of the oncoming vehicle. A holiday drunk, he thought. A kid on speed, getting his kicks wheeling through a parking lot at sixty goddamn miles per—

And then, as he heard Heather scream and felt the impact of the crushing weight of the truck, Marvin caught a glimpse of the driver's face behind the glass, a pale death mask, grinning.

The engine whined into him, into his whirling brain, punching his solar plexus into eternity and he heard Heather screaming:

"Maaarvin!"

And that was all.

1

The phone rang again, but I kept on slicing the onion, five cuts along the grain, then nine cuts the other way, starting from right to left, the chef's knife winking in the light. *Aida* was playing on my vintage RCA stereo, Maria Callas belting out a hefty Italo-Egyptian love tune, and I hummed along, pushing back the December chill with a bottle of good Mondavi red.

It was Wednesday, four days before Christmas, and I was making soup to fight off the holiday gloom. I learned to make soup from my mom, who made it to feed my dad, the Sergeant, who was career army. Winter and summer, Mom kept soup stored in our fridge. The Sergeant had a way of appearing in the doorway by surprise. Honey, I'm home, babe, the tired old foot-soldier, home from the wars, starved as a POW, thirsty as Gunga Din, so what's for dinner, hey?

In five minutes, my mom would have hot steaming soup on the table, corn bread, Tabasco, carrot sticks, black olives, real butter, and an iced mug of Schlitz beer. The Sergeant's favorite soup was goulash, which he claimed was an ancient Celtic recipe stolen by the Viennese. My mom's favorite was bouilla-baisse, with gazpacho a close second. Whatever the type, she made eight quarts at a time, to feed my friends and the Sergeant's bachelor buddies, dragged along to our place for a home-cooked meal. When she died, my mom willed me her soup tureen, a lovely curved piece made in Dresden, inherited from her German grandmother.

So when the phone rang I was in the first stage of creating Minestrone à la Murdock: You braise the beef. You slice four onions. You peel six garlic buds. You pack the beef, the onion, and the garlic into a pot, where the magic is. I paid seventeen dollars for Cal, my pot, after finding him at a garage sale in peaceful Irvine. Cal stands for Calphalon, the gray flannel wonder-metal, swirled at the factory for memorable taste and easy cleanup. You add beef stock, Italian spices, a bay leaf, crushed black pepper, and a pungent Neapolitan clove. You simmer for an hour, maybe two, while you watch sports on televi-sion. You cool the brew overnight, while the grease floats like magic to the top. Stage two begins next day when you—

My answering machine clicked on, the red light winking like a gnat's eyeball. I poured in the beef stock and set the fire on simmer and turned down the volume under Callas and sipped red wine while I waited for the message. Some old flame, I thought, happily married, inviting me over for a chummy family Xmas. Or some Scrooge of a bill collector, grousing at me to pay up or else. Or maybe a rich client. Merry Christmas, Murdock.

"Lancelot," said the voice of Wally St. Moritz. "Wally here. Are you monitoring, dear boy?"

I picked up the phone, heard that hollow echo of the recorder bouncing back at me. "Hey, Professor. I'm on. Where are you?"

"El Toro General."

"Ten days too early for your annual blues," I said. "So they must be treating your tennis elbow."

"Ho-ho-ho, as Santa says to greedy little mall monsters. Can you motor down here? I think I've unearthed a client."

"One with money?"

"And trouble." Wally paused. "All it needs is your presence. Your inimitable persuasive powers."

I stirred the soup. "Who's the client?"

"A state senator from Texas, with a wounded child, who is most impatient with local police procedure."

"I identify with the impatient part. What kind of wound?"

"A hit-and-run."

"Ouch. Where'd it happen?"

"Xanadu Mall, in the parking lot."

"What time?"

"Last evening, nineish."

It hadn't been big enough to make the evening news. "Xanadu's in the sheriff's jurisdiction. What are they doing?"

"Not much. That's why I'm calling you."

"Does the Senator know? Or is this your idea?"

"The Senator became interested when I explained you knew people on the inside."

"Used to know."

Wally sighed. "Be resourceful, Matthew. I assured the Senator you could help."

It didn't feel holiday hopeful. Josh McBride, my deputy pal inside the sheriff's office, had retired to Idaho, where he was running a fishing camp for the tourists. The deputies I'd met on the street were aging jock hotdogs who still hugged dreams about making the jump into pro ball.

I eyed my soup and took another sip of wine. Inside, it was warm and toasty. Outside, it was nasty, cold, and wet. Problem: I needed the work. I'd had a gritty six days in San Diego, doing reference checks for Tritonics, Inc., a software company that was hiring a vice-president for marketing at a base salary of $120,000, plus perks and fringes. Out of four candidates, three had come up dirty as Hell's Angels at an Oakland beer bust. The dirtiest had been handpicked by the Tritonics comptroller, a tightass named Binder, who was busily seeding his little dukedom with fawning supporters. Tritonics owed me two grand for my work, but since checks had to be signed by Binder, it would be Easter before I saw the money. Meanwhile, I had $104 in the checking account and Christmas was closing fast.

Would the Senator be my Santa?

I filled the kettle with water for coffee and turned on the fire.

"Are you there, Matthew?"

"Yo."

"When shall we expect you?"

I needed the work. "Half an hour."

Wally told me the hurt kid was on the fourth floor. We hung up. The rain hammered my roof and I shivered as I tugged on my boots. Bugging the sheriff was not my idea of a hot case. I yawned. Damn Binder. Damn all tightass comptrollers.

Boots on, I spent three minutes deciding about the shoulder harness. Yes. No. Yes. No. They still wore guns in Texas. Was the Senator a hunter? Would hardware impress? I filled the Thermos with travel coffee, antidote to Mondavi red. Drink that on the way. I checked my face in the mirror. Would you hire this man? Circles under the eyes, a broadening swatch of gray in the beard, my mom's straight teeth, the Sergeant's suspicious frown.

With a last look around, I turned *Aida* off, cut the fire under my minestrone, shrugged into my Eddie Bauer rain parka, and walked down the stairs carrying the Thermos and the shoulder harness. The rain slapped down onto the puddles outside my apartment. The pier was deserted. The wind was cold off the sea.

Wheeling south on the San Diego Freeway, you can see only one building, a towering pyramid structure that juts thirty stories into the black California sky. The style, according to an architect friend, is Frank Lloyd Wright neo-Gothic.

This is Xanadu, a combination mall, business complex, convention hotel, and pleasure circus that promises satisfaction for everyone. Moms. Dads. Teens. Yuppies. Tweeners. Seniors. Ethnics. Anyone with a buck to spend on a dream.

Built in the early eighties by Duke Construction, Xanadu crouches on a low hill at the edge of the I-405 freeway, for easy access by shoppers, travelers, tourists, criminals, bums, and assorted mall rats. The hotel has five hundred rooms, including three floors of suites starting at $1,500 a day. The top floor is a lavish penthouse and party suite used by the mighty Dukes to impress visiting dignitaries. The parking lot can handle five thousand vehicles, and last year they built a parking structure to handle three thousand more. Xanadu Mall, which covers three floors connected by shiny escalators and people movers, was the nation's number two retail grosser for the last two years. The foundation slab covers three city blocks.

Last Labor Day, mall management brought in a

big hairy ape, a Fay Wray look-alike, and a television crew. They spent a sweaty afternoon crawling along the exterior walls of the pyramid shooting a beer commercial while down below the crowds gawked and cheered.

Across the freeway from Xanadu, in the booming city of El Toro, sits El Toro General Hospital. I took my ticket to raise the traffic bar and wheeled into the lot. At the entrance sat a vehicle marked with a sheriff's star. I parked beside Wally's Saab, a turbo colored rose quartz. Raindrops spattered my parka as I locked up, leaving the Beretta, and jogged through the rain. When I reached the door, I was breathing hard. New Year's resolution: exercise; cut down on the drinking.

The elevator creaked on the way up. It smelled of smoke, fear, sweat, and something gray and dead. I got off at the fourth floor and made my way past a nurses' station to the far end of the corridor where Wally St. Moritz sat in a pink plastic hospital chair. Wally is the proprietor of The Saintly Silver Surfer. It used to be called Wally's Surf Shop, but two Christmases ago the beach kids persuaded him to change the name. The kids have always called Wally "Saint." Their comic book cult hero at the time was the Silver Surfer. Renaming the place—Wally calls the blend "mythologically and emblematically charismatic"— gave us an excuse for a wingding of a Christmas party.

Wally has a great location for the shop, fifty feet from the Newport Pier, on the Quad, at the southwest corner of Punker's Strip. Customers drift by, stop in. He provides jobs for runaways on the rebound. My place is on the second floor, directly above.

Wally St. Moritz is an author and a scholar. He

taught college for longer than he cares to remember and never lost the habit of critical thinking. He knows people in high places. He's published books and articles, mostly in a field he calls SAEM, socio-anthro-eco-morphology. He's written speeches for local politicians who espouse causes like No Growth and Save the Flora and Fauna. In the middle of a conversation, Wally will drag out pad and pencil to jot a note about something he's working on.

Tonight, Wally wore tennis warm-ups, green with three white stripes up the trousers and along the sleeves, and high-top sneakers. His yellow rain slicker was folded on the chair next to him. He saw me, finished writing his note, and stood up to take my arm. At the end of the short hallway, a woman in a tweed suit was talking to two beefy sheriff's deputies. Her back was to me. She was tall, with wide shoulders and ash-blond hair. Her voice was in lecture mode. Off to her left, a mousey woman with mousey hair and mouse-colored clothes was writing on an executive leather clipboard. Light flashed off her glasses.

"Where's the Senator?"

"Shh. This way, Matthew."

He steered me past the nurses' station and beyond the elevators to a door marked STAIRS. He opened the door and we went through. He waited until the door closed. Then he pulled out a handkerchief and cleaned his glasses, frowning.

"KGB got us bugged?"

Wally listened to the stairwell sounds for a moment, his head cocked to the side. You could hear the elevator whirring behind the wall.

"Nice meeting place, Professor. Will the Senator be along soon?"

"Bear with me, Matthew. The tall, striking, Ama-

zonian woman lecturing the deputies is Senator Jane
Whitney Blasingame."

"A lady senator from Texas?"

"Hmm. Last evening, her daughter Heather was
injured in a vicious hit-and-run. She was rushed here,
to the Emergency Room. Identification was made,
and the child's connection with Texas established. It
took a while to reach the Senator in Austin. On arrival, the Senator found her daughter in a coma and a
distressing investigation under way."

"Welcome to wonderful Orange County."

"The girl fits the profile of the female member of
the San Diego Kids. Blond hair, blue eyes, late teens,
Anglo, wistful, educated."

"Yeah, her and maybe a hundred thousand kids
between L.A. and San Diego, they all fit the profile."

A gang called the San Diego Kids had been on the
news since Thanksgiving. Four guys and a girl, roam-
ing the freeways, running scams on traveling salesmen. They used the female as bait. She'd lure the
pigeon to a motel, pop his drink with a Mickey. When
he was snoring, she'd throw open the door for her
accomplices. The pigeon would wake up minus
money, credit cards, wristwatch, class ring, luggage,
and vehicle. Youth has no heart.

"The sheriff's investigation is being run by a Deputy Emil Hanks. His scenario is the falling out
amongst thieves. The hit, he surmises, was made by a
vengeful angry gang member. This angle made the
Senator angry."

"The scenario slows things down, right?"

"Precisely."

I leaned against the wall, my arms folded. If the
Senator wanted help, I could start at the crime scene,
backtrack the girl, hunt around for witnesses, make a
couple hundred bucks, maybe even turn over a rock

or two. What the hell, it was better than divorce work.

"How did the Senator know to contact you?"

"Horace Entwhistle, a professor at the University of Texas, made the contact. We taught together at Brown in the sixties. Horace knows the Senator. She phoned him. He advised her to call me."

"What's your reading on the deputy, what's his name?"

"Hanks. He's slow-moving, sardonic, straitlaced, very full of himself. A twenty-five-watt brain and the soul of a true Nixon conservative."

"What about the daughter?"

"Heather Blasingame is seventeen, dreamy, inner-directed. The story is, she was on her way north to see her father, traveling alone, hitchhiking. The Senator assures me the girl had a plane ticket home, but none was found on her." Wally paused at the doorway to peer through the window, which needed a Windex swabbing. "In the parking area, she was struck by a vehicle moving at a good speed."

"Any make on the vehicle?"

"Small truck. Van. Car. Hanks won't say."

"Anything in the papers?"

"There was a small squib in the *Tribune*, Metro, page nine. I suppose you failed to catch it."

Wally likes digging at me. He devours information. I avoid it. Some days I don't even catch the sports pages.

"Around nine, you said?"

"Yes."

"No witnesses?"

"The deputy refuses to say."

"Any idea who found her?"

"Same answer."

"Where was mall security?"

"Ah," he said. "You're starting to hum, Matthew."

"Haven't been hired yet."

"Soon," he said.

"Where does the father live?"

"Palo Alto. The Senator tried phoning, several times, only to learn he'll be out of the country until Christmas."

"So the kid didn't know?"

"Perhaps."

"What does daddy do, something impressive and corporate?"

"He's CFO, I think, for an American firm that does substantial business with the Pacific Rim."

"CFO. That's Chief Financial Officer?"

"Correct."

"Was the kid running away?"

"I presume so. So far, the Senator has not verified in so many words."

"What do you think?"

"Youth is frail. Divorce sometimes numbs a child. It's possible she was thinking of changing parents."

"Where did she leave from?"

"Scottsdale. She's in school there."

"Expensive school?"

"I assume so."

"Did you contact them?"

"It's holiday time, Matthew. I reached an answering machine."

It was time to meet the Senator. We left the stairwell and headed down the corridor. The sheriff's deputies were walking our way. One wore an official green slicker, open in front, and carried a black baseball-type cap. The other wore an Eisenhower jacket and a Jack Webb drill instructor hat. His name tag said HANKS. Both deputies were thick through the hams, arms, and torso. Age: early thirties. Experience: police work, probably in the military or a small-town police force. Goals: to look good, to be alive at the end of the day, to retire after twenty years. Baseball Cap had dark hair. The other man looked blond beneath his wide-brimmed hat. They nodded without speaking and headed for the elevator.

The Senator, her legs crossed, was sitting in a pink chair, talking earnestly to Miss Mousey, who kept nodding, yes, yes, I understand, oh, yes, certainly, as she jotted notes. Her face was hidden by heavy-lensed eyeglasses. Her low-heeled shoes rested flat on the floor, for added stability.

As we came up, the Senator shifted slightly to give us her best angle, showing she was at home with cameras, newshounds, gawkers, paparazzi, the press. The movement tightened the skirt across her thighs, displaying nice contours. She was in shape, which meant regular exercise. The tweed jacket was off, revealing a soft yellow blouse with shoulder pads that were not necessary. She had a strong face with prominent cheekbones, and the ash-blond hair was curled spiffily around her left ear. As she gestured, underlining the point she was making, a ring caught the light, and then a gold wristwatch. She wore brown leather boots almost to the knee. The boots had a medium heel. I figured her age at late thirties, her weight at one-forty, her height at five-ten. Viking lady, with a hurt daughter and tired countenance.

She finished talking to Miss Mousey, uncrossed her legs, showing a flash of stockinged knee, and stood up, politico onstage. As I got closer, she frowned.

Wally introduced me. "Senator, this is Matt Murdock, the man who might be able to help. Matthew, this is Senator Blasingame."

We shook. The hand she reached out to me was warm, strong, smooth, and pleasantly slender. Like a lot of professional politicos, she had a quick memory for names. "Thanks for coming out in the rain, Mr. Murdock. Dr. St. Moritz says you have connections inside the sheriff's department. What can you tell me about that?"

"It's a network, Senator. I used to be a cop. I work with cops on cases. We help each other out."

"You have someone specific inside the sheriff's?"

I felt Wally watching. "I can get there via the network."

"How soon can you get started?"

"Can't do much until tomorrow."

The Senator's frown deepened, creasing her forehead. She didn't like people screwing up her timetable. "No sooner?"

"Sorry. The people I know work the day shift."

"How about trying them at home?"

"I could try. But the records are at the station, on somebody's computer."

Her eyes flashed as she gave me a look of stern disappointment. The interview was not going well. She turned away and walked to a chair and sat down, glancing at Wally before she looked back at me. "You're a private detective, is that right?"

"Correct."

"Licensed?"

I showed her my yellow ticket.

The Senator tapped the chair arm with a fingernail. Regal profile, upturned nose—this lady enjoyed control. "Time is of the essence, Mr. Murdock. I'm a stranger here in la-la land, and frankly, this place gives me the creeps. My daughter's been viciously hurt. The law—those people who should be hard at an investigation—seem more interested in putting my baby in jail than in finding out who slammed into her with a deadly weapon. I'm not a detective, of course. I leave that to you. But my father was a judge and I do have a law degree. I know about how the trail gets cold, which is why I'd like to get a running jump on this." Her voice had a cutting edge to it. I could feel her measuring me, a trained lawyer gearing up for interrogation. She kept eyeballing my clothes. Maybe she thought private cops should wear thirties suits, floppy felt hats, and wing-tip shoes. "Would you like to work for me?"

"That's why I'm here, Senator."

"What do you charge?"

"Three hundred a day, plus expenses."

"My, that's pricey."

"It's the going rate."

"It's outrageous, like the rest of this state. How do you feel about written reports?"

"A waste of the client's time."

"Really? How do you account for your time?"

"Results."

"Hmm." She studied something over my right shoulder. The job was slipping away. My hands clenched.

Wally broke in. "Matthew's uncovered some dastardly grime, Senator. Locally. Regionally. He also—"

She gestured him to silence. "Thank you, Doctor. Can you describe your investigative routine, Mr. Murdock? Break down the process for me, step by step? I'd like an idea, no matter how rough, how arduous for you, of where my three hundred goes."

She didn't want to know. The Senator was peering at me, and I looked back. Pale pink lipstick, with a buttery sheen. Worry lines edging the mouth. Smoke-colored eyes, the skin directly behind the eyes creased by crow's feet. We stared at each other, a kid's game of locking eyeballs, he who looks away

first is a dead Injun. Her nostrils flared, a Thoroughbred filly asking to be tamed. Thinking the unthink-
able, I wanted to kiss her.

"I'm waiting," she said.

The interview was over. I wanted to be outside,
breathing in fresh air. "I hunt around, pick up a trail.
Then I follow the trail."

"The trail from there?" She pointed across the interstate at Xanadu, glittery with Christmas lights.

I nodded. "Or before she got there."

Her eyes narrowed and she leaned forward.
"Then, Mr. Murdock, to follow your metaphor of the
hunt—what if you cross two trails? Or, for the sake of
argument, three?"

Miss Mousey spoke. "Jane, I—"

The Senator turned around and waved Miss
Mousey off, like a pesky fly. The air grew close in the
corridor and I had that feeling you get when you
stumble into a movie ten minutes after the credits
have rolled and you have to spend the next three
minutes letting your eyes get used to the dark before
you can figure out where you're at in the story. A
phone rang down the hall and a nurse answered. I
wondered what kind of politician the Senator was. I
wondered what kind of woman she was out from
under the defenses, the snotty remarks, the barrier
reef of mistrust.

"Two trails, Mr. Murdock. Then what?" For some
reason, she was grinding on me like coarse sandpaper
on soft pine.

"One trail at a time, Senator."

The Senator stared at me for a moment, then stood
up and walked to the window. "I'd like to think about
this. You're very . . . expensive. It's been a long day
and I'm tired. Leave your card with Amanda. And
thank you for coming. Good night, Doctor. I'll re-

member you to Horace when my daughter and I return to Austin."

"But Senator." Wally's face was worried. "I can assure you that Mr. Murdock is—"

"Thank you, Doctor. Amanda, would you show the gentlemen out."

Miss Mousey gave me an imploring look, shrugged, and walked with us to the nurses' station. "You'll have to forgive Jane," she whispered. "The Senator. This thing with Heather . . ." She shrugged. "It's an awful weight. Terrible."

"Yes," Wally said.

I nodded, but said nothing. Miss Mousey left us and walked back to the Senator. Wally punched the button to call the elevator. Something was bugging the Senator. She wanted to work it out on me. Matt Murdock, whipping boy.

At ground level, we walked past the information booth to stand in the doorway looking out. I hate to lose. Outside, beyond the glass, the rain had turned to a soft drizzle. I helped Wally with his slicker, and then pulled on my parka. We walked outside. Fine mist tickled my face.

"Well, Prof. Thanks for trying."

Wally shook his head. "What a female, the pain rising up, so palpable you can see it. Quite spectacular, wouldn't you say?"

"Like being on the receiving end of a Soviet laser."

"You triggered something, Matthew. Something from the deepest depths."

"Glad you noticed."

We walked through the puddles toward our vehicles. Across the freeway, Xanadu towered above us. "She was fine talking with me, earlier. Strategic. Knowledgeable. Angered by Deputy Hanks, of course, but still in control. Then you walk in and she's

transformed into a banshee." He fished out his keys
and unlocked the door of his Saab. He got behind the
wheel and rolled down the window. "A troubled
lady, that. But marvelous, like a warrior queen of old.
Heroic, sensual, ero—"

I broke in. "Can you lend me a hundred until New
Year's?"

"Of course." He dug out his wallet and handed me
five twenties. "You're still planning on Christmas dinner at my Balboa bungalow?"

"Wouldn't miss smoked turkey."

"You're bringing the wine, don't forget." Starting
up, he revved his engine. It sounded like a sewing
machine made in Korea. "Are you still seeing Alicia
the Fair? An attorney, wasn't she?"

"An assistant U.S. attorney. The answer is no on
Alicia. She's playing lawyer games in L.A. Why?"

"You need companionship, Matthew. Female
warmth, female sensibility. I thought you might
bring Alicia along to the festivities."

"How about the Senator? She could look down her
nose at us."

"Guilt is a heavy burden, Matthew. Be forgiving."

"Hey. What's to forgive?"

We said good night. I was halfway around to my
pickup door when I heard my name called, a femi-
nine voice, part squeal, part bird shriek, and saw a
figure darting awkwardly across the puddles on the
tarmac, a shiny blue raincoat thrown up to protect
her hair.

Wally opened his window. "A messenger, I trow,
crossing the flood plain from the tented encamp-
ment of the queen."

"Good deduction, Dr. Watson."

The figure got closer. It was Miss Mousey, the com-
panion-secretary to the Senator. Her foot hit a final

puddle, darkening her skirt with spots of water. She came up breathlessly.

"Mr. Murdock!" Between gulps of air, Miss Mousey gasped. "Jane, the Senator, wants you . . . back. She told me to say she needs your . . . help?"

"I'll just bet."

"No. I mean it. She really does." Raindrops spotted her glasses. "Okay. So I glossed it a little. Will you come?"

"This is your idea, right?"

"Yes. But it's Jane's money. You'd be working for her. Helping her." She gave me a lopsided smile. "Hunting."

"Oral reports?" I asked.

"Matthew?" Wally spoke from the car.

"She needs your help. She's sorry for the way she acted. She's tired. She sent me down to bring you back upstairs."

"Why the turnaround?"

Miss Mousey shook her head, acknowledging the paradox. "That's Jane. She's a true . . . Gemini. She changes personalities like other women change clothes. It's not a fault, really. It's just that—" She stopped. "Will you help, Mr. Murdock? This thing with poor Heather is driving her crazy. She's draped herself in blame. She was worn out, ready for Christmas, then this happens. She didn't mean to insult you, I'm sure."

Wally's voice, from the Saab. "Say yes, Matthew."

Miss Mousey eyed me from behind her glasses. "Will you come back? Just try it, for a couple of days anyway?"

"Is that how long I've got?"

"Three days, Jane said."

I grinned. My expelled breath was gray on the moist night air. Round one to the Senator. Round two, all Murdock. "Okay. Three days of hunting. Tell the Senator I'll be right there."

Miss Mousey did a little rain dance, toe, toe, heel, skip, toe and heel, and then scurried back to shelter. A wind blew rain spray into my face and I wondered how I would look in a Jack Webb DI hat. Snappy.

"Man works better with deadlines," Wally said. "More discipline, far more productivity."

"Thanks for the pep talk." I reached into the pickup and brought out the Beretta in its shoulder holster. "Think the Senator likes guns?"

"Try a hauberk and shield," Wally said, revving his Saab sewing machine. "Polish up that tarnished armor. And before you charge the foe, tie a bright orange kerchief to your lance tip."

I watched Wally drive off toward the tollbooth and then I locked the Beretta in the pickup and headed back upstairs. The Senator had me going, all right. Up. Down. Up. Down. Yo-Yo Murdock, on a string. I didn't mind. She was a handsome woman. Sexy. Full of fire. A woman to put some zing into life. If you survived the contact.

In the elevator, going up, I hummed a tune from *Aida*.

2

"You've got your three days," the Senator said. "I want written reports, daily."

"I run the case," I said. "Oral reports when I have something."

"Three hundred a day," the Senator said, shaking her head. "That's beyond pricey."

"That's my rate. Plus expenses."

She spoke to Miss Mousey. "I told you this wouldn't work."

"Jane, please!"

The Senator glared at her, then turned back to me. "All right. Since time is of the essence. And since you come so highly recommended. Three hundred a day for three days."

"Plus expenses."

"All right. All right. Expenses. Where will you start?"

"With your daughter."

Her eyebrows shot up. "Are you clairvoyant? She's in a coma."

"With whatever you can tell me."

The Senator spoke in a dull voice. "She was headed home when she changed her mind. She came to California. Some madman slammed her with his car in a parking lot. She—"

I walked over to stand in front of her. I wanted to reach out and touch her. It wasn't the right time, so I locked eyeballs with her. The stream of words slowed.

"Get some rest, Senator. I'm on your side."

"I've hired a mercenary," she said. "Watch my back, soldier."

"Get some rest, okay?"

"Yes." She nodded. "Rest. I'm very tired."

"I'll check around, call you tomorrow."

"You do that."

There was a long silence while the Senator stared past me at something in her memory. She reached out her hand as if groping for support. Then she nodded, abruptly, and motioned Miss Mousey to write me a check. In the gray hospital silence, I could hear the gold fountain pen scratching the paper. Miss Mousey closed the book and brought the check to me. It was made out to M. Murdock for a thousand dollars. Her eyes swam behind the glasses and her throat worked. There was something she wanted to tell me. Now was not the time.

Miss Mousey excused herself to go to the ladies' room down the hall past the nurses' station, and I sat next to the Senator, who now sat with her eyes closed, legs crossed at the ankles, her head resting on the back of the chair. The tweed jacket was draped across her shoulders.

"All right. What do you want to know?"

"Heather ran away, didn't she?"

The Senator sighed. "You know she did."

"Why?"

"She's young. She's impetuous. We . . . haven't been getting along."

"Has she run away before?"

"Once."

"Why did she run away that time?"

"She had a crush on a boy. It was stupid. I didn't think he was good for her. We quarreled."

"Where did she run to?"

"When we picked her up, she was headed west."

"San Francisco?"

"I presume so. A friend of mine—he's with the Texas Rangers—located her on a bus leaving El Paso."

"What's she like, your daughter?"

The Senator thought about that. "Headstrong. Willful. Stubborn. Bright if she gets interested in something. Dull if she's bored."

"What does she like in school?"

"Classes, you mean?"

"Yes."

"She likes the humanities. Reading and writing. Literature. Drama and the stage. She's quite a good little actress. She's very good at numbers. Her father taught her—and this is the only thing he taught her—to multiply in her head. She can multiply as high as the eighteens without help from a calculator."

"What's your ex-husband's work?"

"He's a lawyer specializing in international finance, a whiz with numbers. He works with banks in Japan and Singapore."

"Did he remarry?"

"Oh, yes. A minute after the divorce decree was granted. A pretty young thing working her way through law school. She dropped her pursuit of the law and gave him two children."

"You didn't remarry?"

She shifted her weight in the chair. "No. Not a chance. Have you been married?"

"Once. A long time ago." I grinned at her and felt my face get hot. "So tell me what happened with you and Deputy Hanks."

"A nasty little man with pig's eyes. Very skilled at taking evasive action."

"What was he evading?"

"Me. My questions."

"Go on."

"I asked a question. He evaded. I came from another angle. He evaded again. I pressed. He brought up the nonsense about this gang of thieves. Would you believe they take this idea seriously? My baby girl as sex bait for traveling businessmen?"

"Cops like simple explanations. It makes writing reports easier."

"Touché. I asked for evidence of Heather's involvement. Not for my eyes, he said. He'd have to interview Heather. I kept probing. He was like an eel, slipping, sliding. I kept having the feeling that . . . something else was going on."

"There are things cops can't tell you. It's policy."

"Of course. I understand that. I just kept having this feeling—it's gone now—that this slippery little man had been sent here, dispatched, to lead me astray. Sounds paranoid now."

"Astray from what?"

She shook her head and pulled the coat tighter around her shoulders. "It's as if there was—I don't know—something in a trash can. Hanks was sitting on the lid, smirking at me from behind the uniform."

"Did you do anything?"

"I asked to speak to a supervisor."

"Did you?"

"Yes. A Lieutenant Rome. He seemed sympathetic, understanding. I mentioned the possibility of a press conference. He said he'd confer with Hanks. His word was 'monitor.' I phoned Austin. I got the name of your friend, Dr. St. Moritz. You're my first detective. Did you know that?" The Senator put a hand over her mouth to hide her yawn. "I am so tired. Do you have enough to get started on? I really need to get some rest."

"Just a couple more questions. How easily did Heather make friends?"

"Heather's a loner. In that, she takes after me. She has one close friend in Austin. And another close friend at school."

"Do you have that name? The one at school?"

"Of course. Rachel Friedman. Heather writes about her in the letters."

"How often does she write?"

A pause. "Once a week."

I pulled an envelope out of my pocket and wrote down the name of Rachel Friedman.

"Any idea where she lives, this Rachel Friedman?"

"Around Denver. One of the suburbs. Littleton. Golden, perhaps. If you really need it, we could phone the school."

"The professor already tried calling. Reached an answering machine."

"I spoke to someone yesterday, about Heather."

"Can you phone them tomorrow and try to find out?"

"I'll tell Amanda." She yawned again, a deeper one this time.

"When did you find out Heather had run away?"

"When her flight came in and she wasn't on it."

"What day was that?"

"Monday. Late evening."

"What did you do?"

"I phoned the school. They thought she was on a plane to Austin. I alerted my friend with the Texas Rangers. He alerted the Scottsdale police and the Arizona state police. I phoned my FBI friend. He said he'd keep me informed, but there wasn't much there."

"So the first real information was when they phoned you here from the hospital?"

"Yes. They wouldn't say much. Only that Heather had been injured. I didn't find out about the coma until I arrived. I was tired from the trip. There was my baby in Intensive Care."

"Did you get any help from the doctor?"

The weary smile again. "They changed doctors. A Dr. Prather admitted Heather. He went home, a bad cold, according to some nurse. Another doctor's in charge now."

"Any help there?"

"I tried speaking to her as she was rushing into surgery. Her name was Ruffin. She confirmed Dr. Prather's findings about Heather. Shock from a blow. Multiple contusions. Head injuries. Internal injuries. I've asked to speak to her again. No luck yet."

"Does it feel like the old runaround?"

"I thought so. Now I'm not so sure. Maybe I'm just tired."

"How long ago did this happen, the thing with the Austin boyfriend?"

"A year or so. Fourteen months. Why?"

"Maybe they got together again. Without your knowing."

"No. I'd have known. Heather's like me. I know her tricks."

"Any idea what she was wearing last night?"

"What she always wore, I suppose. Jeans with slits in the knees. A sweater over a blouse. Her down jacket, a parka with a little hood. I'm just guessing, you understand. When I saw her, she wore a hospital gown."

"What was she carrying?"

"She had a new rucksack. Green. Sort of like a book bag with backstraps."

"Anything in the book bag?"

"A change of clothes. Socks and underwear. Something to write on. I don't have a list of contents, if that's what you mean."

I stood up. My tailbone hurt from sitting in the pink plastic chair. My neck was stiff. I jotted my number on a corner of the envelope, tore it off, and handed it to Senator Jane. "If you think of anything else, give me a call. I'll check back with you after I've worked my network. And I could use a photo."

She dug into her purse and brought out a photo and handed it to me. "Written reports, Mr. Murdock." She gave me a tired smile. A Gemini, Miss Mousey had said. Changes her moods like changing her clothes.

"Oral reports, Senator."

I picked up my parka and headed out. Miss Mousey was at the nurses' station, speaking to one of the nurses, but she paused to say good-bye and ask me for my business card. I wrote out my name, address, and phone on a hospital memo pad. In the elevator, the Muzak played "I'll Be Home for Christmas."

In the lobby, I stopped to phone Webby Smith, my pal on the Laguna Beach police force. Webby groused when I told him what I wanted. He was just back after working a bad traffic accident in Laguna Canyon. Give him two hours, he said. Then call him at home.

* * *

Traffic was light and the rain was still only a slow silver drizzle, so I made it back to my place on the Newport Pier in half an hour. Grease had gathered in little streaks on the surface of my minestrone. Cal the magic soup pot was lukewarm. I carried the soup out to my workroom and opened a window and felt the bite of the chill sea wind. I closed the door that separated the workroom from the rest of the house. I cleaned up the vegetable skins and put the meat trimmings in a plastic Baggie for Leo Castelli's dog, Pavarotti. I poured myself a glass of Mondavi and studied the photo of Heather Blasingame. It was a mug shot showing a girl with blond frizzy hair and granny glasses. Her mouth was curled with the hint of a smile. The blue eyes looked directly into the camera. She wore a crewneck sweater. Actress, the Senator had said. Loves the stage.

I flipped on the television and sipped my wine. What was Heather doing at Xanadu? Had she met up with someone? Picked up a pigeon for plucking? Was she a member of the San Diego Kids? Had she been followed from San Diego? From Scottsdale? Were there any witnesses to the hit-and-run?

Around midnight, I phoned Webby Smith at home. He sounded grouchy. In the background, I heard the lilting tinkle of a girl's voice. Webby has a weakness for college girls, PE majors mostly, with leggy legs and short-cropped hair and tight-muscled arms. Webby's a veteran competitor in the Iron Man in Hawaii. He trains the whole year round. Only a jock can keep up with him. "Let's make it fast, Sherlock. I just spent a bad hour with some grieving parents. And Julie's here, goddammit."

"Anything on the Blasingame kid?"

"If I tell you, will you get off the phone?"

"Scout's honor."

Papers rustled at Webby's end of the phone. "Didn't get much out of the sheriff, so I had to call San Diego."

"Okay. What have you got?"

"There's a holiday scam going down south of here, from Oceanside to San Ysidro, on the border. San Diego PD thought it was one team, now they think it's four, maybe five. Trendy, no? The teams have one woman, two to four guys. The woman is the bait. She waits in a truck stop or a shopping mall or a roadside Denny's, putting on the sad-eyed look, until some mark asks to buy her a cup of coffee. She finds out where he's headed, the mark, then feeds him her story. She's on her way somewhere, going his way, of course. She's out of money, been sleeping in parks and doorways. Is spooked at the danger. Thought when she left home the world was a real safe place. Now all she wants is to get back home. The mark offers her a ride. She accepts. Her *compadres* in crime follow close behind. Down the road she gets flirty, suggests a fast set of motel tennis. He's nice, she says. She wants to be nice too. The mark rents a room. Inside the room, she dopes him with a Mickey Finn—boy, is that shit getting sophisticated—and the mark is out in minutes. Did you know today's Mickeys work like Contac? Would you believe crooks using tiny time pills? Anyway, she opens the door for her pals, who steal whatever's not nailed down."

"Have they connected the Blasingame kid?"

"She fits the MO. Underage, cute as a bug, innocent chickie in trouble."

"Anything solid from Hanks?"

"Not much. They found oil drips on her clothes. She had six bucks on her. Two reefers in her rucksack, along with clean underwear and a notepad and a paperback book of poems. Can't read my writing. Wait a minute." I heard the girl's voice again, from offstage at Webby's place. "Oh, yeah. Traces of marijuana showed up in the Blasingame kid's bloodstream. And she was carrying pills."

"Pills? What kind?"

"Birth control," Webby said. "Cute little package, Hanks said, pink pills for seven days, then light blue, then white, then orange. Evidence, he says, the kid was ready for action."

"What time was the hit-and-run?"

"The best they can do is nineish. The mall was closing."

"Where did it happen?"

"East quadrant, close to the freeway."

"Any witnesses?"

"Someone called it in. Hanks wouldn't say who."

"He must have interviewed them."

"If he did, he's not saying."

"What about mall security?"

"I asked. Got nothing."

"What about the paramedics?"

"They got there a couple minutes after nine. They were loading the girl when Hanks made the scene."

"Where did they find the girl, exactly?"

"Near a van, a Dodge. The paramedic I talked to thinks she crawled under the van. Someone saw her and called in and then split."

"A stalwart citizen who didn't want to get involved."

"Millions of those in the naked city."

"Where's the van now?"

"I mentioned it to Hanks. He says the van was gone by the time he arrived."

"What do you know about Hanks?"

"He's a loner, not too popular with his fellow deputies. Pulls some real soft duty." There was a pause. Then Webby said: "Listen, Sherlock. Since you're working again, does that mean I get that hundred you owe me?"

"How about lunch?"

"You're on. When?"

"Friday. I'll call you, okay?"

I heard the voice of Webby's girl, talking in the background. Webby covered the mouthpiece with his hand. When he came back on, he made me a deal. "Listen, Sherlock, if you're feeling lonely as a shepherd boy tending his flock, Julie's got this really dynamite friend, loves older men, available for the holidays."

"She old enough to vote yet?"

"Listen." His voice was a whisper. "She votes. She dances. She jogs. She writes for the school paper. Her family's loaded. She's—" He stopped. "This is a one-time offer, for the holidays only. If you're interested, call me mañana, hey?"

"Thanks, Iron Man."

After hanging up, I phoned the sheriff's headquarters and asked for Deputy Emil Hanks. A woman's toneless voice told me Hanks worked out of the East County substation. When I phoned there, they said to call back tomorrow. Thinking of Rachel Friedman, Heather's pal from school, I phoned Denver information, area code 303. The operator said there were lots of Friedmans, far too many to count. I asked for Littleton and Golden. How about a first name, the operator said. I gave her three different initials. She doled out two numbers. This was against policy, she said, and hung up. The first number did not answer. The second number got me to an old guy, snorting, angry. "Go to hell, you turd, for waking me up."

I worked for an hour to locate the right Friedman. No luck. Maybe it wasn't Littleton. Maybe it wasn't Golden. I refilled my wineglass and got a blanket and snuggled up on the sofa and watched the news. It was heartwarming.

The Russians had dismantled two Soviet missiles, one in Novosibirsk, the other at a silo in Krasnoyarsk. Our side had paralleled the Russian actions by dismantling missiles in Utah and Oregon.

Angry blacks were rioting in Miami.

Locally, a victim in careful blotto silhouette verified how he was robbed by the San Diego Kids on Monday night. The girl used as bait was dark-haired, sweet, cute, maybe eighteen, a runaway in trouble. Heather with dark hair?

The pigeon was replaced with eerie shots of the accident at Big Bend curve in Laguna Canyon. Two dead, three injured. Webby Smith, raindrops glistening on his yellow slicker, estimated the speed of one vehicle, driven by a teen, at ninety-two miles per hour.

Webby was replaced by the face of Reginald D. Canfield, M.D., of Huntington Beach. Dr. Canfield, a respected physician, was accused of child molestation. The girl in question, now nineteen, had been hospitalized due to severe psychological trauma. There were statements from the defense lawyer and from an assistant D.A. named Harriet Trueblood. According to the assistant D.A., the molestation had gone on for a period of five years, victim's age eleven to sixteen. Witnesses who knew the doctor said he was above reproach, a nice person, a dedicated physician.

The phone rang. It was Senator Jane. She sounded a little drunk. "It's me," she said. "I want a report. Want to know you're working, Murdock, so verify.

Oral reportage is okay. Written report, due tomorrow, zero nine hundred, my desk."

"Where are you?"

"In my room, cozy, recalcitrant, drifting. Where are you?"

"Home."

"Where is that, pray?"

"A gnat's flight from the Newport Pier."

"The humble hut of the humble Neanderthal detective, right?"

"That's about it."

"Is it appropriately cavelike?"

"Only if the buffalo-chip fire wanes. Are you feeling okay, Senator?"

"Right as rain, Mister M, now that I've had my toddy. And you?"

I told her what I'd learned from Webby Smith, omitting the part about the birth control pills.

"What does it all mean, Mr. Murdock?"

"I also called some Friedmans in the Denver area. No luck there."

"Good thinking. Did you try Littleton? Golden?"

"Yes."

"I'll put Amanda on it tomorrow." There was a pause. "Detectives work on hunches, right? Little blips of intuition."

"Yes."

"I thought so. What's your hunch, your trained professional intuition, about this mess with my daughter?"

"Nothing yet, Senator."

She took in a deep breath. "Want to hear my hunch?"

"Sure."

"Something rotten . . . going on. Something evil and foul, right here in sunny southern California.

Maybe it's the rain, all this dark water falling. How does it smell to you?"

"It smells cold."

"It smells dark, like leaves rotting." There was the clink of ice in her glass at her end of the phone.

"Where are you staying, Senator?"

"Zany, convenient Hotel Xanadu. Quite a place. From my window, I can look down at the parking lot where—" She stopped. "What are you drinking, Mr. Murdock?"

"Mondavi red. You?"

"Mondavi red from Napa?"

"Yes."

"That's very interesting. I'm drinking gin and tonic. My daddy drank bourbon and branch water. What did your daddy drink?"

"Schlitz."

"A man's man's drink, right?"

"I suppose."

She switched directions on me. "Who are you, Murdock? Where are you coming from?"

"Just a guy," I said.

"Why did you take this case?"

"Money, Senator. Bills to pay."

"I had the feeling you were sent."

"You mean by Wally St. Moritz?"

"No. Something much more cosmic. You were in Special Forces, weren't you?"

"Good guess, Senator."

"And did you drop out of school?"

"Guilty."

"Just had to get there, right? Had to get over there and play macho man."

"My old man was career army. Runs in the blood."

"My brother was in Special Forces. Did you know him?"

The link, finally. "What was his name?"

"Wade Whitney. He dropped out of high school so he could join up."

"I didn't know a Wade Whitney. What rank was he?"

"Captain, just before he died."

Captain was my rank. "Sorry to hear it. Were you close?"

"Sometimes. Wade was killed in the Tet offensive, in 1968. Before that, he trained at Fort Ord. Napa was his favorite area for weekends. His favorite wine, also, was Mondavi." She paused. "Were you there? For the Tet, I mean?"

"Yeah."

"Were you wounded?"

"In the leg."

She gasped. "Where in the leg?"

"High up, left thigh."

"Wade was hurt in his right leg, about the same place. Did yours heal all right?"

"It only bothers me when it rains."

"You sound like Wade. Just like him." She shifted direction again. "You didn't answer my question."

"What question is that?"

"I asked you why you took the case. Don't tell me it was money."

Money, I thought. And those thighs beneath the tweed. Stirred up by a senator. "What else?"

"Wade would have said it that way, short, clipped. Money. I can hear him, hear his voice, so rascally, so full of deviltry. You have his smirk, you know, that macho man swagger. That's what killed my brother, the old machismo. I miss him, you know, the way he played with surfaces. He'd dig into you, getting under your skin, poking at your mind, probing your soul, until you were happy to open up and let it all hang out. People were like old houses, Wade said, old houses in dusty old towns, and they needed someone to throw open their windows and let some fresh air in. Wade was older by three years. For me, growing up in Bastrop, he was promise and hope. Janey, he'd say, don't let the bastards smother you with crap. Before they do, bust some windows.

"The problem was, he never opened up himself. Or at least not that he'd let you see. Wade's windows stayed closed. He left town so he wouldn't die of suffocation, ran away to war. Just like you. What else besides money, you say. I could name the reasons, but I won't. Are you there, Mr. Murdock?"

She broke off what she was saying about windows and houses and Mondavi wine and her brother, Wade Whitney, the dead army captain, to let out a long, sighing breath. I pictured her on the phone, the tweed suit, the boots, the lonely hotel nightcap.

Or maybe she was in her nighty and sexy peignoir, underwear off, her rich hair caressing her shoulders. I'm a sucker for a smart woman. I wondered what color the Senator painted her toenails.

I had a couple of things to say to her, but at the end of the long sigh she hung up, click, just like that. And I was alone with the burring whir of the sea wind outside my door and an empty wineglass and a bright and glitzy Spuds Mackenzie commercial.

3

The sheriff's East County substation was painted institutional beige. The parking lot held a dozen black-and-whites. I left my Beretta in the pickup.

Just inside the door to the station was a metal detector. While a female deputy watched, I cleaned out my pockets and pulled off the belt with the heavy brass buckle. The deputy smiled when I passed through without a beep. She directed me down along a corridor to a duty room with several desks. At one of the desks sat Deputy Emil Hanks, pecking away at a computer keyboard. The olive drab DI hat was hung on the back of a second chair.

I stood beside the desk. Hanks kept on typing, his face the picture of effortless smug. His uniform blouse was wet under the armpits. In the sickly green light from the overhead fluorescents, he looked thick and squat, glued to the floor, like a stalagmite.

A second deputy came into the room, saw me, and yelled at Hanks: "Hey, Emil. You got company."

Hanks tapped in a final line before looking up. "Something?" he asked.

"Name's Murdock," I said. "They tell me you're handling the hit-and-run over at Xanadu Mall."

"They do, do they?"

"I've been hired to investigate."

"Hired?" His eyes narrowed. He had chubby cheeks, made red from booze. "You a PI?"

"Yes."

He held out his hand. "Ticket."

I handed over my detective's license. He took a long time studying it, then turned to his computer, brought up a new screen, and slowly typed in my number, then my name, mouthing each entry as he punched it in: "Got a *M*, got a *A*, got a *T*, got ano-ther *T* . . ." When he finished, Hanks pressed a last key and sat back to watch the screen, hands folded over his belly. Was he looking for something? Or did he want us both to sweat?

The computer beeped. Hanks sat forward to read the screen. He grunted, then swiveled to face me. "You must be pretty special, friend. Instructor in small arms, it says here, at three police academies. Well, yayhoo for you. Vietnam vet." He squinted at me. "You that old?" Then went on without waiting for an answer. "Purple Heart, a long time ago. Medals out the kazoo. I am impressed. A real hotdog with a smoking pistol, it says here."

"Look, Deputy, I know you're busy. If you could help me out on this, I'll be moving on."

He waved a pudgy hand. "Always happy to help a hotdog. Shoot."

I knew I'd get nothing. But here I was, trying for the whole nine yards. "You reported to the Senator that the hit-and-run occurred between eight and nine."

"So?"

"I was hoping you could pin it down."

"Be more precise, you mean?"

"Yes."

"Sorry. Best I can do."

"Who called it in?"

"That's confidential."

"Where was the victim when you arrived?"

"In the ambulance, getting treated. Same as you'd be if you got bunted across the macadam."

"Did the paramedics tell you where they found her?"

"That's confidential."

"What time did you make the scene?"

He grinned. "Between eight and nine."

"How about witnesses?"

He leaned back and folded his hands on his stomach. "Confidential." He picked up my license and held it out to me. I took it from him.

"Where, in your best expert opinion, did the hit take place?"

The grin widened. "In the parking lot."

"Not the parking building?"

This pissed him off. "Look, Mister Private Eye, an investigation is ongoing. It's official. You're not. What gives you the idea you can come in here and get answers? Now, be a good guy and take your ticket and let me get back to this paper, hey?"

"How about a list of the girl's belongings?"

"Out."

"Does Josh McBride still work at your main facility?"

"Who?"

"Josh McBride. An ace criminalist."

"Never heard of him."

"That's funny. He's been with the sheriff for twenty years."

"Like I said, pal, I never heard of him. Lots of new faces around." He turned back to his computer.

As I left the duty room, I heard the slow tap-tapping of keys. The sound was without rhythm or caring.

I swung by El Toro General to check on the medical reports, but the woman at the information desk couldn't raise either Dr. Prather or Dr. Ruffin. I took the elevator to the fourth floor. Senator Jane and Miss Mousey had not yet appeared, but the nurse at the station said Heather was still in a coma. No change, she said, in a sympathetic tone. I headed across the freeway to Xanadu Mall.

Xanadu didn't open wide its golden doors until ten, so I used the time to scout the parking lot. Sometimes with a hit-and-run the law erects a crime scene barrier, but I circled the lot without seeing any sawhorses and yellow ribbons. Puddles stood in the low spots. Last night's rain made it impossible to look for skid marks. I parked the pickup and walked the vine-covered cyclone fence, hearing the swoosh of traffic on the freeway, not expecting to find anything.

Above me, the tower of Hotel Xanadu rose like a great bird. It was supported on the huge slab by curved struts that gave it an Eiffel Tower look. During construction, a five-year building marathon, the Duke publicity people had touted the decision to build with structural steel, so that Xanadu would flex during an earthquake. Like a supple willow in the wind, they said. The base was big enough to support a building twice as high.

Near one of the support struts and about three feet from the fence I found a piece of clear glass, thick and striated, like a shard from a headlight. It was triangular and about an inch across. I put it into my pocket and spent another fifteen minutes poking around the fence. Cars seeped into the lot and Christmas shoppers climbed out and headed for Xanadu.

I was about to give up when I found a book, a rain-soaked paperback with a cover mottled by rain. It lay at the bottom of the vines that shinnied up the fence. The price tag was from Xanadu Books and the pages were swollen with wetness. The title of the book was *Jungles Burning.* The author was Marvin Holly, a name I did not recognize. The date of publication was back in the seventies.

There was a photo of Marvin on the back, a youngish, bearded man wearing an army shirt and military dress frame glasses. I opened the front cover to find the ink smears of what once had been an inscription. I made out *ravel, Blak,* and *rtex.* The other words were smeared beyond reading.

I tucked the soggy book into my pocket and headed across the lot to the mall, glancing upward when I felt someone watching me from above. Five hundred rooms up there, with two hundred windows staring out and down on this side. Maybe I was being watched. But from which room?

The doors whispered open. I smelled happy Christmas smells and was bathed in happy Christmas tunes. Pretty women passed. Handsome children raced down the jeweled corridors. The whole world looked healthy, prosperous, in gear. Yeah, Santa Claus was coming to town.

It took me a half hour to work through the security maze to Ward Bigelow, head of mall security. He was a beefy ex-cop with gray hair that had once been red. He'd heard an oral report about the hit-and-run from his night man, but when he asked his secretary to check the computer, nothing came up on the screen.

"Maybe the goddamn machine ate it," Ward said.

"Was there a written report?"

"Supposed to be." He swung around in his swivel chair to call through the door to his secretary. Her name was Della and she was not happy at having her phone conversation interrupted.

The security office needed a good cleaning. Papers lay in heaps on Ward's desk. Fuzzballs decorated the corners of the room. Della hung up with a bang. Drawers opened as she started her search. Ward Bigelow made a face at me. "You really an eye?"

I showed him my ticket.

"I knew an eye once. Tossed some brews with him at Halloran's. You know Halloran's?"

"Sure." Halloran's was an Irish pub in Orange where cops came to drink with each other.

"Well, this guy, he said the nookie would line up for him. Rich broads, he said, dressed to the nines, bored out of their skulls. Sometimes they'd stand in line for it, three-deep, four, begging."

"Sounds like paradise, all right."

Ward leaned toward me. "That ever happen to you?"

"Never," I said.

"Shit," he said. "You wouldn't tell me if it had, would you?"

"Paradise," I said, "is all in the mind."

He licked his lips and sighed. "So, while we're waiting, what can I do you for?"

"Tell me what you know about night before last."

"The hit-and-run?"

"Yes."

"Just what Billy told me."

"Billy's the night man?"

"Yeah. Billy Hargrove. Young, good-looking, full of himself. Anyway, he was making rounds when he got a call on his handy talkie saying someone was hurt in the parking lot. The call came here, to our switchboard, which was being manned by Oscar Smith. Billy hauled ass outside, but was a while getting to the scene, because Oscar had told him the ocean side when it was the freeway side. By then the victim was in the ambulance, and the sheriff had taken over—major crimes we switch to them like hot potatoes—so all Billy got talking to the paramedics was that the victim crawled underneath a vehicle, which was where she was found. She was unconscious and pretty beat up."

"What kind of vehicle?"

"Van. They thought it was a Dodge, maybe or Chevy."

"Anything on the color? The model? License plate?"

"Nothing more. Like I said, something like this, it's out of our territory. Once the law gets called, it's all theirs."

"Any idea who called your switchboard?"

He shook his head. "Probably a customer, going home. This time of year, we get a ton of calls. Shoplifting's on the upswing. I got three men out with the flu."

"Do you log in the calls?"

He nodded. "Sure. The sheriff took the log."

End of the trail. Bigelow gave me Oscar's home phone, which I wrote down on the back of an envelope. "When does Billy's shift start?"

Bigelow consulted a schedule clipped to a clipboard. "Today's his day off. That means he'll be lifting weights up in Muscle Beach. Because it's Christmas, he's taking tomorrow off too, which means he'll work Christmas Eve, when we close at five." Bigelow snapped the clipboard back on its hook.

"Muscle Beach, as in Venice?"

"Right again," the old man said. "Kid thinks he's the next Mister America. You going up there?"

I said maybe I would and got a description of Billy Hargrove. I thanked Bigelow and shook hands and said I'd be in touch. His phone rang and he turned to answer it. The secretary was on the phone again, talking to someone about turkey and dressing. In a glass ashtray on her desk, a cigarette smoldered. She glared at me as I left the outer office. There was no sign of Billy Hargrove's report on the hit-and-run.

I used a pay phone to call the number of Oscar, the night man on the switchboard. The phone rang a dozen times before I hung up.

Xanadu Books was downstairs on the first floor, next door to a restaurant with a CLOSED sign on the door. Business was brisk inside the bookstore, so I had to wait to speak to the manager. When she was free, I showed her the copy of *Jungles Burning*. She did not remember selling it. She told me her inventory control went through the computer to headquarters in San Jose. It would take her a couple of hours to get through and she wouldn't have a couple of hours until the day after Christmas. "Come back when it's dead around here. I'll have nothing but time."

A bearded guy with an earring passed. He wore sandals with no socks, a Hawaiian shirt, and jeans. His name tag said Paul. "Oh, Paul," the manager said. "Did you remember selling a copy of . . . what was it again?"

"This." I showed Paul the book.

"Who wants to know?" he asked.

"My name's Murdock. I'm a private investigator on a case."

"What kind of case?"

The manager excused herself and hurried away. I brought out the photo of Heather and showed it to Paul. "This kid was a victim of a hit-and-run last night. I'm trying to find someone who saw it happen."

He studied the photo. "We haven't heard anything about a hit-and-run. What time was it?"

"Around closing time, Tuesday night."

"I worked Tuesday. What do you need?"

"I'm backtracking the victim, hoping for a witness. Did you see her?"

"Yeah. I think so. Lemme tell you what happened." He pointed to the name Marvin Holly. "Around eight or so, this guy walks in, asking for this book. I think I know him because I heard him give a speech in seventy-four in Oakland. He's older now, but then aren't we all, right? Just happens it's a great book, one I always keep a couple copies of. I walk him back and is he pleased, seeing his book on the shelf. We shoot the breeze a minute about old times and I'm ringing up the sale when in walks a kid. It could be this kid. Or it could be some other kid."

"What was she wearing?"

"Kid clothes. The acid wash. The high-tops. The baggy down jacket. The only thing different was, she carried a rucksack and looked like Little Orphan Annie."

"Ragamuffin?"

"Yeah. This is Orange County, man. Your average Xanadu teener dresses spiffy. The girls have clean hair and heartbreaker smiles. The guys know which Reeboks are in. Anyway, Holly sees this kid and goes into shock. He calls out to her. I don't catch the name. He beelines for her, sees it's the wrong kid, and zips out the door, leaving his purchase. I give the kid fifty cents to run him down and hand over the book."

"Did she hand it over?"

Paul shrugged. "I went back to the register."

"Would you know her if you saw her again?"

"If she did the Orphan Annie routine I might." He indicated the photo. "Kids these days. The fourteeners seem twenty. The sixteeners are ripe for marriage and childbirth, not necessarily in that order. They work the mall in packs, flashing their goddamn grins, strutting their stuff. I'm forty-five, man, with a steady lady, and some of them turn me on like a three-hundred-watt bulb. For example. . . ."

With his chin, Paul directed my attention to the front, where two teens had just entered the store. Age: fourteen or so. Dress: jeans, high-tops, identical blue parkas. One was dark blond, with a pretty face and detective's eyes. Her pal was a redhead, more jolly than pretty, with a permanent smile. They came toward us, the blonde leading. She saw me, saw the book. Her mouth opened and her eyes got wide and she plucked her friend by the sleeve and whispered something. Their footsteps quickened as they hurried past, trailing wisps of soft perfume. "Jailbait," Paul said. "And ripe as a Modesto peach." He stuck out his hand. "Well, got to get back to work."

Paul walked up front. The teens had stopped at the literature section and the blonde was whispering as she showed a book to her friend. The book had a green cover. The friend took the book and the blonde stared at me again, her eyes narrowed. I dropped Marvin Holly's rain-soaked book in my parka pocket and started for the door, nodding at Paul on the way out.

In the crowded corridor, I heard someone call my

name. "Mr. Murdock? Wait up, please! Mr. Murdock?"

I turned to see the blonde from the bookstore, then her tagalong friend, then Paul. The blonde was waving at me with a green book. I stopped. Did I know this kid?

"Don't you remember me?" she said, coming up. "I'm Cindy. Cindy Duke. The stables? In Laguna Canyon?"

Her face was longer, the body leaning toward maturity, but I remembered all right. A dark night in March, the rain slashing down, me with a bullet hole in the left shoulder, and brave Cindy behind the wheel of my pickup, careening down the wet canyon road, chauffeuring me toward a rendezvous with Philo Waddell and his sicko goons. That had happened a couple of years ago, which would make Cindy thirteen, maybe fourteen. And back then, her last name had been Martin.

"Hey, Cindy the horsewoman." I stuck out my hand and we shook. "You've grown up, kid."

Before she could answer, Paul caught up to us, his eyes angry as he grabbed Cindy's arm. "Okay, sweetheart. Either pay for the merchandise or I'm calling security."

"What?" Cindy blushed. "Oh. I'm sorry."

"Leave her alone!" the friend said. "She wasn't doing anything!"

Across the corridor, two women with bulging shopping carts stopped to watch.

"Stealing is something," Paul growled.

And then Cindy turned the book faceup and I saw the book was the last copy of *Jungles Burning* and I hauled out a ten. "Here." I handed it to Paul.

"I have money," Cindy said. "Don't."

Paul's chest was heaving. A ten-yard run had him

breathing like a beached whale. "Okay, okay," he said, staring down at Cindy. "Okay." He looked at me. "Come back to the store. I'll make change."

We walked back to the store, where he rang up the purchase and made change. He placed the book into a paper sack. He handed it to me. "Sorry, kid."

"I'm no thief," Cindy said.

Cindy grabbed the book and hurried out, followed by her friend.

Paul saluted me. "Kids," he said. "They drive you bats."

In the mall, Cindy introduced her friend, whose name was Phyllis. I handed her the book and she dug out a roll of money—a fat roll with twenties on top—and peeled off a ten. The friend watched as Cindy stuffed the roll back into her front pocket. "Thanks."

"Pretty heavy reading," I said.

She wagged the book in my face. "This was written by my dad."

"Marvin Holly?"

"Um."

"I thought your name was Duke."

"That's now," she said. "But first it was Holly. My mom, she—"

Her pal Phyllis interrupted the conversation by tugging on Cindy's sleeve. "Cyn. What about that shopping?"

"In a minute, Phyl, okay?" She turned back to me. "Are you a fan of my daddy's?"

I hauled out my copy of Marvin's book.

"It got all wet," she said.

"Yeah."

Cindy opened it and read what was left of the inscription, then handed it back to me. "I can't read what it says. Can you?"

"Cyn," Phyl said. "I don't have all day, okay?"

Cindy shook her off.

"Is your dad in town, Cindy?"

She nodded. "Yes."

"Have you seen him?"

"Not yet."

"Cyn!" Phyllis pointed to her wristwatch and whined: "Please come on! You know I've got to get home by twelve-thirty!"

Cindy excused herself and walked away a few steps. They argued for a couple of minutes, two miniature almost-adults. They were a team, a twosome, and Cindy was the leader. She was also cuter, smarter, tougher. Without Cindy, Phyl was a wanderer in the wilderness of Xanadu. The argument peaked as Cindy handed over a bill from her money roll. Phyl walked off with a dirty look at me, trying her best to saunter. Cindy came back to me.

"I'm supposed to meet her at the bus stop at twelve."

"I didn't mean to ruin your day."

Cindy shook her head and blew her nose with an embroidered handkerchief. A tear appeared in one eye, then the other. She wiped them away. More tears followed. She tucked the handkerchief away. "Phyl doesn't understand."

"About what?"

"About finding Daddy."

"Here?"

She nodded. "Um."

"You had an appointment?"

"Not exactly. I had a . . . feeling."

She said she was hungry, so we walked to the Choc Shoppe, where we ordered hot chocolate. We found seats against the window that looked out onto the mall. She placed her copy of *Jungles Burning* on the white Formica. She had pretty eyes and a ripe mouth. "Are you still a policeman?"

"Not a policeman. A detective."

"Like Magnum, on TV?"

I smiled. "Not that rich. Never that lucky."

"But you help people, don't you?"

"Sometimes."

"And they pay you, right?"

"Sometimes."

She hauled out the roll of bills again. "Is this enough?"

"For what?"

She grabbed my sleeve. "Mr. Murdock, will you help me find him?"

And then she burst into tears.

4

———————————

Outside the cloying cocoon of the mall, the air was moist and wintry, with the ugly tang of exhaust drifting across the fence from the freeway. Cindy snuffled as she walked, pulling out her handkerchief to blow her nose, then stuffing it back into the pocket of her blue jacket. We stopped at the spot along the fence where I had found the book. She stared down without speaking, then turned and walked toward my pickup. I caught up to her.

"This is it, isn't it? The one I drove, I mean."

"A magical Ford," I said. "Nineteen seventy-three vintage. This is it."

"You were hurt pretty bad," she said. "So was your friend."

"Yeah."

"Did she get okay?"

"Yes."

"I was hoping you two would, well, you know."

"Yeah. I know. But things didn't work out."

Cindy looked at me. "My mom was really happy

when you didn't tell the television or anything. So was Gramps. Did she phone you, like she said?"

"I don't think so."

"She's like that. She says she'll do something, promises, but then she forgets, my mom. Because she's so busy." Cindy pointed with her arm at Xanadu Tower. "Gramps built this, the whole thing. His company, I mean."

"Wheeler Duke is your grandfather?" I asked.

"Yes. Do you know him?"

"We've never met."

Cindy hugged herself and shivered. It was breezy in the parking lot, the wind dropping down off the pyramid, so I suggested we sit in the pickup. Cindy nodded okay. I unlocked the doors and we climbed in. I cracked the window so we wouldn't fog the glass. "What can you tell me about your dad?"

"Why do you want to know?"

"Someone got hurt here, a couple of nights ago. Your dad might have been a witness."

"Really?"

"Really."

Cindy squirmed around, trying to get comfortable, and the jeans tightened across her rump. One minute she was a kid, all teeth and hair and wide innocent eyes. The next, she was a young woman on the road to maturity, curves and promise and mystery. A precarious time. "Daddy came to the house to see me. He lives in Madison, Wisconsin, where he teaches at the university. I didn't know when he was coming, the exact day, I mean, and I wouldn't have known except for—" She stopped. "Can you keep a secret, Mr. Murdock?"

"Give me a buck."

"Huh?"

"Give me a dollar. From your stash."

She hauled out her money roll and opened it to the center. The dollar bills were in the center, under the tens, the twenties. She peeled off a dollar and handed it to me. I wrote a receipt for one dollar, C. Duke to M. Murdock, for services rendered, and handed it to her. Rich kid.

"That makes you my client. Everything's confidential."

"Like on TV," she said.

"Yes."

"Okay. This is the secret. I eavesdropped on my mom talking to my uncle. They were talking about Daddy. Since I didn't know he was in town I was surprised, I guess."

"When was this?"

"Tuesday. I'd just gotten home from the mall and I was trying to call Phyl when I heard them talking."

"What did they say?"

"Well, my mom, she goes something like, 'He was here. Marvin was here.' And then Uncle Jamie goes, 'That's not news, Sissy.' That's what he calls my mom when he wants her to do something, Sissy. And she says, 'What?' And Uncle Jamie says, 'Who do you think broke out my windshield?' And so she goes, 'Your windshield? Where?' And he goes, 'Where do you think, Sissy? The Benz was parked in my regular slot, at the HQ, emblazoned with my name and everything. I come out. An alarm's whooping away, but I can't believe it's mine, and then who comes along but Marvin the Madman, wielding his vicious little Little League baseball bat.' And then my mom goes, 'Jesus, what did he say?' And Uncle Jamie, he goes, 'Not on the phone, Sissy. Use your head. Not on the phone. Christ. He was there, wasn't he? He came to Carcassonne?' And she goes, 'Of course he was here.' And he goes, 'Hunting for her?' And my mom says yes. So then he asks where Daddy went, only before I can hear anymore, Alicia comes in, she's our maid, and I have to hang up."

"But you came to Xanadu."

"I knew she sent him here, to get rid of him, but all she said was he'd call me at the house. When I asked about the mall, she wouldn't answer. But I could tell from the look on her face she'd told him I was here, all right. I would have come yesterday, but I had to hang around the house waiting for him to call. Then when he never called, I phoned Phyl this morning to help me hunt for him. This was the place to start. Phyl has never believed me about him being an author. That's why I showed her the book. Mom tossed my other copy, last summer, or I'd have shown her that one."

"Carcassonne. That's your house? In Jamaica Cove?"

"Um. We moved there after Mom got divorced from Charley."

"Charley was Mr. Martin?"

She nodded. "I got tired of changing my name, so I made her promise I could stay with Duke, no matter who she marries. Gramps likes it better, anyway."

"Good thinking."

I remembered Carcassonne from a walk-through during the construction phase, fifteen years back, when I was bidding for some cabinet work. The house, a monster Mediterranean palace, was being built by Wheeler Duke for one of his wives, number three or number four, and I was a struggling subcontractor with no local juice. Duke Construction had gone with a lower bid. I'd moved on to other work.

"Does your mother know you're here?"

"Probably."

"How did you get here? Bus?"

She cut her eyes at me and grinned. "We hitched."

"Does your mother know about that?"

"She thinks I take the bus."

I smiled. "Any idea what time your dad came to visit?"

"He'd been there by the time I got home, after five. Alicia told me when I walked in the door. Then I went to call Phyl and that's when I heard the phone conversation. Do you think you can find him, my dad, I mean?"

"I can try."

"What if he saw something?"

"Then maybe he can help me out."

"Who got hurt, Mr. Murdock?"

"A girl named Heather."

"Oh. How old was she?"

"Seventeen. She was running away from home."

"Where was she from?"

"Texas."

Cindy was quiet for a moment. Then she said it again: "Oh."

"When did you see your dad last?"

"In the summer. I visited him in Madison for three weeks. He hates coming to California, so I visit him at his house."

"Does he live alone?"

"Sometimes he lives with a girl friend."

"What was her name?"

"Sue. He called her Susie. I liked her. We took a trip to the Dells, the three of us. It was great."

"Does he still see her?"

"I don't think so."

"Why not?"

"He's stopped talking about her. She used to answer the phone when I called. And when I asked him about her, he said they were having a tiff."

"When did you talk to him last?"

"Monday."

"And he was here by Tuesday."

"Yes."

"Pretty fast trip, for a guy who hates California."

"Um." Cindy folded her arms and stared out the front window. Her face was a mask.

I waited for more. When nothing came, I started the Ford. "Want a ride to the airport?"

"Are we going someplace?"

"Hunting," I said.

"Oh, wow." The mask fell away as she blew her nose again.

At John Wayne Airport the first problem was finding a place to park. After making five circles on the roundabout, we finally found a slot in the thirty-minute lot, where I plugged in two quarters. Cindy didn't say much as we headed for the terminal. The sky was dull gray and moist mist tingled my cheeks.

It took us twenty-two minutes to work our way up through the line of Christmas fliers to the American terminal, where we learned the only connection from Chicago to Orange County was through Dallas. A flight that could have ferried Cindy's dad had arrived Tuesday at three-sixteen, but no one at the ticket counter would give out more information. It was hot inside the terminal. Travelers stood in snaky lines, gray-faced from waiting. I sent Cindy out to the lot to feed the meter and went to find a better way.

I found him drinking coffee in the airport café. His name was Frank Whisner, a retired cop now working airport security, and I'd known him to speak to for a dozen years. Whisner was thirty pounds over his fighting weight. There were greenish circles under his eyes. I identified myself and he remembered me.

I told him what I needed and he nodded, left a quarter for the waitress, and we went downstairs, where Cindy was waiting. I introduced them. Then Frank led us to a door marked AIRPORT PERSONNEL ONLY, which he opened with a six-digit combination.

"Oh, boy," Cindy said.

We followed Whisner down a corridor and into a room packed with computer terminals. He led us to the only window in the place and introduced us to a woman wearing a headset. I gave her the name of Cindy's dad and the approximate time of arrival, early or midafternoon on Tuesday. She punched in the information. Wheezing, Whisner pulled up a chair and sat down.

"Here he is," the woman said. "Marvin Holly, passenger, departed O'Hare at 5:03 on Flight 619. They were late getting away, then had to set down in Dallas, engine trouble, it looks like. Arrived at John Wayne, 2:46."

"Did he have a return flight?"

"Let me check."

Again the keys clicking. The waiting. Cindy sneezed, pulled out the handkerchief, soggy now from much use, and blew her nose. The computer lady handed Cindy a box of pink Kleenex and Cindy took one. "Thank you," she said. The screen blipped and the lady said:

"Yes. Here it is. Return departed LAX Wednesday at 12:04 A.M."

"Back to Madison?" I stared at the screen. There was the name, Marvin Holly, on a United Airlines flight out of LAX.

"O'Hare," the lady said. "Arrival at 4:08, Wednesday morning."

"Brrr," Whisner said. "I grew up in Des Plaines,

outside Chicago. Cold as a witch's—" He coughed to cover himself.

"He's gone back?" Cindy said. "My daddy?"

"Looks like it, hon."

"But he just got here!"

"Are you sure?" I asked the lady.

"Computers never lie," she said.

"But he wouldn't!" Cindy cried. "He came to see me!"

Whisner pushed himself out of the chair. "That about it, Murdock? I got to get back."

"Sure." It didn't make sense. Cindy had called Marvin on Monday. Early Tuesday morning, he hops a plane to California. Tuesday night, without seeing Cindy, he hops a plane back to Madison. "How did he get to LAX?" I asked.

More key-punching by the lady, this time with irritation added. "Puddle jumper," she said. "From John Wayne. Now, if there's nothing else, like the man said, I should get back to work myself."

We were finished here. I thanked the lady and we followed Whisner back out and down the stuffy corridor to the security door, back away from the world of computers and electronic information to the sweaty hustle and bustle of the crowded airport. Cindy's nose was red from crying. Whisner nodded at her and touched the brim of his cap in a final salute.

But I wasn't finished. "You know anyone at the car rental places, Frank?"

"Hey, Murdock. Come on."

I reached into my pocket and pulled out a twenty and he took it, furtively, and walked us over to the Hertz desk, where a young woman with a dazzling smile checked her records, finding nothing, and then passed us on to Avis, same story there. Avis passed us along to Dollar, who passed us along to Budget, where the smile was one-half as dazzling, and where I felt more comfortable. The clerk's name tag said VERONICA.

Cindy was yawning now, her shoulders rounded with disappointment. Her daddy had deserted her. She'd been counting on him. Grayish circles had appeared under her eyes and she slumped on a bench beside the Budget alcove. "I'm tired, Mr. Murdock."

"I know, kid. Hang on."

"He's gone," Cindy said.

"Here it is," Veronica said. "A vehicle was rented by an M. K. Holly on Tuesday. An eighty-seven Chevrolet. That vehicle was returned the same day, so the surcharge was bypassed."

"Were you on that night?"

"No. Sorry."

"Any idea who was?"

"Mrs. Considine."

"Is she on tonight?"

"Is this police business or something?"

I showed her my license. "I'm a private investigator. We're trying to locate this young lady's father. It's an emergency."

Veronica checked a roster on a clipboard. "Mrs. Considine called in sick yesterday. And before you ask, I can't give out her home phone, or her address."

"Don't blame you. Did Mr. Holly pay with a credit card?"

Veronica peered at me. "Have I seen you in the newspapers?"

"I hope not. I try to keep a low profile."

"Well, you're certainly persistent. That's good for your profession, I bet." She gave me a nice smile, not a neon dazzler, but something warmer and more honest, and checked her computer one last time. "Cash, it says here."

"How much?"

"One day, mileage comes to eighty-two miles. The total, with tax, is $73.05."

"Any chance of examining the vehicle?"

"No," she said. "I know where I've seen you. On television. That cop show, the one on Thursday night. I can't remember the name right now, but there's a guy on there who looks like your twin brother."

"Magnum, P.I.," Cindy said.

"No. I know him. Someone else. Give me a minute and I'll come up with the name."

I plucked a card from the card holder in front of her and wrote down my phone number. "If you come up with it, call this number," I said.

"Hey," Veronica said.

We stopped outdoors near the entrance to phone Cindy's dad in Madison. Of course, she knew the number. We let the operator place the call and then when a connection was made I pumped in three dollars in quarters. "It's his answering machine," Cindy said, holding out the phone so I could hear the recording.

"Hello. This is Marv Holly. I'm not at the phone right now, but if you leave a message at the end of the beep, I'll be sure and get back to you. Be sure you tell me your name and numero and the time you called. Here's looking at you, kid."

There was a beep. Then Cindy spoke into the phone. "Daddy, it's me. Call me at home, okay. I miss you, Daddy. I—"

And then the operator cut in, asking for more quarters. Cindy stared at the phone before hanging up angrily.

In the parking lot, a deputy stood with one boot on

my bumper, writing me out a parking ticket. He turned as we came up. "This your vehicle, sir?"

I nodded.

"Any idea how long you've been parked here overtime?"

I shook my head. Cindy tugged at my sleeve.

He finished writing, ripped the top copy off, and handed me the original. "Have a good day, sir."

When we were in the car, stopped at the light on MacArthur, Cindy asked: "Why didn't you answer that policeman back there?"

"He was recording me."

"You're kidding!"

"Nope. Cops carry little cassette recorders. They tape your smart remarks so they can use them in court."

"The dirty stinkers!" Cindy said.

I waited for the light. When it changed, I headed across MacArthur and drove onto the San Diego Freeway. We cruised along in silence until we reached Laguna Canyon Road.

"Do you still carry a gun, Mr. Murdock?"

"Sometimes. Why?"

"Could I see it, please?"

I looked over at her. She was sitting against the passenger door, her arms folded, her face tight. "How come, kid?"

"Gramps has been teaching me to shoot. Okay?"

"Okay."

I swung the Ford over onto the shoulder and rolled to a stop. I cut the engine and used the key to unlock the glove box. I brought out the Beretta and ejected the clip. I racked the slide back twice, to make sure there was nothing in the magazine. Then I handed the piece to Cindy. Cars slid by us, heading toward Laguna Beach.

Cindy held the gun in front of her, using both hands as she tracked a car going past. "Could I shoot it sometime?"

"Sure."

"This is lighter than Gramps's six-shooter."

"How many times have you shot?"

"Oh, six or so. Gramps takes me out to the ranch. He let me use his shotgun some, but I like the six-shooter better. And I like this even better. May I cock it?"

"Sure."

She thumbed back the hammer and then let it back down softly, to show me she understood how the mechanism worked. She hefted the piece before handing it back to me. "Thank you."

"You're welcome."

I shoved the clip back in. Then I holstered the piece and locked it back into the glove box and then we continued on our way down Canyon Road to peaceful Laguna.

5

The main gate to Jamaica Cove is on the inland side, and the private gated community is protected from the real world by an eight-foot wrought-iron fence and twenty-four-hour security guards. The cute brick gatehouse looks as if it was imported from Hollywood, from a movie set starring Stewart Granger as the Prisoner of Zenda. We stopped at the gatehouse in front of a candy-striped traffic control barrier that had been recently repaired in the middle with stove bolts and a clumsy length of one-by-three pine. The guard, a beef-head muscle boy in a carefully tailored uniform, stepped out wielding a clipboard.

"Happy holiday, sir. Help you?"

"Hey, Lance," Cindy said. "Come off it, okay?"

Muscles flexed in Beef-Head's face as he leaned down to verify. His name tag read WOOLFORD. "Well, Princess Cynthia Duke, prettiest girl in Laguna. Who's your new chauffeur, Princess?"

Cindy sighed. "Save it for Mrs. Mather, Lance. Lift the bar, will you?"

A flush of red appeared along Woolford's thick

neck, moving up into his jawline, reddening his cheeks and ears. "Be nice, Princess. Be nice to your uncle Lance."

Cindy gave a huff, folded her arms, and looked away from the guard. He reached beneath the papers on the clipboard and handed me a piece of yellow paper with a big black number 18 on it. "Windshield," he said. He walked back into the gatehouse and pressed a control and the traffic bar raised up and we went through. Cindy directed me to turn right and I was impressed.

The houses on the inland side started at a million. There was a mixture of styles—Spanish, French Riviera, Cape Cod, California Mod. The road curved around and down, past a well-kept park that contained four well-kept tennis courts. Rain kept the courts empty today and made the dead leaves look brown and sad.

"Who's Mrs. Mather?" I asked.

"His latest conquest. She lives up there, on the hill, and she's older than my mom, and he can't be more than twenty-five. Lance, I mean."

"Seems like a nice enough guy. Handsome. Well-built."

Cindy stabbed me with her eyes. "Him? He's a creep."

"How so?"

"He comes on to everything female. Thinks he's God's gift to the girls. If he weren't so boring, I'd really hate him. Into the tunnel and then along the road to the right. You don't really think he's nice, do you? Tell me you're kidding."

"No." I chuckled. "I think he's a squid."

Cindy laughed. "A squid! Oh, perfect. Wait until I tell Phyl. He is a squid."

We went through a tunnel that took us underneath

the Coast Highway to the beachfront side and the houses climbed up to two million, zip, right up the economic ladder, three million, four million, five million, and then out of sight as you got closer to the water. Down below, on the beach, a woman walked her dog. She wore a white jumpsuit and carried a cherry-red umbrella and her bare feet made Robinson Crusoe tracks in the sand, which the rain had turned a dark gold. Between the cliffs and another well-kept tennis court, we had a view of the horseshoe bay that some movie producer had named Jamaica Cove.

It was magnificent.

"That's Carcassonne, out on the point." The street was narrow, with room enough for one big car or two small ones. It twisted in between the sumptuous houses like a dragon lane from a medieval city in Europe. The street had no name and the houses had no numbers. In the front of each house was a stone plaque with the name carved on it in Gothic letters. We passed Tour d'Argent and Bimini on the left. We passed Rififi and Roncesvalles and Bordeaux on the right. Out at the end of the arm of the horseshoe, Carcassonne angled in splendor down the cliffs toward the gray Pacific.

"You know what it means? Carcassonne?"

"It's a walled city in France."

"Hey. How'd you know that?"

"I have smart friends," I said.

I wheeled into the driveway beside a fancy silver Mercedes coupe. The license plate read DUKE II. On the wall of the house was a blue shield with gold letters that said HORVATH SECURITY. I knew Horvath's work. They glue tiny orange cross wires across your windows, and last time I checked they were experimenting with infrared grid stuff for a wireless perimeter.

"I'll check the phone. Maybe Daddy has called. Wait here, okay?"

"Okay."

Cindy was out of the pickup before it stopped rolling. The door was opened by a young Chicana in a maid's dark skirt and white blouse, and Cindy went on through. I turned off the ignition and climbed out for a stretch. After a long, suspicious look at me, the maid closed the door. Suddenly, it opened again and a woman stepped out into the gray morning. She wore a pair of silver warm-up pants, tight as a second skin, and a wide-neck sweatshirt that bared her right shoulder. The shoulder was very tanned. Her hair was cropped short in the fashion of a London punker. It's the kind of haircut that reminds me of those movies about Nazi collaborators during World War II, the ones that got their heads shaved by partisans. The woman had a narrow, sculpted face, photogenic cheekbones, and silver-blue eyes. The hips and legs looked tight and firm. I guessed her age at thirty-eight. Her stance was a model's pose. Since I was the only one there, I assumed she was posing for me.

"Mrs. Duke?"

"I'm Barb Duke. You're the man who brought my daughter home?"

"Yes."

"Just a moment, please." Barb Duke turned to the maid and said something in Spanish. The maid went away and Barb Duke turned back to me. We were four feet apart and I could feel vibes coming off her, an overripe sexual heat. "She was at the mall, correct?"

"Yes."

Before we could say any more, the maid handed

Barb Duke a silver handbag. She brought out a wallet, also silver, and handed the handbag to the maid to hold while she dug for money. She stepped forward to hand me a twenty. "For your trouble."

I waved it off. "It's okay, Mrs. Duke. My pleasure."

"I insist." She eyeballed my 1973 Ford like a used-car dealer and shoved the money at me.

I shook my head. "Mrs. Duke, I'd like to ask you some questions."

The twenty wavered in her fingers. Her hand and forearm were very brown. Either Acapulco or the local tanning booth. "Questions?"

"About your husband."

"Who?" Her hand went to her throat.

"Marvin Holly. Cindy's dad."

She backed away. Behind her, the maid's eyebrows went up. "Señora?"

"Who are you?" Barb Duke asked, edging closer to the door.

"My name's Murdock. I'm a private inves—"

Before I could finish there was the squeak of tires on the road and a car wheeled around the corner, bouncing into the driveway. The vehicle was a Mercedes, an expensive four-door, with a license plate that read DUKE VII. It was a large car to accommodate the large man who climbed out from behind the wheel. He stood six-three, maybe bigger, and he had the look of a weight lifter who'd stopped lifting, letting the muscles slide into fat. Black hair, thick, with a slight upward curl at the nape. The face was dark and pocked with acne scars. Italian shoes and a three-piece pinstripe that set him back two grand.

"Jamie?" Barb Duke said. "What—?"

"Hey, Sissy." He eyed me. "Plumbing out again?"

"Mr. Murdock was . . . just leaving."

Jamie's mouth twisted into an ugly grin. "Job's

over, pal. Whatever it was that brought you, the road's that way."

I turned away from him and spoke to Barb Duke. "Cindy wanted me to wait."

"No, Mr., ah, Murdock. I think it's better if you leave."

Out of the corner of my eye I saw Jamie reach back into the Mercedes. When he straightened up, he was holding a shiny black Ninja stick, maybe eighteen inches long, with a leather thong at one end. Jamie was beefy in the jowls. He outweighed me at least eighty pounds. His hair was jet black, while mine was showing some gray. He swaggered like a bully and I was to be his morning workout.

He slapped the stick against his fat palm. "So. I count to five while you start for your Chevy. One."

I thought of the Beretta, locked in the glove box. "It's a Ford."

"Hey. Two for the Ford."

"You're James Duke, aren't you? Of Duke Construction?"

"Hey, Sissy. Surprise. The bozo can read. That's three, bozo."

I looked around for a weapon, but saw nothing. "And your brother-in-law is Marvin Holly?"

"My ex-brother-in-law. By a dozen years, hey, Sissy?" He took two steps away from the car. "Four. Time's about gone, bozo. Better split while the splitting's good."

"I'm tracing Mr. Holly, as a witness in connection with an accident at Xanadu Mall."

He stood fifteen feet away, three long steps, five short ones. *Slap, slap* went the Ninja stick. "Five."

Barb Duke spoke from my left. "Mr. Murdock, you'd better leave now, please, before there's trouble."

He cut his eyes over at his sister. "I get it now. Little Cyn-Cyn's been hitching again. The bozo brought her home."

"Jamie, please. Not here."

He took another step toward me, closing the distance. "I'll ask the bozo. You drove her home, right?"

I nodded. My head hammered. How would I parry his attack?

His eyes were narrower. A drop of drool appeared at the right corner of his mouth. "You picked her up on the road, Mr. Bozo. It didn't take much to see she was underage, did it?" He waggled the stick at me, pointing at my eyes, one-two, as if he planned to poke them out. Then he turned to his sister again. "Let's bring her out, Sissy. Ask her what the bozo did to her in the truck there."

"She's fine, Jamie. Nothing hap—"

"Look, Mr. Duke. Your niece was at the mall, hunting for her father. That's how we met. I'm hunting for him too. I was heading this way, so I offered her a lift home."

"Call the police, Sissy," Jamie growled. "I bet this bozo's got a record."

Jamie was a creep. I didn't think he'd call the cops. I decided not to mention the name of Webby Smith.

"Okay," I said. "I'll go."

And it was time to go. Technically, I was trespassing. Jamie had ordered me away. The law said I had to go. But there was something rotten here in Duke territory. You could smell it filling the air with stink. I didn't like leaving Cindy. I didn't want to tangle with Uncle Jamie, his bullying bulk, and his black Ninja stick.

Then the front door opened and Cindy burst through, brushing past the maid, coming to a stop as she saw what was going on in her driveway. She caught my eye and shook her head, meaning there had been no word from her dad.

"Mom," Cindy said. "What—?"

"Cindy, dear. Go inside." Barb Duke grabbed her daughter and shoved her back toward the door. Cindy yelled. And Jamie Duke chose that minute to charge, grunting with the effort of getting his bulk in motion, lunging, all two hundred and eighty pounds of him, cursing me as he swung the stick at my head.

I pivoted, alarm bells ringing, *ding, ding,* and waited for him in a half crouch, arms out in a karate stance, hands open and on edge, knowing if I hit him the hand would swell up and I'd be married to an ice pack until Christmas. As the fear rose in his eyes I feinted with my left, watching him break stride and lose his momentum, stepping in close, crowding him while giving him my face as a target, seeing the triumph rise in his eyes, noting the white knuckles tight on the black stick, timing the arc of the swing as he brought it up over his shoulder like a Cro-Magnon club, and then sliding out of the way as he brought it down to crunch my face. I felt the wind of its passing, heard it catch the zipper on my parka, a small ripping sound. I stabbed his shin with my boot toe, making him grunt with surprised pain, and then as he fell sideways hammering his ear with the side of my hand, the pain ripping up through my tendons because I'd put a little more into it than was necessary, and then dancing out of the way, hearing a woman's bright scream cut the air as Uncle Jamie went down like a bull in the ring. Matt Murdock, *torero.*

The big man hit the driveway, making the ground shake. Barb Duke rushed past me to cradle her brother's head in her lap, the loose-fitting sweatshirt falling open to reveal the fact that she was tanned a long way down. "Jamie, Jamie," she crooned. Then she glared at me. "Get the hell away from us!"

The maid had vanished back into the house, where she was, no doubt, calling the cops. My hand felt like I'd made contact with a slab of concrete instead of Uncle Jamie's ear. I looked at Cindy, shrugged, and headed for the pickup. Cindy hurried over, her face working with sympathy. "Need a driver?" she asked.

The dilemma again. She was fourteen. She had to stay at home. "Thanks, kid. Now that you're home, you better stick." I wrote my number on the back of someone else's business card and handed it to her.

She looked at the number and then glanced over at her mother and her uncle. "Did you tell them?"

"I said we'd met at the mall. We were both hunting for your dad."

She gave me a half smile. "Thanks," she said.

Over the top of her head, I saw Uncle Jamie sit up, with help from his sister. A thin trickle of blood ran down the side of his head, staining his white shirt collar. The maid rushed out, carrying a wet washcloth, but when Barb tried to use it on Jamie, he snatched it away and held it over his wound.

"I'm pressing charges, bozo!" he called. "You can't mess with James Duke and get away with it!"

"I'll keep in touch," I said to Cindy. I climbed behind the wheel, started the Ford, and felt a knifing pain in my hand as I shoved the gears into reverse, and then I was out in the narrow street, clutching and shifting and feeling like a medieval knight in shining armor who had just aced a fire-breathing dragon in full view of his smiling lady fair. I swallowed some Arnica, to take down the pain.

In the rearview mirror, I spotted Cindy on the road, hands stuck in her pockets. Good luck, kid.

By the time I reached the gatehouse, the hand felt

better. Beef-Head the guard was a dark shape behind the windows. I parked the pickup and walked to the door and looked in. Beef-Head was on the phone. He saw me, then turned his back and went on talking. I rapped on the glass and he made me wait. It was raining again, a light coastal mist drifting down, cooling the emotions. After a couple of minutes, he slid the door open. "Help, you, sir?" he asked.

I flashed my license. "You sure can, Mr. Woolford. I'm a private investigator working on a case and I was hoping you'd give me a peek at your entry roster."

"Sorry. That's confidential. Even if you're a real cop, it would take a court order. What we got here's a private community. What that means is, people like their privacy." He paused to hook his thumbs inside his belt, gunfighter style. "Now, was there something else, sir?"

I grinned, peaceful Murdock, and tried again. "That would have been Tuesday afternoon, around three-thirty, maybe four. The party I'm interested in drove a Chevy, brown, eighty-seven. He was a mid-size man in his mid-forties. His name was Marvin Holly. Were you on duty then?"

"Tuesday, let me see. Who was on Tuesday, in the afternoon, was it? Yeah. I was working that shift. Didn't see anything like that, nossir."

"You were the only guard on?"

He took in air to expand his expansive chest. "Read my lips. No car like that came through."

"And I can't check the roster?"

"Correct. You can't check my roster."

"Marvin Holly is the father of Cynthia Duke. She was with me a half hour ago."

He took his time checking the clipboard. "That would be number eighteen." He held out a hand. "Could I have your transit pass, sir? It's yellow, for visibility. We have to account for all vehicles at the end of our shift."

I turned on my heel and started back for the pickup.

"Sir?" Woolford called. "Sir?"

I opened the door and climbed behind the wheel and started up. I drove in low gear over to where Woolford stood, his chest puffed up like a recruit on parade, and then I handed him the yellow transit pass and went down the ramp onto the Coast Highway.

Back at my place on the pier, there were four phone messages waiting on my machine. The first one was from Wally St. Moritz. He was in bed with a cold. Dorene Wilson, his current female interest, was in charge of Christmas dinner. She would be calling me with a list of errands.

The second call was from Senator Jane. Her voice had an edge that grated. She wanted a report.

The third call was from Doug Blaisdell, an old buddy from Vietnam, reminding me of our dinner date tonight. Doug, nicknamed "the Blazer," was the founding president of CEO Security, Inc. Doug was a southerner from South Carolina, a rich kid, a track star, an honors student. He came from a long line of soldiers who had attended the Citadel and was on his way to brigadier when he'd decided to resign his commission and go into the bodyguard business. "Foxy, old son," his voice drawled. "Don't you forget our date, now. The Côte d'Azur at six. Tahitian Room. Try a uniform that won't spook the fillies, hear?"

The fourth call was from Cindy. "Mr. Murdock, thanks for bringing me home. My uncle's gone now, but boy, was he mad about his ear. Please keep trying to find my daddy. The number here is 555-4000. It's unlisted, but I thought you should have it. I have to go now. Bye."

I played the tape again. When it was finished, I made a call to Scottsdale School in Arizona and reached a recording. The school was closed for the holidays, the recording said. Please leave a message at the end of the beep. If you are a parent, or in case of an emergency, call this number.

When I tried the emergency number, I reached a security outfit in downtown Scottsdale. They were not authorized to give out any information on any student enrolled at the school. The school was due to open again the second week of January. They gave me the name of the Dean of Students and I hung up before I could ask how their weather was out there.

I poured myself a glass of Mondavi red and brought the soup in from the workroom. I scraped off the slabs of grease and put Cal on the fire to heat. I chopped carrots and white cabbage and half a leek and a turnip. I added another cup of Mondavi red. When the soup was steaming hot, I added the carrots and set the timer for five minutes. When the timer rang, I added the other vegetables and opened up the cans of beans. One can of white navy beans, one of bumpy garbanzos, and two of red kidneys. Kidneys and cabbage give my soup that distinctive minestrone taste. The beans thickened the soup. I adjusted the seasonings and was about to add three dollops of red wine vinegar when I heard footsteps on my stairs.

6

I opened the kitchen drawer where I keep the Colt Diamondback. I turned off the flame under Cal and moved the bottle of Mondavi red to the floor, and then I moved to the wall beside the door and looked out through my special inspection hole. My visitor was a lady.

She was slightly built, five-three or so, wearing tan corduroy slacks, a cable-knit sweater, and a matching muffler. The tails of a khaki raincoat, it looked like a Burberry, were flapping in the breeze. Her hair was wet, her cheeks red from the cold, her glasses dimpled with raindrops.

Miss Mousey.

Keeping the Colt at my side out of sight, I opened the door to her knock.

"Oh?" she said. "You're home?"

"Amanda, right?"

She nodded. "Good memory. Yes. Amanda True."

"Come on in out of the rain, Amanda True."

"Gosh." She peered past me. "It's okay? You're not expecting someone? I don't mean to pry, only—" She stopped. Her chest was heaving, maybe from the climb, maybe from approaching my door. "Oh, heck."

She entered in a rush, did a quick little twirl, took in the room, the soup on the stove, the homemade entertainment center, the door to the bedroom, the 180-degree view of the beach, Punker's Strip, the pier, the gray-blue Pacific, turned back to me, her eyes widening when she saw the gun in my hand, putting one hand to her throat, then the other hand, sticking out her tongue, rolling her eyes and saying: "Don't shoot! I'm an innocent Bryn Mawr lit major! Don't shoot, please!"

A change of clothes, a walk on the beach, some time away from her boss, and Amanda True took on a new personality. Her face was mobile as a gamine's and she had a sense of humor. I laid the gun on the table by the door.

"What is that smell?" She lifted Cal's lid and smelled. "Mmm. It's wonderful!"

"Minestrone."

"Homemade?"

"Sure. Want some?"

"You cook?"

"Soldier's trick."

"Oh. I'd love a taste!" The wide eyes again. The delighted face. "Just a taste, and then I'm off."

The soup still needed five minutes over a hot fire. Without removing her Burberry, Amanda walked around the room, checking out the photos on my wall, nodding. I poured her a glass of wine, which she sipped daintily. I crushed some garlic and made a paste using raw butter. I sliced some French bread and spread on the paste and sprinkled cheese on top and put the bread in the broiler.

"Can I help?"

I showed her the silverware drawer. By the time
the soup was hot, she had the table set. We sat down
across from each other at my kitchen table overlooking the beach. She still wore the Burberry and muffler, eating fast, quick bites, tearing the garlic bread
with her sharp chipmunk teeth. After the first bowl,
she sighed, removed the Burberry, unswirled the
muffler, and drained her wineglass. I refilled her
bowl and her glass. When I returned to the table, she
said, "This soup is wonderful. Do you always greet
guests with a loaded pistol?"

"Only at Christmas."

She smiled knowingly. "Crazy Christmas, right?"

"Right."

"Madness on the highways, stress at the hearth.
Have you found anything?"

"Senator Jane does that."

"Does what?"

"Shifts topics in the middle."

"That's why we get along, Jane and I. So, any
progress?"

"Is that why you're here?"

"Oh, no. I needed some R and R. Heather's still in a
coma and Jane's found a private hospital here in
Newport Beach and she's pulling strings to get
Heather moved. I had a couple of hours, so I took
off."

"Is that good for Heather? Moving her, I mean."

"That's what they're deciding now. Jane phoned a
friend of hers, a specialist at Baylor Med in Houston.
She had him speak to the doctor in charge."

"Dr. Ruffin?" I asked. "Or Dr. Prather?"

Amanda shook her head. "There's a new one on
the case—Dr. Arfazi—Egyptian, I think. Quite handsome." She blushed. "Jane was very distressed about

it. He seems competent enough. He says he'll bring fresh eyes to the case."

"Doctor number three," I said. "Musical chairs at El Toro General."

"They say it's the holidays. Anyway, I was walking along the beach and when it started raining I stopped downstairs at Leo's Café for a coffee and asked the proprietor if he knew you, and he directed me here, grinning, I might add, from ear to ear. I took it to mean you are a man of many conquests."

"Leo's Italian. He exaggerates."

"It's so lovely here. And who would have thought a man like yourself would cook."

"It's cheaper than marriage. Fewer strings. Less heartache."

"So, anything new on the case?"

"Might have a witness."

"Really?"

I ladled more soup into my bowl, took it back to the table, and sat down. "The trail is thin. The minute I get something solid, I'll let you know."

"So I shouldn't tell Jane, right?"

"I was hoping you'd say that."

She finished off her second bowl, put down her spoon, sighed, patted her tummy twice, and puffed out her cheeks to show how full she was. "The reason I came, I wanted to talk about Jane, tell you about her, where she's coming from."

"What about her?"

"Well, you got to her, last night, in a very big way. It wasn't anything you said, exactly, it was more the fact that you were *there,* a presence. Jane's awfully stage conscious. She adores control. Without it, she speeds along too fast. She thought she'd use you to get inside the law enforcement apparatus, but one look told her that couldn't be. Then you came on so, well, frontally, and that made her blow sky-high."

"I wasn't trying to come on at all."

"Of course. That's what made it so perfect. Jane's amazingly strong. So are you. The clash was inevitable."

"You like her, don't you?"

"Oh, yes. Like. Love. Respect. She took me under her wing when I was fresh out of Bryn Mawr, an English lit major with a busy first novel and a grocery sack full of rejection slips. She gave me a job and taught me about poise and the subtext of backroom politics."

"Is she liberal or conservative?"

Amanda True thought about that one before replying. "Neither. And both. She's a Texas Democrat. She's very tough and she's hurting for her state and her constituents."

"Are we leading up to why Heather left home?"

Amanda nodded. "You don't miss much, do you?"

I clinked glasses with her. Her cheeks were flushed and the wine was giving me a nice buzz. "Neither do you."

"After you left last night, with the professor—what a nice man he is, those sad old eyes, reminds me of my dad—anyway, Jane was furious after you left. She felt physically bruised, she said, physically assaulted. All she'd wanted, she said, was for someone to open a door, just one lousy little door, and she would do the rest. She's used to making her own deals, her own connections. She had no intention of hiring a peeper —that's her word, not mine—and especially not one who would insult her with every breath and every gesture."

"So you intervened," I said.

Amanda nodded so vigorously that her curls shook.

"She needs people. She doesn't know it, of course. Thinks she can go it alone, do everything herself. Under stress, she gets very clutchy, like a mother hen gathering her chicks. When Heather's home, she takes the brunt of Jane's mothering. But with Heather lying there in a coma, it falls on me."

"So you decided to spread the stress."

"The professor said it. This is your turf, your territory. I suggested a trial period, a test. Jane decided on three days, probably because Christmas made a convenient deadline. I knew you'd find something. Now you have."

"Maybe."

"Did you know Jane was in line for a cabinet seat?"

"Which cabinet?"

"The one that advises the President," she said carefully. "In the White House in our nation's capital."

"She'd make a hell of a secretary of defense. Not so great at State."

Amanda True laughed. "You're joking. No. Secretary of education. The one that they reserve for members of the fairer sex. Surely you read about it."

"Sorry. I keep my reading to the sports pages. How close was she?"

"Runner-up. The current appointee's presently out of favor, so she's being considered again."

"Does she want it?"

"She hates leaving Texas, with the economy and all. But there are things she could do in Washington."

"Rock some boats, you mean?"

"Set things right. The world's in a mess. Jane wants to heal things."

"Would you go with her?"

Amanda True nodded. "We make a super team."

I pushed away from the table. The pain in my hand

was back, so I popped in more Arnica. By the time we had the table cleared, the hand felt better. "Tell me about Heather," I said.

"She's a tricky one. Her eyesight's fine, but she insists on wearing glasses. She's bright, manipulative, confused. At fourteen, she lost her maidenhead. At fifteen, she was in trouble with the law."

"The law. What for?"

"Stealing car stereos. Most of the victims were moneyed friends of Jane's. Heather studied the scene —I think you'd call it 'cased'—made sure the coast was clear. Then her pals committed the actual thefts."

"Is that the reason for the private school?"

"Yes. Things have gone swimmingly until this holiday. Her grades have been up. No scrapes with the law. Jane was planning on a warm, homey Christmas. I remember waiting at the airport with Jane, waiting and waiting, and then Jane taking my notebook to start writing out names of people to alert. That was bad. The next day was worse."

"Any specific reason for running away?"

Amanda True sighed. "I could be wrong, but I think she's got a boyfriend."

"Have you told Jane?"

"It's only a guess."

"How about the San Diego thing?"

She shook her head. "Anything's possible. Heather's a Gemini, like her mom. One side of her is stable. The other is wacko adventurer. Girls that age, they sometimes—" She looked at my kitchen clock. "Oops. Time for me to scoot." She got up and opened the front door to check the weather, then closed it again while she wrapped the muffler around her throat. I helped her with the Burberry. "You're a nice man, Mr. Murdock. Jane likes you a lot. Know how I can tell?"

"She's pinned up my mug shot to use as a dart board."

"Not really. She's staring into space a lot. When your name comes up, she turns away." She buttoned the Burberry. "Know what that means? For you, I mean?"

"Tell me."

She smiled behind the glasses and I wondered what her novel was about and how she handled being rejected. "When someone likes you, it means you have a connection and an obligation."

"To do what?"

"Why, to take care," she said. "Thank you for the soup."

And then she was out the door, tripping across the porch and down the stairs.

After she'd gone, the place felt empty. I washed the dishes. I phoned Webby Smith. He had nothing new on the hit-and-run. I phoned the hospital, where they told me Jane had left a message to phone her at eight this evening. There was a seven-digit number and an extension, 745. I dialed Oscar Smith, the man on the Xanadu switchboard. His phone still did not answer. I phoned Marvin Holly in Madison and got his recording again. Twilight gathered darkly on the beach. My quest was at a standstill. I finished the last of the Mondavi red and took a nap.

At six-eighteen I parked the Ford in the lot of the Côte d'Azur Hotel and headed in through the soft drizzling rain to meet Blazer Blaisdell. I was dressed to impress, semi-new Levi jeans with a sharp laundry crease, an off-white shirt from Malaysia, my Eddie Bauer safari jacket, and new cowboy boots I had picked up on sale working a case in Texas. I was not wearing a tie. Ties were for CEOs, cops on the take, politicians, TV preachers, CIA guys, FBI guys, and door-to-door Bible salesmen costumed to look like either FBI or CIA.

The maître d', a suave, dark-faced penguin in a form-fitting tuxedo, gave me the snide once-over and was about to direct me to the rear entrance for deliveries when I dropped the Blazer's name. A miracle occurred. Gears meshed silently into place and I was escorted with fanfare and bustle to the Tahitian Room, a restaurant with fake island decor where the entrées started at a hundred bucks a pop.

"M'sieu Blaisdell," whined the maître d', "your party is here, sir."

The Blazer jumped up when he saw me, breaking off his conversation with two *Playboy* playmate types so he could pump my hand and slap me on the back. "Thank you, Roberto. Stand by for orders, would you? Foxy, how the hell are you? You look wonderful. Not a day older, son. Not a goddamn day."

Blazer had lost weight since I'd seen him last. He still wore his hair short. There was more gray than I'd remembered and the high Indian cheekbones—Blazer claimed Cherokee blood in his family history—were more prominent. For the president of CEO Security, Inc., I'd expected a coat and tie, but Blazer had fooled me and donned a flight jacket of soft brown leather, epaulets riding the shoulders, the waist nipped slightly, like a thinner John Wayne in the Flying Tigers movie. The shirt was soft, my guess was Egyptian cotton. The trousers were cavalry twill. Blazer always wore boots, dress Wellingtons, imported from a bootmaker in London.

"God damn, boy, it's good to see you again, shake

your hand. Here, son, pull up a chair and meet these pretty lassies."

I felt the edge of sarcasm in his voice, bright and commanding, like a razor. The blonde was Pattie. The brunette was Karen. They were handsome fillies, all right, mid-twenties, expensively costumed. Both carried those compact evening purses, the kind with the gleaming metal and the shiny beads.

Pattie, the blonde, wore a green dress with a deep V neckline that rendered a brassiere useless. Her hair fell just below the shoulder. An old-fashioned girl with a Hollywood smile and a peachy Coppertone tan. Standing there, erect as a British color sergeant, Blazer let me know without a word or the flicker of an eyelash that the blonde was his for the evening.

In contrast to the blonde, the brunette, Karen, my lady of the evening, had creamy white skin. Her dress was a form-fitting cocktail sheath, black and strapless, with just enough body in the material to make you guess about her underwear. I liked that, keeping the mystery alive. Her eyes were blue and her lipstick was a pale gloss. "Hello," she said. "You must be Foxy."

"That's me." I sat down.

Blazer grinned, then raised his hand to signal the maître d', who appeared, followed by a tuxedoed waiter, as if they'd been beamed down from the USS *Enterprise.* "Roberto, Verdi awaits and we-uns is in a kind of rush. How about some of your fastest service?"

Roberto nodded like a man facing the firing squad. We ordered drinks, martinis for the fillies, bourbon and branch water for Blazer, a beer for me. Blazer, who was not a beer drinker, insisted on Beck's.

"Sorry I was late."

"No problem, Foxy. We've got tickets for the Verdi,

over at the P.A.C. Curtain at eight-thirty." He checked his watch, a chrome chronometer from Switzerland that he'd been wearing that first day when we met in the jungle. "So we can be fashionably late at nine. Hope you can join us."

"Maybe."

"Maybe?" His eyebrows arched.

"I'm working, Blazer. Got to check in with the client."

"Front and center, troop. Front and center."

The drinks arrived. Roberto handed menus around. With a perfect French accent, the blonde ordered beef bourguignon. Blazer ordered Idaho pheasant. The brunette, a vegetarian, ordered a Mandarin dish. My choice was poulet Provençal, from the low end of the menu, at ninety-five dollars. With a hiss, Roberto hustled the waiter away.

"All right, Foxy," the brunette said. "Douglas made us wait until you arrived before he'd tell us about your name."

The blonde chimed in. "He christened you, he said. A religious ceremony in the jungle that made you blood brothers. But he wouldn't say why. He also called you a hound dog."

"A term of endearment," Blazer said. "Foxy is my dark side of the moon."

The brunette held her hands out facing me, thumbs touching, index fingers pointing up at ninety degrees to make a television director's frame. She framed me first, then Blazer. "Not twins, exactly. How about the flip side of an old LP record?"

"Karen, honey." The blonde was smiling. "I think Foxy needs checking out."

"I'm willing," the brunette said. "And able."

The scene had me blushing. "Blazer," I said. "God damn you."

"You ladies should know, we both dress to the left."

I felt the brunette's hand on my leg. "That will have to be verified. My, my."

"Foxy looks heavier," the blonde said, squeezing Blazer's arm. "You'd have to pork up, hon."

A waiter set Blazer's drink down. Eyes glittering, he grabbed the glass and took a long swallow. "Best bourbon this side of a Kentucky distillery, ladies. A toast to America's heroes." Blazer held out his glass and the four of us clinked. "To heroes," he said. "To heroes and the scintillating damosels who send them into the infernal wasted lands to do heroic deeds."

I took a sip and watched while Blazer set the scene, a rice paddy in the Mekong, his troop under fire, men falling, the enemy getting reinforced with Soviet armaments, the bugs, the blood, the rats, his topkick getting killed by an antipersonnel device, no artillery support, no response from chopper command when he called in his position. "And then," Blazer said, "who should arrive but Foxy, with his bully boys, a tiny armed band of *guerrilleros*—pardon my Spanish, old son—to quell the dastardly foe and set us free." Blazer drained his bourbon and signaled for a refill. He was drinking too much. "There we were, a hundred boys from Georgia and New York and Minnesota, about to become another MIA mystery statistic, and Foxy does the impossible, cutting through the swamp and coming up behind old Charley, raking his yellow ass with fire and—"

The food arrived, plates steaming under those fancy chrome covers, and Blazer broke off his story long enough to order more drinks. The waiters, two of them, walked away. "Now, where was I?"

"Killing Charley," the blonde said, scooting close, pressing her arm and one pneumatic breast into

Blazer. "Getting out of there. Saving your command. Christening Foxy."

"Yeah." He launched into a description of the firefight, embellishing it, making it better than I remembered, longer, more heroic, and three times as fierce. The brunette brushed my leg with hers underneath the table, gave me a warm smile, and grazed my leg with one fingernail. Near the climax of his telling, on his third bourbon now, Blazer became the hero of the story, and I wondered how often he'd gone through this scenario, building himself up with pretty women he didn't know.

The ladies had the appetites of healthy young animals. I had no trouble eating my poulet. The way Blazer picked at his food showed me how he stayed thin. While I ate, he asked me questions about my work. Where did I find clients? How much did I make? What cases was I working on now?

Leaving out names, I told him a little about the Xanadu hit-and-run and my search for a witness. He seemed interested, but not curious. He knew people in the sheriff's department, he said, and would make some calls tomorrow. The brunette kept brushing up against me, light touch of her elbow, easy fluid movement of her leg against mine, no pressure, no insistent lingering, the whole act coming about as if by accident.

At eight, I excused myself to call Senator Jane. There was no answer at room 745, but when I queried the operator she gave me this message: "Message to Murdock from Xanadu on your machine six P.M. Signed J."

To pluck the message off my ancient machine, I'd have to go back home. As I hung up, I recalled a richer time in my life, when I'd had a real live person at an answering service, and I vowed that a remote-access machine would be my next purchase, after I'd paid my bills.

My second call was to the gatehouse at Jamaica Cove. I identified myself as Lt. Webster Smith of the Laguna police and asked for Woolford.

"I'm sorry," the guard said. "Who did you say?"

"Lieutenant Smith, Laguna Beach PD. I'm the watch commander. What's your name?"

"Jackson, George T. What's up, Lieutenant?"

"Holiday gang," I said. "They've gone over the fence at Corona Del Mar, Crystal Cove, and the Irvine Cove, knocking out the alarm systems, hitting the houses for Christmas treasures. Looks like they're working their way down toward your territory there at Jamaica. Wanted to alert you."

"Let me make a note."

"What's your strength on this shift, Jackson?"

"Two of us, sir. We rotate on the gate and the patrol vehicle."

"Hour on, hour off?"

"Yessir."

"When's your shift over?"

"Overtime tonight. Six A.M."

"Let me make a note, trooper. What's your partner's name?"

"Allen."

"Look, Jackson," I said. "We've got hot info coming down the wire every minute. You alert your partner. Anything breaks tonight, I'll get back to you."

"Roger, Lieutenant," he said briskly.

"Be ready to roll," I said.

"Red alert," he said.

As I hung up the phone and started for the men's room, a college boy stumbled past me, smelling of alcohol and rancid sweat. Behind him, to my right, I heard laughter. The college boy pushed on the door at the same time it opened and he collided with a man coming out. "Hey!" the man said. The college boy stared at him, clapped a hand over his mouth, and threw up, splashing the man with vomit. More laughter behind me as three of his pals came up to grab their buddy by the arms. Two wore letter sweaters, CSUF on their beefy chests. The third, a no-neck about the size of Uncle Jamie, wore a corduroy jacket with leather elbow patches. College jocks, out for a good time at Christmas. Their eyes were mean with drink. "Let's hurry it up," one said. "And get back to the great nookie hunt."

The man cursed them. "Crazy kids." And went back inside. I followed.

Inside, the kid who had thrown up leaned over the lavatory, splashing water on his face with one cupped palm. The victim of the vomiting was wiping at his suit coat with a wet paper towel. One of the lads in a CSUF sweater gave me the eye and whispered to his pals, who smirked, their comment, no doubt, on my choice of clothes for the evening. I used the facilities. The door opened and another college boy came in. Red face, ugly grin, weight around two-thirty, the kind of guy who bounces people around for fun. "Hey, Chuckie," he said to the vomiter. "A guy who can't hold his booze is a pussy."

"Lay off, Groucho," said the vomiter.

I zipped up and started out. The two lads at the door were slow in getting out of the way. "Excuse me," I said.

"Hey, dad," one said. "Excuse *us!*"

They made room for me, just enough. When I got through, my hands were clenching and the hairs on the back of my neck were stiff. Yeah, it's great to be young and full of your own piss.

Blazer was checking his chronometer when I got

back to the table. A fresh bourbon sat before him. He was finishing up a story: ". . . so I took him out for a gin sling and christened him Foxy Murdock, named for Francis Marion, born 1732, died 1795, buried under a stone along the edge of the swamp of the national forest that bears his name. Isn't that right, Foxy?"

"Fought the redcoats to a standstill," I said, "and then vanished into the swamp."

"A toast to Foxy," Blazer said, in an overloud voice.

We drank. After a couple of questions, the ladies excused themselves and hurried off to powder their noses. People at neighboring tables turned to watch. The blonde's dress was backless and her bare brown back gleamed dangerously.

Blazer raised his bourbon. "You need a refill, Foxy."

"No more for me. Got to work."

"Crudball hours you keep, old son." He drank. "What do you think of your date?"

"Expensive," I said. "And beautiful."

Blazer leaned toward me, his eyes narrowed. "Let's drink to us, Foxy. Let's drink to friendship and old times and women shared."

"These two in particular?" I said.

"Huh," he grunted. "Just a little test drive, Foxy. They've had their tune-ups. They're both clean, and there are the medical records to prove it. Yours is better in the rack, but mine's, well . . . she caters to me."

"I'm on a tight budget, Blazer."

"My treat."

I shook my head. "Don't buy women for me, okay?"

"Remember that line from Philip Roth in *Letting Go*? 'I am a man yet.'"

"Sorry. I didn't read it."

"Read it," he said. "We've got to define and redefine, Foxy, and females are here for that purpose." He slammed his hand on my shoulder. "I've missed you, Foxy. Missed your humor, your tightassed ways." He gave me a brotherly squeeze and I remembered the times we'd had in Vietnam, in the jungle, in the bars along Rue Catinat. Then he grinned. "Well, they're paid for. You don't want in, that means a ménage for Dougie."

The ladies came back, looking flustered. In the foyer, I saw one of the college boys handing money to the maître d'. "Something wrong?" Blazer asked.

"Just mashers," the brunette said. "Boy-bees with the hots. Pattie draws them like flies."

Blazer's eyes narrowed into gun slits. His nostrils flared. I helped the brunette into her wrap and we started out, Blazer and the blonde in the lead.

"You're not coming, are you?" the brunette said. "To the Verdi? And then after?"

"Got work to do."

She brushed me with her hip and put her hand on my arm. "Can't change your mind?"

"Not tonight."

"I'm sorry," she said.

"Me too," I lied.

"How about later? After work? Or tomorrow? Christmas Day is wide open."

I could take her to Wally's house for smoked Christmas turkey. "Maybe."

She slipped a business card into my hand. It had her name, Karen Hix, and a phone number with a Los Angeles area code. "I'm a pro. I know you know, so I want you to know this is not business. It's purely personal, between us."

"Thanks. I'm flattered."

"You should be. It doesn't happen for me much, but tonight, for some reason, I—"

Up ahead, Groucho and two of his jock friends had stepped in front of Blazer and the blonde, blocking their way.

"That's them," the brunette said. "The mashers."

Blazer had stopped. The blonde still held his arm.

"If I give you a push," I told the brunette, "get clear."

She gulped, and let go of my arm.

We came up as Groucho was saying he'd like a dance with Pattie. ". . . just one quick dance, dad, we're old friends, haven't seen one another since like high school, isn't that right, doll?"

"I never saw you before in my life," Pattie said. She turned to Blazer. "Can we go now?"

"Of course, my dear," Blazer said as he hit Groucho in the nose, pivoting nicely, driving up with the heel of his hand, using the tensile force of hips and knees and shoulders and torso to get everything into the shot.

We were trapped for a moment in dead time, that moment just before the pebble lands in the water and the ripples start, and then Groucho grabbed his face and screamed and a college boy made a lunge for Blazer, who stepped aside like a bullfighter, clipping the kid on the back of the neck. The blonde screamed, going to her stockinged knees as Blazer shoved her aside. The brunette, heeding my warning, had already shimmied out of the way. I collided with a college boy before he grabbed Blazer from behind. His breath stank of alcohol and after-dinner mints. I belted him in the gut and he went down.

Someone grabbed me from behind. Strong muscles, all that flexibility of green youth. I twisted, jabbing up with an elbow, hearing the hollow sound as I caught his chin. He grunted with pain as I turned and grabbed a handful of sweater, using my hip as a pivot point as I slung him away from me onto the jade-green tiles. He skidded into a wall, cracking a vase, and I turned to rescue Blazer, who was just finishing up and did not need my help.

Groucho lay on the tiles, hands covering his face and nose. Blood ran down the side of his face. The vomiter was crawling away from Blazer, who was poised like the king of kung fu, hands on edge. Five college boys against two old men. Four were down. The only one left standing now tried a swing, which Blazer deflected, dealing out two punches to the kid's abdomen, *pop, pop,* and then two more to the face, the kid wobbling now, hating the pain, fear widening his eyes as he backed away, taking Blazer's kick on the leg, going down to one knee, arms up for protection.

"Hey, mister," the kid said. "I surrender."

But Blazer kept after him, the chrome chronometer flickering in the warm restaurant light, chopping and knifing with murderous accuracy, cutting the kid down with a methodical overkill that knew no stopping.

"Blazer?" I called. "Cool it!"

He whirled on me, his eyes glowing with the fire of battle. "No retreat, Captain," he growled. "Take no prisoners. Pass the word, you hear?"

The blonde tried to lead him out, but he shoved her away and tossed some bills to Roberto, the maître d', and then marched past the gawkers into the rain. When we caught up to him, he was standing with hands on hips, his lean face staring up at the dark sky. He handed over his keys and sent the ladies on to the car, and then he got to the reason for the evening.

"Come to work for me, Foxy. I'm expanding the

office here in Newport and I need someone I can depend on. A hundred grand a year to start, a company car, expense account. You'll head up the operation here in Orange County—that includes San Diego County—with seven operatives reporting to you. The perks are better than fantasy." And here he used his thumb to indicate the ladies in the car.

"Would I have to wear a tie?"

Blazer's laugh had a ragged edge. "I liked the way you backed me up in there, Foxy. No bullshit. No committee meetings. No need to radio the base for assistance." He grabbed my arm and stared into my face. "I need you on board. Say you'll do it."

The money was a surprise. More than I'd make in three years. What did Blazer really want? "When would I start?"

"Now," he said. "Tonight."

"Got a meeting with a client. How's tomorrow?"

"You disappoint me, Foxy." Headlights rammed through the night, throwing us both into silhouette against the wall of the Côte d'Azur. Above us, the outdoor elevator whispered up the side of the wall. He bopped me on the bicep. "Forget I said that. Tomorrow's all right, old chum. If you change your mind and want to join the fun, I'm at the Xanadu. Suite four."

The car, a new black BMW with windows tinted midnight, slid to a stop. The window rolled down and the brunette said: "Going our way, soldier?"

Blazer chuckled, held out his hand, and we shook. "Be a man, Foxy. Remember Phil Roth. Be a mensch."

I watched the BMW pull away. A client of mine owned a similar model. With the dollar weak against the mark, Blazer's black car would retail at fifty-five thousand, maybe higher. Nice wheels. Glitzy ladies.

Hundred-dollar entrées at fancy restaurants. I was working for a kid who carried more cash than I did. Maybe I should think about Blazer's offer.

I jogged to the Ford. As I was driving out past the entrance to the Côte d'Azur, an ambulance arrived and two men hauled out a stretcher on wheels and hurried inside, to tend the wounded.

7

The message from Senator Jane was waiting for me on my answering machine when I reached home at nine-forty. Her voice, slurred by alcohol, said: "I called for a report, preferably written. I know you've found something. I'll be at the hospital until ten-thirty or so, and then Amanda will relieve me. I have some ideas I'd like to kick around. Could you come to the hotel? Room seven four five."

I ground coffee beans and put the teakettle on to boil. I splashed cold water on my face. I rummaged in the closet until I found my police officer's uniform from my days in Hollenbeck Division, up in wonderful Los Angeles. The pants were tight in the seat, thighs, and crotch. The blouse buttoned, but with care. The billed cap—it said LAPD—was too obvious. I posed in front of the mirror wearing the uniform, and over it my yellow police rain jacket. How many cops these days wore beards? I removed the rain jacket and strapped on the policeman's harness. Equipment for a young man, a hard guy. The holster was cowboy. So were the little boxes built for cop survival: a spare clip, the walkie-talkie, the notebook to calm the witnesses.

I rummaged in the gun drawer until I found the fake police shield, Mexican silver, slightly tarnished. On the front there was a peace officer's star and pale blue letters that said BAT MASTERSON, SHERIFF OF LINCOLN COUNTY. On the back, in tiny letters, it said HECHO EN MEXICO.

Dressed, a steaming cup of coffee in my hand, I made two phone calls. The first one was to Wally St. Moritz, and Dorene Wilson answered. Wally was watching television, she said.

"That's okay, Dorene. I need a favor."

Dorene was a graduate student in philosophy at UC-Irvine. She'd been married and divorced. Now she worked for Wally in the Saintly Silver Surfer, downstairs. "Okay."

I checked the time: nine fifty-nine. "Thanks. At ten-thirty, make a call to this number"—I gave her the number of the gatehouse at Jamaica Cove— "identify yourself as Mrs. Mather, up on the hill. Tell them prowlers are in the house and to get a car up there fast."

She repeated the instructions back to me. "Are we making an action flick, or what?"

"The second favor," I said. "Wait two minutes. Have Wally call the same number, identify himself as Sergeant Stone, of the Laguna Beach PD, and alert them."

"Alert them about what?"

"Break-ins," I said. "An officer has been dispatched."

"What if the line's busy? What if we can't get through?"

"Keep trying."

"How will you know? Can we call you?"

"Just keep trying, okay?"

She covered the mouthpiece with her hand while she spoke to Wally. She came back on. "Ten-four, General. Is that it?"

Then I told her how to make the third call.

"Convolutions," she said, when I'd finished.

"Not for a grad student at UCI."

"Thank you for your patronage, sir. And good luck."

We synchronized our watches. I finished the coffee and filled the Thermos and added a shot of brandy. I unlocked the gun cabinet and pulled out a shotgun, a Winchester pump, and a box of shells. I took a last look around and then, wearing the yellow jacket, I went down the stairs to the pickup.

At ten twenty-one, at the traffic signal just south of Jamaica Cove, I made an illegal U-turn and headed back up the Coast Highway to park sixty feet south of the gatehouse. My plan was B-minus. The purpose was to get me inside the gatehouse for a peek at the log without hurting anyone. There were two guards. I wanted both of them away from the gatehouse for a couple of minutes. If Woolford had been on duty, I would have been tempted to bust him a good one. But these lads were strangers, innocents. Until they walloped me, or threatened to, I would avoid trouble.

At ten twenty-eight, I slipped up the exit ramp to crouch in some bushes by the gatehouse. The guard was on the horn. I couldn't make out the words, only the rise and fall of his voice. The cadence was social. At ten thirty-two, he was still talking. I visualized Dorene and Wally trying to get through. I was sweating inside the yellow slicker. At ten thirty-eight, he finally hung up. I had counted to thirty-seven before the phone rang. The guard answered. His voice became sharp. Okay, he said. Ten-four. A pause as he connected to his counterpart in the security vehicle. I heard Mrs. Mather's name. It sounded like he was arguing with the other guard, some procedural thing. Then he hung up and there was silence.

Counting again, forty-seven, forty-eight, forty-nine, damn the sweat, remembering the long days patrolling the streets of Los Angeles, the dirt, the perps, the sad, blear-faced victims. There was the work, procedure and rules and writing reports, and then there was the dead time, the space in between, like a green lily pad on a storm-tossed sea, when you sat like a zombie in front of the television, still wearing the yellow police slicker, the boots, your clothes soaked all the way out from the skin—sweat, blood, water, grief—your bones so weary you didn't have the energy to strip, shower off, lie down, and dive into sleep.

The phone rang again inside the gatehouse. Gambling that it was Wally, I jogged down the exit ramp, past the row of imbedded metal shark teeth and the sign warning you not to back up, severe tire damage, it said. Headlights looped past me, heading north on the Coast Highway. I counted to ten and headed back to the gatehouse, manufacturing a limp and hauling out my fake police shield. The guard, looking like a cavalry fort under attack, was staring out through the window and up the hill. I held the shield up to the window and rapped on the door with my riot stick. The guard grabbed for his piece, turned wild eyes in my direction. A jumpy one. Young. Mustached. Mid-twenties.

He opened the door. I held the shield for a beat longer, covering up the lettering, before putting it away.

"Are you Jackson?"

His hand was still on his gun. "No. I'm Allen. Who the fuck are you?"

"Haberstam," I said, using a Texas accent. "Down to Laguna station. Didn't the Sarge call?"

His eyes were suspicious. "Just got the call. Where's your vehicle?"

I gestured back toward the road. "Sumbitch just died on me. Had to leave her in the bar ditch and hoof it on in here. Turned my goddamn foot. Hurts like hell." I paused to unbutton the yellow jacket so he could see my police hardware. It was fifteen years out of date, but to a guy raised on television, it might look like the real thing.

"Well, okay. What's up?"

I limped to a chair and sat down. I propped the Winchester against the wall and heaved a sigh of relief. The logbook, what I had come for, lay on the desk near the door. "Seems quiet enough around here."

"Semi," the guard said. "You want me to call for a tow truck, or something?"

"I'll do her," I said. "Gimme a minute. We got a special number for a special towing service. The Loot, he hates it like hell to spend tax dollars—"

The phone rang again. Answering, Allen came close to jerking the cord loose. His knuckles tightened on the receiver. "Yes, ma'am," he said. "I know the house. We'll have someone over there right away, ma'am." He hung up, rolled his eyes at the ceiling, and said: "Shit!"

A car wheeled in. Allen took a quick look to verify and then raised the traffic bar.

I stood up, giving him my best grimace. "How about I make that call?"

"Oh, sure. Dial a nine and you're out of here."

I limped to the phone, picked up the receiver, dialed a nine, and then punched in my home number. While it rang, I looked over at him. "Anything I can help you with, Allen?"

He shook his head. The phone was on its third ring. Then number four. My answering machine clicked on with its cheery message. Hello, you have reached the heart of Murdock Country, at the edge of the ocean on beautiful Newport Pier. Please leave a message at the end of—

"Do you think you could take a quick drive to check out a reported prowler?"

"Just a minute," I said to my answering machine. I turned to Allen. "Where's he at?"

"A prowler's been reported, out on the hook, a home called Carcass Song, something like that. My partner's on the mountain. This lady who called, Mrs. Duke, she's, well, she pulls a lot of weight. If I don't get out there, the garbage could fly. I could get buried for this."

"Call you back," I told the answering machine as I hung up on myself. "With this foot of mine, I can't brake, can't punch the foot feed. How about I watch the store here while you do your check."

"No," he said. "That would be—"

Outside, a horn tooted and a Jaguar wheeled in. Allen didn't know the car, so he stepped outside. I eyed the logbook. Times of entry ran along the narrow left-hand column, but I couldn't see the rest.

Allen came back inside to make a quick call. When he had the party verified, he pressed a lever to raise the traffic bar. The Jaguar slid through, the bar lowered itself, and he turned to me. "Okay," he said. "If my partner calls, tell him I've gone out to Carcass Song."

I tried not to grin at his pronunciation. "How's that?"

He shrugged. "Carcass Song. The houses in here, they all got foreign names."

I saluted. "Go along then. I'll hold the fort."

Some soldier. It took him ninety seconds to gather up his rain jacket and riot stick, check his piece to make sure it was loaded, grab a clipboard, and get down to his vehicle. Before his taillights had disappeared around the curve I was reading the log entries for Thursday. My name was penciled in, along with the pickup license: 12:59, Murdock in; 1:32, Murdock out. Mr. James P. Duke entered at 1:12 in his Mercedes. He was logged out at 2:40. I flipped back to Tuesday, hunting for a trace of Marvin Holly.

Nothing. The guard's initials were in a narrow column on the far right. On Tuesday, *L. W.*—I assumed that was Woolford—alternated with *R.R.U.*, the initials of a second guard. I zeroed in on the afternoon. Two slots had been changed between 3:00 and 5:00, the lead smudged by an eraser, then written over with a thick lead pencil. According to Cindy, Marvin had been here. According to the log, he hadn't. So. The log was precise, times recorded by bored guards down to the minute. The initials *L. W.* were printed in the right-hand column next to the erasures, which meant Lance Woolford had been busy. Marvin's visit made two people jumpy. His ex, Barb. And her brother, Uncle Jamie. Was Woolford doing the Duke twosome a favor? Or was he picking up an extra buck working for them on retainer? Officially, Marvin had not been here.

A horn sounded outside. I opened the door but stayed in the shadow. The car was a big square-bodied Lincoln with a JC sticker inside the windshield. I could not see the driver's face.

"Hello?" the driver said. "Where's the—"

I flashed my fake tin. "Laguna police, sir. Are you a resident, sir?"

"Me? Hell, yes. What are the police doing at this—"

I cut him off. "Could I see some ID, sir? Sorry to have to ask you to do this. Robbery team's inside the compound. Only residents admitted."

Grumbling, the guy pointed to his JC sticker, then handed over his registration. His name was Roger Sturm, of Jamaica Cove Properties, Ltd.

"Very good, sir."

"And I'd like your badge number, officer."

"Of course, sir. My number's—oops, there goes the phone."

I bounded back into the gatehouse and picked up the phone. My badge number was HECHO EN MEX-ICO. I counted to ten while I pretended to talk on the phone. Then I raised the traffic bar and waved the Lincoln through. Any minute now and the second guard would be calling in. I didn't have much time.

The first erased entry was at 4:06 on Tuesday. Mather, blue Lincoln, California license. Did residents have to sign in? The second was at 4:21, Gingrich, green Porsche 911, California license. The times were about right for Marvin Holly's visit to Carcassonne. But if Holly had been here, why had Woolford bothered to alter his log?

A horn honked outside, where three cars waited. Two of them had JC stickers. One was an outsider. Sweating, I verified all three, then raised the traffic bar to let them through. I looked at the logbook once more, hoping to find a clue, then turned the pages back to Thursday.

Helpful Murdock.

Headlights appeared at the curve as I jogged down

the exit ramp toward the Coast Highway. I slipped
into a shadow of the brick wall that surrounded the
perimeter of Jamaica Cove. There were two vehicles.
The first was a white security vehicle, a squarish
truck with a yellow roof light and the Jamaica Cove
pirate logo. It parked in the slot and I saw my pal
Allen jump out and run into the gatehouse.

The second car was a Mercedes coupe, the windows tinted dark so you couldn't see the driver. It
paused for a break in the traffic, then slipped across
the highway to join the cars heading south. The license plate said DUKE II.

Barb Duke, out for an evening spin.

Where was Cindy?

From the gatehouse, I heard the guard curse like a
man who'd been had, and then I jogged back down
the shoulder to my Ford.

I'd hoped to have more for my report to Senator
Jane. I grinned. I was like a high school jock trying to
impress the head cheerleader.

And it was not a bad feeling.

8

─────────────

With the Gothic ramparts of Hotel Xanadu towering above me, I parked in the lot, near the spot where I had found Marvin Holly's waterlogged book earlier in the day, and then I made my way through the rear entrance that served both the mall and the hotel. The time was after eleven. Marvin Holly's book was in an inside pocket.

The corridor swerved around the mall to a bank of elevators in the high arched dome of the front entry. Behind the wide glass doors of Xanadu Mall, a smiling, red-cheeked Santa Claus, some two stories tall, sat in a giant chair talking to a huge fat-faced youngster, filling his head with tales of giant sugarplums. Let's keep the Santa myth alive, all through the night.

In the elevator, two couples in evening dress hugged and chatted while they eyed my police uniform, making me feel dumb for not bringing along a change of clothes. A soft bell bonged and the door opened onto the hotel lobby. This was the end of the line. From here, you had to take a second elevator to your room in the tower.

The couples drifted away in a flurry of Technicolor slow motion and I stepped into a world of oily wealth and sweet pleasure. Perfect white tile led to a perfect white rug, which led to a perfect reception area, white on gold, which was staffed by a pretty lady and a handsome man, both wearing perfect smiles. Playing James Bond with entry logs is thirsty work. At the perfect desk, I asked for the bar.

"Which bar would you prefer, sir?" In a long-delayed double take, eyelids sharply arched, Mister Perfect noted the uniform. "I'm the night manager. Is there something wrong, officer?"

"No. Nothing wrong. I'm off duty. Haven't had time to change."

The perfect teeth glimmered. "Holiday hours, eh?"

"That's right, sir. Are you a driver?"

"Yes."

"Like a hot tip on a sobriety checkpoint?"

"I certainly would." He leaned close his perfect ear.

"Heading north," I said in a stage whisper, "watch for the Laguna Canyon exit. That's a biggie. Southbound, they're checking at Crown Valley."

He wrote the streets down in a perfect hand and gave me two chits good at any bar in the hotel until New Year's Day. The names of the bars were printed on the chits in gothic letters: the Marco Polo, the Scheherazade, and the Genghis Khan. The first two were packed tight with singles trying their best to be doubles. I headed around the corner along a shimmering corridor to the Genghis Khan. Dark in here, the darkness made thicker by smoke. I stood at the entrance, waiting for my eyes to get accustomed to the light. A woman at the bar caught my eye as a man lit her cigarette. The planes in her face were accented by a recessed cone light in the ceiling. She saw me. We locked eyeballs. She raised her chin an inch, blew smoke slowly through her nose, and indicated, with her cigarette hand, the empty seat to her right.

I was about to head for the seat beside the smoker when I saw Blazer Blaisdell. He sat in an upholstered booth at a curved table at the far end of the room. The brunette—I like you, she'd said; I'm free for Christmas—was next to him, sitting close as a Siamese twin. Next to her was a man I didn't know. Heavy eyelids, nasty mouth, blue shadow of a beard scoring his shiny jawline. And next to him, Blazer's blonde, who was touching shoulders with the mystery man.

Two things had happened since our chummy dinner at the Côte d'Azur. Murdock had been replaced by a swarthy guy with a heavy shadow of beard. And the girls—fillies, Blazer had called them—had changed guys.

A waiter started toward them but was waved off by Blazer. My brunette leaned against Blazer, turning up her face to nuzzle his neck. Blazer spoke to the mystery man, who took a drink and nodded. His left hand was hooked around the blonde's shoulder, fingers digging into bare flesh. The blonde sipped her drink, followed by a heaving of her bosom as she took a deep breath, nodding, fluffing her hair with her left hand. Her face wore a dreamy smile and I knew she was on something more than booze and holiday cheer.

The woman at the bar saw me watching Blazer's table. She slid off the stool and came toward me, carrying her purse. She was five-five, slightly overweight, and mature enough to know what she was doing. She smiled at me and blew smoke in my face. "Evening, officer. Are you on duty or just slumming?"

"I'm interested in the man at the far wall. The one with the two pros."

She turned to stare at Blazer's table. Blazer and the brunette were getting out of the booth to make way for the mystery man. The blonde had not moved. She lay, half reclining in her seat, eyes dreamy, her head resting against the cushions. The woman with the cigarette plucked at my sleeve. "Sorry. I know one of the girls. Don't know either of the boys. When are you off?"

"Half an hour. Which girl?"

"The little brunette. She's pricey, if you ask me. I'm in seven fifty-five. How about dropping up?"

Blazer and the mystery man were coming my way and there was nowhere to hide. "Okay," I said, taking the lady's hand. Her skin was smooth. I stepped back a couple of paces, until I felt the wall at my back, pulled her close and buried my face in her neck as Blazer and his guy walked past, huddled in conversation. Her hair smelled strongly of cigarette smoke. Blazer had to stoop down to talk, the guy was so short.

The mystery man was talking softly. I heard the words *Douglas-baby*, *General*, and *shipment*. A man in a business suit left his station at the bar to trail after them. Goon, I registered, fresh from Vegas or Chicago or a black-and-white movie about Prohibition days.

The woman broke free. "Well, officer," she said in a throaty voice. "Welcome to Xanadu."

"Sorry." I let her go and she grinned at me, showing one crooked tooth.

"Hey, no problem." She straightened her dress. "I like a man who knows what he wants and goes for it."

Blazer and the mystery man were around the corner and out of sight. "How about a rain check?" I said. "I'm still on duty."

"Room seven five five," she said. "Hotel Xanadu."

"I'll try."

We both knew I wouldn't. I squeezed her hand for helping me out and followed Blazer out to the perfect lobby, where I spotted a second goon, heavier than the first, and definitely packing a piece. Goon One, from the bar, took up a flanking position while Goon Two, from the lobby, pressed a button to call the elevator. From behind the reception desk, the two perfect clerks watched from behind two perfect smiles. The elevator arrived. As Blazer and mystery man got on, followed by Goon Two, I found a door marked STAIRS and went down them two at a time. By the time I got down to ground level, they were strolling out the mirrored entrance underneath the groined arch to the parking area, with Big Santa still yakking to the kid behind them in the mall. Goon Two spotted me in my uniform and smiled.

The door opened and Blazer and mystery man walked through, into the night, their heads close together. The mystery man brandished a cigar. Goon Two jogged over with a light. Flame brightened the world for a brief moment. Since there was no way I could get close enough to hear what they were saying, I turned back to the hotel and my report to Senator Jane.

Before I rang the buzzer to room 745, I slipped my dark glasses on. I heard movement behind the door, footsteps, rustlings. I held the fake shield up near the security peephole, hiding my face but not the uniform. There was a long moment when I thought she wasn't going to open up, but then the locked clicked and Senator Jane stood there, wearing the tweed skirt, the elegant boots, and a pumpkin-colored turtleneck sweater. Behind her I saw the living room of a suite, and a half-filled glass on a table beside the sofa. "Yes, officer, what is this all—"

Her attention was on the shield. My head was lowered. The dark glasses were working. "Trouble, ma'am," I said. "You'll have to come with me, down to the station."

"Trouble? What kind?"

I lowered the shield and grinned. "It's me. Murdock."

Her face went from pale white to deep pink. "Good God, and I was thinking that—"

"Can I come in, Senator?"

"Of course." She stood aside. Her breath smelled of alcohol. She closed the door and locked it and walked over to pick up her drink. "Moonlighting, are we?"

"Working for you, Senator."

"Where I come from, Mr. Murdock, impersonating an officer is an illegal act."

"It's my own uniform."

"Really? Where from?"

"Los Angeles. I spent eighteen months working out of Hollenbeck."

"How long ago was this?"

"Fifteen years."

Slight smile as she assessed me. "You've filled out a little."

"Life."

"Makes you more human. Can I get you something?"

"Is there beer?"

"Sorry. There's vodka and then there's vodka."

"Vodka's fine."

She tossed cubes into a glass and poured vodka over the cubes and walked toward me, her hips swaying nicely, to hand me the drink. She told me to sit down. I shrugged out of the yellow rain jacket and took the easy chair. The room was furnished in white and gold, like the lobby. In one corner was a wet bar and a Mr. Coffee maker.

The Senator mixed herself a fresh drink and sat down on the sofa, crossing her legs. The tweed skirt bared her knees and she didn't pull it back down. The vodka bottle was down to the one-third mark. I wondered how many she'd had tonight.

"Time for your report, Mr. Murdock."

"Okay." I took a swallow of vodka and told her about the bearded bookstore guy who'd sent Heather after Marvin Holly with the book. I handed over the book. She studied the inscription, then questioned me about Holly. I told her about Cindy hunting for her dad at the mall, what we'd learned on our trek to the airport, the phone calls that hadn't gone through to Madison.

"A goose chase," Jane said.

"I'm not through, Senator." I told her about Carcassonne and Barb Duke and Uncle Jamie giving me a hard time when I asked about his ex-brother-in-law. I went through the stuff with Lance Woolford, the security guard, and how he wouldn't let me look at the log. Finally, I told her about the erasures in the log.

"So we're back to my cover-up theory?"

"Maybe."

"I told you I could smell it." She sipped her vodka. "Who are these Dukes? What have they got to hide?"

"They're the heaviest family in Orange County. They deal in power and money. The first Duke got here a hundred years ago, just in time to cheat the Mexicans out of their land grants. Duke Construction's the second biggest employer, after the county itself. Rumor has it they buy politicians, here on the local scene, in Sacramento, and in Washington. The old man—he's had four or five wives—lives in a castle on Duke Island."

"You seem to know a lot about them."

"Just rumor and legend."

"No. There's something more, something with an edge. I can hear it in your voice."

"Okay." I drank some vodka. "They ran me out of business."

"Really. What sort of business?"

"I had a construction firm, back in the seventies, when interest was running over twenty percent. Duke Construction kept undercutting my bids."

"They had cash. You didn't. Am I right?"

"Right."

"Hmm." Senator Jane set her glass down and leaned back against the sofa. Her chest expanded, tightening the sweater, outlining her breasts. She stretched her arms over her head and let out a lazy yawn. Then, still asking me questions, she leaned over and began unzipping her boots. "Any idea of their net worth?"

"In the billions. In seventy-four, the year I went broke, Duke Construction did a billion in southern California alone. That doesn't count the Sunbelt, the rest of the country. Or foreign sales."

"A castle, you said?"

"Yeah."

"A real castle?"

"Imported, stone by stone, from France."

"Impressive. Who did that?"

"The first Duke. Sometime around 1902."

The first boot came off. Senator Jane rubbed her toes and started on the second one. "And who heads up the family today?"

"Wheeler Duke."

"What's he like?"

"Tough. Some say ruthless."

"Age?"

"Early seventies."

The other boot came off. She sighed, stretched her legs, and rested her stockinged feet on the coffee table. "I never met a rich man who didn't have something to hide. And they have the machinery for an elaborate cover-up." She began massaging her feet on the edge of the coffee table. "Ahh. That feels good."

I finished my drink and felt uncomfortable. Maybe it was the tight uniform, pinching me to remind me I wasn't a kid anymore. Maybe it was being this close, watching the Senator knead her feet. A strand of hair came loose to trail down her left cheek. She held out her glass. "Freshen us, would you?"

I poured silver vodka over cubes. When I handed her drink over, she clinked my glass with hers. "The Duke family cover-up," she said again. "I like it. I like it a lot."

"Not much to go on."

"It's the hidden agenda, don't you see? It explains why the sheriff's people were so twitchy about telling me anything. It explains the events at the hospital— three doctors on the case, and a third one who barely speaks English. They probably own the newspaper. I forget the name."

"The *Trib.*"

"Yes. And a television station or two. Control the media and you control the world." She drank her vodka, set her glass down, and looked at me without smiling. "I have a deal for you, Murdock."

"What kind of deal?"

"Foot massage. You go first." She stuck out her feet, the toes pointing at me.

"Foot massage?"

"Hmm. An ancient Greek custom. Surely you grasp the concept."

"Well, I—"

She sensed my hesitation and patted the sofa. "All right, so I'll do you first. You sit here. Take off your shoes."

"Careful of the smell."

"I grew up in Texas, remember. It's a veritable nation of smells."

"It's a deal."

"Take off your pistol, Murdock. You're safe with me."

I unbuckled the holster and laid it on the chair. I moved to the sofa, where I pulled off the boots. Senator Jane sat on the floor in front of me, skirt above her knees. Another strand of her hair had come loose. The vodka was taking hold, making her slur the occasional word, strengthening her accent. She took my foot and began kneading the muscles. Her hands were strong. When she found a tight spot, she dug in, using her thumbs to probe. "Crystal here," she said, digging deep. "Crystal there. Crystal everywhere."

Pain zinged through my foot. And pleasure. "What kind of crystal?"

"Bad news crystal. Another word is deposits. Am I hurting you?"

"Sometimes."

"Poor baby."

Her work on the right foot made the left foot feel isolated, like a third leg. Maybe the vodka was getting to me, too. Or maybe it was the day, getting slapped around by strangers. I could feel myself relaxing, Murdock on the slide, defenses wobbling like sand castles melting in the rain. She shifted to the left foot.

"Tell me about the women."

"What women?"

"The little girl from the mall. And the mother. Tell me about them."

I closed my eyes. "The mother's name is Barb. She's late thirties, brittle, and very rich. She gets what she asks for."

The thumbs dug in, making me squirm. "Is she attractive?"

"Depends on your taste."

"Taste in what?"

"Reptiles."

The thumbs dug deeper, probing for crystals, finding them. "Did she come on to you?"

"She tried. I fended her off."

The rubbing stopped and I opened my eyes to see Senator Jane scowling at me. "Rascal," she said, gouging me.

"Jesus." I closed my eyes and the pain lessened.

"Tell me about the little girl."

"She's fourteen. Her name's Cindy. I met her in the bookstore in the mall."

"I don't understand how you connected."

I gave the Senator a brief synopsis of Ambush Night in Laguna Canyon, when Cindy had guided me up and down the mountain and then had piloted my Ford into Bluebird Canyon, to Philo's house.

"She drove?"

"Yeah. I was hurt, couldn't handle a stick."

"How did she handle it?"

"Cool as a commando."

"Did you recognize her in the bookstore?"

"Not at first. It's been a couple of years. Kids grow fast."

"So let me get this straight. Why did her father fly out to see her?"

"It's Christmas. Wanted to see her."

"Of course. But why did he leave town without seeing her?"

"I asked the same question."

She stopped rubbing. My only wish in the world was to have the foot massage go on forever. She stared past me at the wall. "Where did you say he was from? The father?"

"Madison."

"Wisconsin?"

"Yes."

She got up and walked to the phone. "Do you have the number?"

"Not with me."

Standing hipshot in her stocking feet, Senator Jane punched in some digits and asked for the number for Marvin Holly. She dialed the number. "Is he at the university there?"

"He teaches some courses, Cindy said."

"It's ringing." She nodded at me. I rubbed my feet against the edge of the coffee table. "His phone machine is answering." Frowning, she listened through to the end of the phone machine, then left her name and the number of the hotel and asked Marvin to call her. She hung up but did not return to the sofa. "I know some people at Madison. Let me make some calls."

I feared my foot massage was over. "Is there anyplace you don't know people?"

She nodded. "Here. In wonderful Orange County C.A."

"You know me."

"Only to speak to on the street," she said. "You're a strange one, a man without a business card. I don't even know your first name."

"Matt," I said.

"Matt," she echoed. "A good, strong name. I like it. My turn. Would you excuse me for a moment?" She headed into the bedroom, closing the door behind her with a soft click. The toilet flushed. I heard water running. I checked my watch: 11:58. I wondered where Blazer was. Who was his short friend, the mystery man with the blue-shadowed cheeks? Had Blazer's job offer with CEO Security been for real? Would the Senator send me north to Madison to check on our mystery witness? Was Holly a witness? Or was this another dead end?

The door opened. Senator Jane had changed clothes. She now wore a terry cloth robe, soft, peach-colored, and tightly belted. She had combed her hair and freshened her lipstick. Bare toes peeked out at me. The toenail polish matched the robe. "Turnabout," she said.

"A stiff price, Your Honor."

"Don't call me that."

"Okay."

She picked up the vodka bottle, eyeing its contents, then set it down with an awkward thump and settled herself on the sofa. The robe fell away from her legs, to mid-calf. Slender curved ankles, hinting at nice legs above. She presented me her left foot. "Now," she ordered. "Do me."

I sat on the floor at her feet, working my hands along the muscles, along the fine bones. After a minute or so, her feet began perspiring, a thin film of sweat that made my work easier. There was no talking. When I found a hot spot and dug in, she grunted, rested her head on the sofa back, and closed her eyes. When I ran my thumbs from her heel to that soft spot up near the ball of her foot, she twisted on the sofa. As she twisted, the belt loosened and the folds of the robe slid open, revealing shaved knees and nicely rounded thighs.

"Uuhhh," she said.

"Too much?"

She opened her eyes. "No," she whispered. "Never. Keep . . . probing. Always. Keep. Probing." She pulled the edges of the robe up around her legs, covering herself, but at the same time I gave her an extra dig with my thumb that made her twist and the robe came open again.

The Senator was not wearing panties.

"God damn you," she said, but softly.

I kept on digging. The time for words was over. She was a handsome woman, mature, built for the long haul. She was carrying around a heavy burden of guilt about her daughter and God only knew what else. She was half drunk and so was I. We were two strangers, alone in a hotel room high above a California freeway, where the traffic never stopped moving. It was Christmas, the loneliest time of the year, and we were plowed on good Russian vodka.

"Stop," she ordered.

I stopped.

"Don't stop," she ordered.

I dug in my thumbs.

"No," she said, reaching out to me. "No."

I gave her my hand. She leaned over and grabbed both of them and pulled me onto the sofa beside her, where she took a long time staring into my eyes. "Who are you?" she asked.

"Santa Claus."

She grabbed my shoulders and shook me, the

schoolteacher routine again, keeper of chicks, angry mother. "You're a Neanderthal. A cave creature, up out of the swamp. God damn you, Mister Neanderthal, waltzing in here behind a fake police uniform. Don't get funny with me!"

"It's not fake."

She shook me again. Then she laughed, giggly at first, then hysterically.

"Hey," I said, shaking her. "Hey. You. Senator."

The laughter stopped. Her eyes widened in sudden recognition. It was as if we'd known each other sometime in the past, and had lucked into a chance meeting in a revolving door in a strange hotel in a strange gray city. It was the dead of winter. We were locked in twin pie-shaped cubicles, her quarter of the tubular door separated from mine. Hot in here. Smell of sweat, the numbing rubbery tug of fear on meeting a stranger who is not a stranger. Across the glass, her face stared at my face.

Faces swam around us, gray faces, empty faces, pale white faces, and we were the only two spots of living color in the bare wintry urban landscape. The revolving door was stuck. To get us past this point, someone had to give it a push. Sweat on my face, armpits, chest, the uniform squeezing me, choking. Then the Senator smiled, her eyes blazing with flickering fire as she pulled my hand close and bit me hard on the finger, sharp white senatorial teeth drawing a small dot of blood, then grinned impishly as she settled back to wait, knees together, peach robe coming undone, for my opening kiss. And as our tongues met in a heated gasping rush I remembered our phone conversation from last night when she had told me, through a series of carefully paced statements, that I reminded her of her dead brother.

9

I woke up to the smell of coffee, my feet tangled in sheets. From the other room came the clink of crockery. The bedroom door was open a crack. I was alone in the bed. I padded to the bathroom, used the facilities, and found a towel. Wrapped in the towel, I made my way to the sitting room. The Senator, carrying a coffee tray, met me at the door. The coffee smell was overwhelming.

"I was thinking of lettuce," she said.

"Lettuce?"

"Lettuce wedges, actually. Where were you born?"

"El Paso. On the army base."

She handed me the tray. "You've lost your accent."

"My old man was career army. We moved around."

Working quickly, she straightened the bedclothes. We climbed back under the covers. The coffee was not up to the quality level of Murdock Blend, but it would do. I lay propped against Xanadu pillows, eyes closed, cradling the cup with both hands.

"Head lettuce?" I asked.

"Um. I remember on Sunday after church Daddy would take us to lunch at Smith's on the Austin highway, where the fried chicken was out of this world. My mouth would be watering all through church, and always before they brought the chicken there'd be these little tan-colored bowls, each one holding a lettuce wedge, and all the wedges with exactly the same dollop of French dressing. And we'd eat the lettuce and nothing could taste as good until the chicken came. Childhood. My God, how good it was."

"I remember biscuits and butter melting into the honey."

"Those were the days." She climbed out of bed to refill our coffee cups. When she handed my cup over, the peach robe fell open in front and she did not rush to close it. Her hair was tousled. "Have you known many women?"

"No."

"It was a stupid question. I'm sorry."

"Forget it."

"I guess I'm feeling a little vulnerable, now that the heat of passion has waned." She pulled the lapels of the robe closer.

"Waned for you, maybe."

"Oh, you." She bopped me on the arm, then lay back against the pillows, her mouth in a half smile. "It's been a while for me, you see. Quite a while. After Jason left me, I lost my taste for men. For males. For their companionship. For their very sight. I had a father, a brother, droves of boy-cousins hunking around. So I knew what they were all about, the male anatomy, the general direction of their male drives. But Jason wounded me with his rejection, then yipping off with a younger female. Oh, I know all the anthropological theories, old bull apes going for young girl apes, but when your own husband does it to you it ceases to be an intellectual problem. I picked up the pieces, pasted them together. I kept going."

"Listen," I said, touching her cheek. "You were terrific. You were warm and wonderful. You don't have to say a goddamn word."

"Thank you. Yes. I do. If you're willing, that is."

"Fire away."

"What's your birth sign, Murdock?"

"Taurus."

"I'm a Gemini. My symbol is twins. An astrologer told me I had two distinct personalities. Spirits, she called them. Two distinct spirits. First, there's the public Jane, the steady senator, the speechmaker, the vote-getter, the lady politico who engineers bills through the good-old-boy Texas legislature. Second, there's Jane the Dark, Jane the Lustful, Jane Full of Shame. She surfaced when I was thirteen, when I noticed boys following me with their eyes, and when I understood about the boys, what they wanted, I discovered power. Not only boys, of course. Men too. Bankers and sheriff's deputies and the tight-collared Baptist minister and even Mr. Lilienthal, my sissified, henpecked English teacher in junior high. I was smart in school. I made all A's. I had beaus. I played tennis and set a new record in the hundred yard dash. And then, at fifteen, I fell in love and lost my virginity."

"Who was the guy?"

"A senior named Brick Henson. Brick, beautiful Brick, was captain of the baseball team, a track star, and an all-conference quarterback. Bookish Jane Whitney tumbles for football hero. I thought he was the handsomest man I'd ever seen. A macho man with a Clark Kent profile, dark hair, straight teeth, and a beautiful, wicked smile. When Brick came into a room, my heart stopped beating and I couldn't breathe. One Saturday after a baseball game he gave me his brother's fraternity pin—the brother, Jimmy, had been Phi Gam at Austin—and two hours later, in his family's Chrysler, beautiful Brick stole my maidenhead."

She paused to place the cup on the bedside table, then resumed her story. "It hurt, but not for very long. I was out of phase with the moon, so I was lucky and didn't get pregnant. It was the middle of May and Brick was about to graduate. That summer, he worked in the oil fields, and then that fall he galloped off to a football scholarship at OU, up in Norman. Bastrop's a small town. Word about us got around fast. And I learned a lesson about men, how they operate. Brick had seen me as prey, my virginity as a hunter's trophy. Jane Whitney was a mere tick-mark on Brick's fuselage. And he became my metaphor, and my yardstick, for judging the other half of humanity.

"I studied hard, but refused to date. I locked up my heart, vowed never to fall in love again. No more men for Wounded Janie. But life goes on. My senior year in high school, I developed a crush on Mr. Ridley, my high school English teacher. I was already reading Ginsberg and Ferlinghetti, so Mr. Ridley introduced me to marijuana and free love. Lust rose up. I fought it, shoved it into a dark corner, struggled with the demons, stopped wearing perfume, stepped up my athletics, sweated a lot. But when love grabbed me, I needed someone to talk to. Daddy was too old-fashioned. Mama, well, I think she'd known about Brick, maybe even had a crush on him herself, but she was a churchgoer who held tight the image of Daughter as Eternal Virgin Vessel. I didn't dare tell her about Mr. Ridley. I remember I'd be sitting at my desk, studying, and all of a sudden there'd be this terrible terrible heat, as if the light bulb had turned into a sun, and then the fire would pour through my body like a fever of molten lava, forcing me to bathe my face in cold water to stop the trembling.

"At the university in Austin, I was doomed. Jane the Lustful, surrounded by good-looking men with brains and money and fast cars who had access to beer and pot and fraternity parties. One side of me is quite social. I wanted it all, the books, the privacy to read, and the parties and the music and the fun. I explored birth control. I flirted. I retreated. I fell in love with George and Harry and Timmy. Each time it was forever. Each time it didn't last. That was my weakness. I fell hard and fast and for always. I was always hurt when love crumbled away. I married Jason the day after I graduated from law school. Nine months later, Heather was born. And guess what?"

"What?"

"Love is not forever, and my poor daughter's a Gemini, just like me."

I asked if she wanted more coffee and she said yes. I refilled our cups and brought them back to the bed. She took a couple of sips and went on with her story.

"I saw it happening to Heather the same way it happened to me. The little girl losing her innocent, twiggy girlishness, her body suddenly becoming lush and curvy. The significant looks from the men. The slow flush of blood flooding across the throat, the neck, filling you with the knowledge that here it is, here's what makes the world go round, this, kid, is the power. I saw it happening and it made me afraid, the inevitability of it, the mirrored memory coming around again, as the world turns, Janie, my mama would have said. And so I did what any mother would have. I talked to my baby, counseled her, tried to warn her. Only it didn't do any good. The pull of the moon was stronger. She fell in with a group of kids, local baddies. They were into drugs, into kicks, into petty theft. And there were boys. The worst one was four years older, a rake, handsome and cocky, a younger Brick full of his own machismo but without the leavening of high school athletics, and way too mature for my baby. I found out when they called me from school, saying she'd been caught with marijuana in her Emily Dickinson book. A teacher reported it before they called the law. I called people around town, a lawyer and a judge, and managed to fix it."

"This is when you sent her to the school in Scottsdale?"

"Soon after. She kept having crazy ideas. She met a man—a graduate student at UT—and swore she was running away with him when he finished his work. She fibbed about where she was. At the movies, she'd say. But she'd be with her crowd, or with some man or other. Then she turned up with birth control pills."

I remembered the report from Webby Smith. "When was this?"

"Three weeks ago, when she was home for Thanksgiving. Her grades were good at school, so I thought everything was fine. I found the little package. Nine pills were left out of twenty-eight."

"Where?"

"In the pocket of a shirt."

"Maybe she put it there so you could find it."

"A call for help. Yes. I thought of that."

"So what did you do?"

"What any mother would. I confronted my daughter. She admitted she'd been seeing someone while she was at school, but swore to me that it was all over. I shouted at her. She shouted at me. She flew back to Scottsdale School, but now there was a terrible breach between us. Our phone conversations were short. I would ask questions. She would give curt answers. I imagined all sorts of awful things happening to her. Things seemed better that week before she was to fly home, but I realize now she was still hurting." Senator Jane paused to sip her coffee. "And that's where we were when she didn't show up at the airport in Austin. An impasse over the arts of love. Like mother, like daughter."

I put my hand on top of her hand. "Things will work out."

"I hope so," she said. "I hope and pray they will."

She gave me a brief hug and a soft, sad kiss, and then she went in and took a long shower. It was after three on Friday morning. I finished the coffee and watched the news on television.

The President had left Camp David and would spend a day at the White House before flying in Air Force One to California. He and the First Lady would spend Christmas with friends in Palm Springs. Frank Sinatra would also be a guest in Palm Springs, singing the old songs. The Arabs were meeting in Brussels on the price of oil. New York had twelve inches of snow. Washington, D.C., had fourteen inches. Congress had adjourned for the holidays.

Locally, here in California, the mayor of Los Angeles had put out an appeal for food for the homeless. And here in Orange County, the Coastal Commission was clearing up some last-minute items before final approval for Duke Harbour, the development of the golden strip, that last slice of coast between Laguna Beach and Corona Del Mar.

There was a two-minute interview with Wheeler

Duke at the Duke Harbour construction site, where work had been stalled by new concerns from the Coastal Commission. The camera picked up the old man coming out of a construction shack on wheels, wearing safari pants, a plaid hunting shirt, a down vest, and a blue hard hat. Wheeler Duke, the grand old man of Orange County, grinned into the camera, winning us over, and then got serious about the real purpose of Duke Harbour. "What we're doing here at Duke Harbour," he said, "is creating jobs. Four thousand new jobs at the hotel. Three thousand more in the new small businesses that will come in as support services. To make it easy on entrepreneurs, we're keeping rents at bargain-basement levels. Our main goal is to give the medium-sized American merchant a slice of paradise on the California beach."

He did not want to talk about his twenty-year battle with environmentalists and slow-growth activists. And when the reporter asked him about the latest setback with the Coastal Commission, he sandwiched in this statement: "Things are going real great up there at the Coastal Commission. They're cleaving to their rules and regs. We're bending over backwards to comply. Duke Construction's not here to deface the last real stretch of beach in the great state of California." He waved back toward the hills. "Twenty-three acres are being kept in a virgin state for local wildlife. Hellfire, as one who grew up in this country, I'm not about to let it get chewed up with bulldozers and backhoes."

Cut to the reporter, a pretty lady with a microphone, thanking Wheeler Duke, chairman of the board of Duke Construction, for taking time out of his busy holiday, yadda, yadda, and then smiling with envy as she dropped some names of celebrities from last year's Christmas Eve party at Duke Castle: Frank Sinatra. John Glenn. Pilar Wayne. Ron Reagan. Jimmy Stewart. Burt Lancaster. General Westmoreland. On and on with her list from last year, the teaser followed by a sly winking invitation to tune in tomorrow, folks, for Channel Three's coverage of this year's bash, with who only knows what wonderful guest list.

I could hardly wait.

The bathroom door opened to reveal Senator Jane, nude, hair slicked down, her shiny skin pink from the heat of the shower, smiling a hooded smile. Steam billowed behind her. I climbed out of bed. She retreated, taking one backward step, then another, leading me into her steamy domain.

We kissed in the shower, the torrent raining down. "Now do you see, Mister Neanderthal?" she asked, her mouth against my throat. "Now do you see?"

I said yes, and we kissed awhile, our bodies made slicker and younger by the magic of fast-flowing water, and then I led her back to the bed, and we made love.

She was gone from the bed when I woke. The sheets were damp. I felt drugged with the power of her. Wrapped in a towel, I stumbled into the sitting room. There was coffee, a soft-boiled egg that was still warm, and a note from Senator Jane.

Had to relieve Amanda, the note read. *May move Heather today, to South Bay Hosp., Newport B. Will call if anything turns up in Madison. I like you, M. Mucho. Call me. J.*

The coffee revived me. The time was six-fifteen. When I pulled on the police trousers, they seemed less confining. Let's hear it for a night of heated exercise. I found I was interested in the egg. The egg got me interested in the toast. I ate it all, then sopped up the rest of the egg with the last bite of toast. I stood at the window of room 745 thinking about how nice it would be to stay here all day, drinking coffee and watching television, Murdock the couch potato, and not have to plunge back into the world. Should I ring room service? Should I take a shower? Should I phone Deputy Hanks?

Too early.

Yawning, I finished dressing, and then I took the elevator down to the lobby. In the gray morning light, it looked less like Nirvana. Across the white tiled floor, I saw an OUT OF SERVICE sign on one elevator. In the second elevator, a Chicano was swabbing out the floor. In front of his elevator was a little yellow traffic triangle that said CLOSED. PLEASE EXCUSE OUR DELAY.

"How do I get down?" I asked.

"Servicio," he said, and pointed around the corner.

"Where does it go?"

"Al garaje."

"My car's in the lot."

He shrugged and went on mopping.

The desk clerk was apologetic. Take the service elevator to L-1. Turn left as you leave the elevator. Follow the green line to the red door. They don't make it easy, getting back into the world.

I followed the clerk's directions, L-1, green line, red door. The parking garage was gloomy. I noted three burned-out ceiling lights, the only flaw so far in the perfection of Xanadu. I opened the red door and stepped out into a chill winter morning, gray clouds, pale hint of sun. I came around a corner in time to see a Mercedes coupe, silver-gray, easing up out of the garage. The license plate read DUKE II. I stepped back behind the corner and waited. The Mercedes stopped and the passenger door opened and a man got out. It was the Blazer. He wore running shoes and a black running suit with a hood. He flipped the hood up and walked around to the driver's side. The driver's window lowered and I knew where Barb Duke had spent the night. The spiked hair was now frizzy punk. The face was in need of makeup. Blazer squatted down to say something to her. She leaned across the open window to give him a kiss.

What had Blazer done with his fillies?

With a wet squeak of rubber, Barb Duke pulled away. The Blazer stood, hands on hips, watching her go, and then he set off, jogging west. I counted to twenty, looked to make sure he was gone, and walked to my pickup. As I pulled out of the Xanadu lot, I saw a tall figure moving toward the hills. He was running now, moving at a good clip, just one more reason we'd called him the Blazer back in the jungles of Vietnam.

10

Back home on the beach, the red light was on, meaning I had messages. I put on the water for a pot of Murdock Blend. Then I changed clothes, sighing as I squirreled out of the tight uniform, and checked the phone machine.

Webby Smith had called last night to invite me to the Bal Musette, a twenties-type dance hall and bar in Corona Del Mar. He had a treat for me, he said. Jasmine, her name was. She was half French, half Chinese. Beautiful face and gorgeous legs. A dancer, Webby said. Your kind of girl, Sherlock. Dance your troubles away.

On the Heather Blasingame case, Webby had nothing to report. "My goddamn contacts over at the OC sheriff's won't give me the time of day. Maybe something's up, like you said. If you hear anything, buzz me. Wally's invited me for Xmas turkey. See you there, pal."

The second call was from Senator Jane. The room at South Bay Hospital would not be ready until tomorrow morning, so Heather was stuck at El Toro.

The good news was that she'd come awake for a minute or so this morning. Jane was excited. She hadn't told anyone yet, not even the doctors. If Heather stayed awake long enough to talk, Jane would call me immediately.

The third call was from Cindy Duke. It was after midnight, she said, and she just wanted to talk, and had I found out anything about her daddy?

Poor kid.

The fourth call was from Wheeler Duke. "Murdock?" he said. "Wheeler Duke here. Got a proposition for you. Like to talk to you about it, just me and you. Call me at this number before noon Friday." There was a click. I wrote down the number.

The fifth call was from Kristi Flamingo, a lady barber with a one-chair shop called Kristi Flamingo's Hair Emporium. "Sherlock?" Kristi breathed. "A hot news flash from the Coast Highway. Le Club's been sold. They're revamping Grogan's Grogerie and changing the name to something real dumb, and I want to buy you a memory-drink before everything goes kaputski. Call me at the shop before three. You're due for a cut."

I ground beans for Murdock Blend, which changes depending on the world situation and which coffee caravans are running. This Friday, the eve of Christmas Eve, it was one part Kenya, one part Colombian dark, and one part Viennese. The smell of ground beans always pleasures the senses, but today the joy was less intense. I made the coffee and poured a cup and called Deputy Hanks, at the East County station. They switched me around four times before I locked on to Lieutenant Rome, who made me wait seven minutes before coming back on the line. "I'm sorry, sir. Deputy Hanks is on vacation. I'm Lieutenant Rome. Perhaps I can help."

"Vacation? You sure about that?"

"Yes, sir. Took his family up north, I believe. Wanted an early jump on the holiday traffic, the lucky guy. Was there something I could help you with, sir?"

"I'm a private investigator working on the Xanadu Mall hit-and-run. Hanks said to call today. He'd been very helpful. Said he might have something for me."

"Did he say anything specifically?"

"Something on a witness," I said. "Maybe you could find his file."

There was a long pause. I heard voices murmuring, then a click, as of someone picking up a receiver. Lieutenant Rome came back on: "Could I have your name, please, sir? Last name first, then the first name, then the middle name."

I told him my name. He made me spell it out. I heard him punch it into the computer.

"And the number of your investigator's license, please?"

I opened my mouth to give him the number, and then I realized I was getting the runaround. There would be no help with witnesses. I hung up.

When in doubt, make a list.

Fortified by the coffee, I brought out a ballpoint and a yellow legal pad left behind by a lady. I jotted down names—Heather, Holly, Cindy—but nothing came to mind. So I drew a circle around *Holly* and connected it with lines to *Cindy* and *Heather*. I connected *Heather* to *Jane*, *Cindy* to *Barb*, *Barb* to *Uncle Jamie*, *Uncle Jamie* to *Wheeler Duke*. I connected *Blazer* to *Barb*, and then to the *Mystery Man*. I drew a box around all the names and labeled it *Xanadu*. I added towers and a clock. I wished I could draw. I connected *Wheeler Duke* to *Duke Construction* and *Duke Harbour*. I wrote *Duke Family* and added a question mark. I wrote down *Deputy Hanks* and connected him to *Heather.* I wrote *parking lot, hit-and-run, night.* In the opposite corner, I wrote *Carcassonne, Jamaica Cove, log, Woolford, lies, erasures.*

Two trails, Jane had said. What happens if there are two trails? Or three? Which trail does the tracker track? I folded the yellow paper, tucked it into a shirt pocket, and phoned Wheeler Duke. He answered on the second ring.

"Wheeler Duke," he said. "Who's got me?" His voice had humor. He sounded close, like on my roof. We made a date for eleven, the construction shack at Duke Harbour. "I'm not armed," he said, with a chuckle. "No lawyers. No secretaries. No seconds with spare pistols and clean white towels. I've heard about you, Murdock. They say you're tough. You know how to hang on. I like that. Otherwise, we wouldn't be talking. This is personal, just between you and me." Again, that edge of humor, the voice of big-time power, the confidence that only billions can bring.

"I understand."

"Looking forward to it," he said, and hung up.

I phoned Wally St. Moritz, to ask him what he knew about the Dukes. He said he'd make some inquiries. Then I gave him the rain-smeared words from Marvin Holly's inscription: *Blak, ravel, ortex.* Interesting, Wally said, and hung up.

While I waited, I doodled on my name diagram. A writer I know, a lady named Corinne who pens romance novels, does cluster diagrams every morning before she tackles the word processor. Swears they help clear her head. What could clear my head? I was standing at the window, staring out at the Pacific, when the phone rang. I could feel something building, but it was probably the storm contained in the black clouds out over the Pacific. I answered.

"Lancelot," Wally said. "I have a source."

Wally's source was a UCI professor in social ecology. His name was Roth. He was doing a book on Orange County, its money, its power. A whole chapter was devoted to the Dukes.

"One chapter's not much."

"I think he had trouble clearing that much," Wally said.

"Is he in town?"

"Yes. He can see you tomorrow afternoon, at four. He'll be in his office on the UCI campus. He's flying east tomorrow evening, so don't be late."

"Timely Murdock," I said. "What can you tell me about these words?"

"They're from William Blake, a variation on a quotation from one of the Prophetic Books. The works are fragmentary. I recall the line, but not the exact reference. Ortex is *vortex*, Blake's favorite symbol. *Ravel* is *Traveller*, spelled with two *l*'s. The image in question is of Blake's Traveller, a sort of spirit of confused movement, standing at the crossing of the vortices of Time and Space. *Vortices* is the plural of *vortex*."

"You talk about Blake like he lived next door."

"You don't read enough, Matthew. Blake was a good poet and a masterful engraver. Late eighteenth century, early nineteenth."

"What's that got to do with Holly?"

"We are surmising Holly gave the book to Heather, correct?"

"Correct."

"It's clear he was complimenting her."

"How so?"

Wally sighed at my lack of culture. The sigh

merged into a cough. When he had finished coughing, he blew his nose and said: "He attached her to a lofty image, Matthew. He sensed the presence before him of a poetic soul, a kindred spirit. Writers do communicate by metaphor."

"You just whipped past me, Professor."

"Think about it, Matthew. *Vortex, Traveller.* A metaphor can do noble work."

While Wally gave me his interpretation of Marvin's motives, I jotted some notes. *Ravel* was *Traveller* with two *l*'s, and referred to Heather and her trip up the coast. *Vortex,* according to Wally, was the swirling state of the poetic soul. Very appropriate, he said, for a writer's view of Xanadu.

"Think we could take this to the cops, Professor?"

Wally snorted. "You're bringing white wine for Christmas. And don't forget your meeting at UCI."

My next call was to Oscar Smith, the security guard who'd been on the switchboard at Xanadu Mall. No answer. I phoned Ward Bigelow, who said Oscar had been called out of town, back east somewhere, Yonkers, he thought, or maybe Syracuse. The only thing new on the Xanadu hit-and-run, Bigelow said, was that a guy from the sheriff's office had come by asking for Billy Hargrove, who was still up in Venice, hefting weights. I thanked Bigelow and phoned Roald Swensen in Chicago. Roald's an army buddy who has his own detective agency out in Oak Park. The phone was on daytime rates, so I talked fast. I asked Roald to drive up to Madison and check on Marvin Holly. Roald had a case to finish up today. Saturday was the earliest he could get to it. I said okay and dialed the number for Marvin Holly.

This time the answering machine didn't pick up. After a dozen rings, I hung up.

* * *

At ten-fifty I made a left turn across the oncoming traffic on the Coast Highway into the construction site at Duke Harbour. A light rain fell on the foundation forms, turning them dark gray. Framing timbers were laid out in stacks, enough, it looked like, to rebuild the city of Carthage.

I stopped in front of a gate and beeped my horn. The sign on the gate announced this was a project by Duke Construction. A security guard appeared. Under his slicker on the right hip I saw the bulge of a handgun in a holster. Water dripped off his cap as he swung the gate open. I drove through and he waved me on up the hill, through the maze of stacked building supplies where no one was working.

The pickup ground up the gravel road to the trailer office on wheels. I parked alongside a white Range Rover. Wheeler Duke, wearing his blue down vest, filled the doorway. He was bareheaded. His hair was silvery. I slammed the door and climbed the wooden steps to the office. He shook my hand and pulled me inside, out of the rain. "Wheeler Duke." Strong handshake, and the same silver-blue eyes as his daughter, Barb.

"Matt Murdock," I said.

"You're on time, Murdock. I like that."

I nodded. He waved me to a chair and walked to a coffeepot on a hot plate. I figured his weight at two-twenty. Even with the stooped shoulders, he had to be six feet three.

He handed me a mug of coffee and then fished in a desk drawer and brought out a bottle of VSOP. He poured a shot into his coffee and passed the bottle to me. "So you won't think it's poison," he said, grinning.

I added brandy to my coffee. Aromas wafted up.

The old man sat down behind the desk in a wooden swivel chair. Behind him on the wall I saw a blanket-covered desert canteen, a .30-.30 Winchester lever-action saddle gun hanging in a wall mount. Eighteen or twenty photos showed desert scenes, street scenes, and a building that looked like the Taj Mahal. Some of the people were in uniform, shorts and puttees. The photos were time-yellowed. He toasted me with his coffee mug and we drank together. Not bad.

"India," he said. "And Burma. I was over there during the war, with an intelligence outfit called the OSS. Great times we had. Great booze, good singing, three pretty women for every joe in uniform."

"Am I here because of Cindy, Mr. Duke?"

He grinned. "I like a man who gets right to it. She showed me your receipt for one dollar. That smacks of honesty. Said you wouldn't tell her mama on her, now she was my client. Kids love secrets, don't they?"

I rested the coffee mug on my leg. "She helped me out. I thought I'd help her out."

"You can help her best by leaving town."

I grinned. "I like it here."

He grinned back. "Thought maybe you'd like it better in another state."

"Any state?"

"Texas." He drank from his mug.

"Where in Texas?"

"Bastrop. Little burg near Austin. Lots of pretty women, I hear, and your money goes a long long way in the supermarket."

Bastrop was Senator Jane's hometown.

I let out a long breath. "I like it here."

He nodded. "I hear you. This move would be temporary. Six months, maybe a year. I understand you know people in Austin, in the government there. It's

a half-hour drive, Bastrop to Austin. You could up-
grade your vehicle, get yourself a fancy new Jeep
four-by-four."

"You've got me under surveillance?"

He waved away the charge. "A man has a right to
know who's driving around town with his teenage
granddaughter."

I set the coffee cup on his desk and stood up. "I
understand your concern, Mr. Duke. Why don't you
ask Cindy to fire me."

"I already did. Seems she's real high on you. Thinks
you're some kind of television hero. Wants you to find
her daddy."

"And you know where he is, don't you?"

Instead of answering, he reached down beneath
the desk and hauled out a battered black briefcase. It
was made like a saddlebag, straps, old silver buckles,
a stitched flap cover. No fancy attaché case for
Wheeler Duke. While I watched, he unfastened the
buckles and opened the case and hauled out a stack
of bank notes. Then another. One, two, three, four,
five. Each stack was bound with a white paper strip.
On each strip, someone had printed the number
10,000, with no dollar sign. "Half a year," he said.
"Maybe only a couple of months. Either way, we pay
you the full fifty for relocating."

I gripped the edge of the desk and leaned closer. "I
could have used that money in the seventies."

"The seventies were a tough time," he said.
"Blame the Demo-Rats for that. Blame the Fed, the
Washington bureaucrats. Lots of builders went un-
der."

"Not you. Not Duke Construction."

"Luck of the draw."

"No. You had money contacts. You squeezed people out."

He shrugged. "A grudge can wear you down, Murdock, grind your soul to a nub. Why not play this one smart?" He shoved the fifty thousand at me.

"Where's Marvin Holly, Mr. Duke?"

"Home in bed, sleeping it off. Drunk in some bar in Chicago. Lost in a Midwest snowstorm. Marvin's a grown man. Grown men lead their own lives. How the hell should I know?"

"He was here in town, trying to see Cindy."

The old man nodded. His face was sad now, the lines deeper. He shoved another ten thousand at me, raising the bid to sixty. "I don't want Marvin around here. Drives my Barbi-gal wild, turns her into a banshee. He signed a paper agreeing to that."

"His phone doesn't answer."

"Too drunk, probably." He ran a hand across his silver hair. "Don't get me wrong. I like old Marvin. He's got sand. I like the way he used to stand up to my daughter. Not very damn many men could do that for long. Also, I trust my Cindy-gal, and she likes him. But politically, the man's a total moron. This isn't the first wild hair he's had up his ass. It won't be his last."

"I want him as a witness."

"A witness to what?"

"The Xanadu hit-and-run."

"What makes you think he was there?"

"Evidence, for one thing. For another, you've put me under surveillance."

"Do me a favor, Murdock. Marvin's not here. If he was here, I'd convince him to go away."

"The good of the project, right?"

"Yes. Nothing's right until those morons on the commission give me final clearance on this beach."

"What about Cindy?"

He stood up then to face me across his desk. "Okay.

If you were me, how would you play it? My hophead
ex-son-in-law comes busting into the cove, crashes
the goddamn gate, bulls his way into my daughter's
home, scares the little maid half to death. Next thing
we know, he's taken a Louisville Slugger to my son's
vehicle and threatened my son with bodily harm. We
throw out the net, but no one can find him. An airport computer check says he's gone back home. We
heave a sigh and try to get back to work, coddling
that mare's nest of commissioners. Next thing we
know, you show up at the house, hunting for Marvin,
throwing your weight around."

"That's your version."

"My boy, Jamie, he filed a complaint on you. We
can have those papers served any minute, have you
spend Christmas in the pokey. But I wanted to talk to
you first. Know how long you could get tied up in
court around here?"

"The message is, don't mess with the Dukes."

The old man waved a hand at nothing in particular
and sat down again. "Look, Murdock. You're an honest man trying to make an honest dollar. I'm an old
builder trying to put in one last building site. You got
time on your side. My hourglass has about run out of
sand. That lady senator from Texas is no ordinary
female. She's angry about her daughter getting hurt.
Don't blame her one bit. And between me and you,
we're turning over rocks hunting for the prick that
did it. But right now the last thing I want is for the
liberal goddamn press to make a possible connection
between that accident and my ex-son-in-law."

"Why should they?"

"Because they make dirt, Murdock. They find it
where it's not because they're in the business of selling papers and dirt sells papers. So some nut makes a
call to the papers. I can see the headline now: 'Mys-

tery Witness Sought: Estranged Duke Ex-Son-in-Law, Missing in Action, Could Supply Evidence in Shopping Mall Hit-and-Run.' How's that?"

"Very professional."

"Thanks. I ran a newspaper once. The point is, Marvin's got a screw loose. He's a nut-case hippie draftee who got his fingers burned fighting for his country and he'll carry the hurt all the way to his grave. If the press found him, no telling what he'd say to get custody of his kid. To you, it's just another detecting job. But if Marvin starts jerking off for the press and if they start poking around, stirring things up, before you know it we'll have a tense situation here and those weak sisters on the Coastal Commission will give me another six-month delay and then the bankers will—" He stopped, stared at me. "Hell, man. You're a builder. You know how important it is to get rolling and keep on rolling! God damn it, this is my biggest project, and I am not about to allow a hangdog hippie sob sister liberal blow my chances by bleating to a bunch of crap-can environmentalist bleeding hearts!" Red in the face now, he shoved more money at me. Seventy thousand. Eighty. "Take the money. Go away for a while. Sit on your laurels. Tell the Senator the truth."

"What is the truth?"

"The trail's run cold. That's plain enough."

"How well did you know Marvin Holly?"

There was a long pause before the old man spoke. "Not well. We broke bread together a few times. I bailed him out of the drunk tank. After the divorce, I saw him over the years, maybe five times, when I'd be in Chicago on business."

"You think he loves Cindy?"

"Hell, yes. Who doesn't?"

"If he loves Cindy, why would he go back home before he sees her?"

"He broke the law. Assaulted my son. There are warrants out. Even Marvin would have realized that."

"He's not answering his phone."

Wheeler Duke ran a hand through his silver hair. "Par for the course."

"Why?"

"You read his book? The one about soldiers?"

"No. Not yet."

"Interesting yarn in there called 'The Chains of Christmas.' It's Marvin all over. Starts out in Vietnam, where his foxhole buddy's just been wounded the day before Christmas. Then shifts to childhood. The kid in the story is twelve, a kid watching the lights on the tree. His daddy's left home. His mama's in bed with a stranger. Two years later, his granddaddy dies on Christmas Day. In high school, his best girl jilts him two days before Christmas. In college, his fiancée gets killed in a car crash on Christmas Eve. We get back to Vietnam, his wounded buddy's just died and the story ends, just like that, on a low note, with Marvin sitting by the bed of a dead man singing 'Silent night, holy night.'"

Wheeler Duke sighed. "It was a crazy, depressing story, and in real life, Marvin was just as crazy, just as depressing. I'll never forget the Christmas he was around here, back in the early seventies. Drunk as a sailor, talking like an agent straight from Moscow. The man goes nuts at Christmas. My Barbi-gal calls it Xmas Bonkers. Maybe that's why he's not answering his phone."

The old man was logical, and in a way his scenario made sense. Marvin had left town because he was afraid of Duke power, Duke law. He wasn't answering his phone because he hated Christmas. They didn't want Marvin to surface for fear of jostling the

Coastal Commission. They wanted Murdock out of town so he wouldn't find Marvin. The money was good. It had a smell like no other and it would take me three years, working steady, to earn eighty thousand dollars. And in this business, you seldom worked steady. But there was too much urgency, too much push. And there was that slim connection between Barb and Blazer and Blazer and the mystery man and something going on with Uncle Jamie and down deep I knew the old man wasn't telling me the whole truth.

"Was Marvin there, Mr. Duke?"

"Where?"

"Was he there, at Xanadu, the night the girl got run down?"

"Christ, man! Haven't you heard a single goddamn word?"

I shoved the money at him. I stared at him across the table. "Cindy was carrying quite a money roll, Mr. Duke."

"So?"

"Four hundred dollars. Maybe more. I thought you should know. Lot of money for a kid her age."

"She's a Duke," he said.

For him, that was enough.

I walked outside, into the silver-gray drizzle. I climbed into the pickup and made a crunchy turn on the wet gravel drive. All those words from the old man. All that bluster. His last big development. His view of Marvin. The caring look in his eyes when Cindy's name came up. Telling me about the surveillance. His offer of eighty grand, for me to leave town. A lot of money. Was it a bribe? Or a warning shot?

In the rearview mirror, I saw the door to the construction shack open. Wheeler Duke stepped out. He did not wave good-bye.

11

The sun was out for a change as I drove north on the Coast Highway past the yacht brokers and the yacht outfitters and the fancy restaurants to Le Club of Newport Beach. I pulled up to the gate at the parking lot. A uniformed guard stepped out, holding a clipboard, and I could see this same scene taking place at this exact minute at Jamaica Cove—the control gate, the glassed-in gatehouse, the curled lip of the guard, the clipboard, the storm-trooper stare—and then all across southern California, the Sunbelt, America, the World.

He did not try to conceal his merriment at seeing my Ford. "Yes, sir?"

"I've got an appointment."

"Yes, sir. Name, sir?"

"Murdock."

He read down the names on his clipboard, lipping each one silently. It took a while. Cars lined up behind me. Two sleek Porsches. A Jag. A Mercedes. A Rolls. "Is that a member, sir?"

"No."

"Members only in the lot, sir. You can turn around here. It'll be tight, sir."

"I'm meeting Chick Vardeen," I said.

"Could you spell that for me, sir?"

I spelled it. He lipped down through the names again. A buddy with an identical smirk came to help with the traffic while my guard double-timed to the gatehouse to make a phone call. Colorful foursomes and twosomes strolled up from the tennis courts to the side entrance where a sign in Irish Gothic lettering directed thirsty members to Grogan's Grogerie. One of the tennis players was an old buddy—Uncle Jamie Duke, wearing mint green shorts and a bulky cable-knit sweater. Uncle Jamie was smiling down at a cute girl in a cute dress who looked maybe half his age. To my left, the fancy cars slid past me into the lot.

A tight smile from my guard. A smile expecting trouble. "Sorry, sir. Mr. Vardeen is no longer a member here. Now, if you'll just make your turn around that pylon there—"

I made the turn around the pylon and parked on the Coast Highway and walked back through the intermittent sunshine to the main entrance to Le Club. The door was new, much glass, much shiny metal. The entry was new, black tile, mirrors on the walls, scarlet drapes dripping, like a Berlin whorehouse. The woman at the desk was new, a narrow-faced brunette wearing purple leather that almost matched her lipstick. With a snide smile, she eyeballed my clothes and asked if she could help me.

"I've got an appointment with Mr. Duke," I said.

"And your name, sir?"

"Marvin Holly," I said.

Ms. Leather picked up a phone and stabbed the buttons. Without waiting for her okay, I nodded and headed down along the black tiles toward Grogan's. I turned a corner. The Grogan's sign was gone. In its place was a spiffy silver-on-black-plate sign that said THE PLATINUM ROOM. Times were changing at Le Club of Newport Beach.

I dropped Uncle Jamie Duke's name again to the maître d', a fussy fellow wearing a double-breasted blazer and a club tie. He asked for my card. I handed over one that identified me as Bob Travers from Prudential. He told me to wait and bustled inside to alert Uncle Jamie. I was still waiting when I smelled perfume and felt arms go around me from behind and a husky female voice said: "Sir Sherlock, you do need a trim!"

Kristi Flamingo lives up to her flamboyant name. She possesses vibrant red hair, vibrant green eyes, and a smile to be envied by any game show hostess alive. Kristi is thirty-three. I've known her for six years. She was thirty-three when we met and she does not believe in birthday parties. Thirty-three is a good year, she says. It has symmetry. It has balance.

Kristi's not tall, but she's curvy and sweetly built. Today, in honor of the season, she wore a lime-green jumpsuit and matching cowboy boots.

We hugged. She held me at arm's length. "You're broke again, is that it? Is that why you haven't stopped by?"

"I've got three days' work."

She shook me gently. "On the cuff, Sir Sherlock. In your profession, meeting the public, you've got to keep that image in high polish."

I grinned. She was a delight. The maître d' whispered up to hand me my Bob Travers card. "So sorry, Mr. . . . ah . . . Travers, but Mr. Duke has no recollection of an app—"

Kristi flashed him a platinum card. "He's with me,

Georges." The maître d' blinked, started to say something. We sailed past him into Grogan's—or the Platinum Room—arm in arm.

"We're too late," I said. "Change is afoot."

"Isn't it awful?" she said.

The old Grogan's had been outfitted like a sailors' tavern—stout wood tables, portholes for windows, captain's chairs you could get drunk in. The Platinum Room was being done in Thirties Decadent. Purple chairs, green curtains, that same black tile from the entry on the floor. We found a table across the room from Uncle Jamie and his party, a gaggle of folks in tennis clothes gathered at a table near the bar. Uncle Jamie was the oldest guy there. Three of the girls and one of the guys had to be under the drinking age. The prettiest girl, a California blonde with a pretty tan and a dazzling Hollywood smile, rested the toe of her shoe on Uncle Jamie's bare knee. The blonde was drinking a margarita. So far, Uncle Jamie had not acknowledged my presence on his turf. There was a small bandage on his ear.

Our waitress wore fishnet hose and high heels and a purple leather minidress, sleeveless, with maximum cleavage. The hair was mini-punk, like Barb Duke's. The lipstick shimmered like platinum.

Kristi ordered a gin and tonic. I ordered a draft. No draft, the waitress said, looking bored. I ordered Budweiser. No Bud, she said. Coors, I said. Sorry, she said. No Coors. You can play this game a couple of ways. You can ask them to list the beers. Then you give them the podium. Or you can keep naming beers they don't have. Schlitz, I said. Sorry. Old Milwaukee, I said. Never heard of it. Blatz, I said. Sir? Carling Black Label. Sir, she said. Would you like me to tell you what we do have? Could you do that, I said. She named the beers. I waited for the count of three,

Murdock the Great Decision Maker, and then ordered a Beck's. The waitress left in a huff.

"You feeling all right?" Kristi put a hand on my arm.

"Makes me testy, all this change."

She nodded and looked around at the decor. "I feel the same way. We had some good times here. I guess that's why I called. Around Christmas, for some reason, I always feel a little blue."

"Yeah."

Across the room, Uncle Jamie Duke was watching me. He leaned over, put his hand on the blonde's thigh, and spoke into her ear. She nodded, gave our table a smirky look, and walked trippingly out.

The drinks came. Kristi handed over her membership card. The waitress shimmied away, hips working like pistons underneath the tight leather, to speak to a second waitress. They looked like space twins. Identical outfits, identical hair, identical platinum smiles. I sighed and clinked glasses with Kristi. The beer was ice-cold.

"Help me out, Kristi."

"Anything."

"How old do you think our waitress is?"

"Twenty-two. Twenty-three." She sipped her drink. "You?"

"Not a day over seventeen."

"You're showing your age, Sir Sherlock."

I grinned and toasted her with my Beck's. "And you're a member of the Platinum Club."

She shrugged. "You just have to know the right people."

"And who would that be?"

"One of the new owners."

The blonde came back, followed by the maître d'. She sat down. The maître d' bent over to heed Uncle

Jamie. He nodded, yes, sir, Mr. Duke, and walked out. Two of the tennis players left. One of them called over his shoulder: "See you at the party!"

"So," Kristi said. "What was all that business at the door?"

"What business?"

"Georges, the maître d', said something about you meeting with Mr. Duke. Now he keeps looking over this way."

"Probably wants a date with you."

Kristi snorted, flicking her gaze at our waitress. "Even Miss Leather Hips is out of his age range."

Uncle Jamie's blonde came back to the table. She sat down, crossed her legs, and leaned over to whisper in Jamie's ear. "He's a creep." Kristi sipped her drink and stared across the room at Uncle Jamie's table. "Have you heard about the party?"

"Heard about it on the television. The annual Christmas Eve bash. At historic Duke Castle."

"That's the one. Well, a girl friend of mine is working it tomorrow. She's a waitress trying to break into the movies and she's heard that more deals go down at Duke Castle on Christmas Eve than all year long in Tinseltown and—" She broke off in midsentence to look over my shoulder. "Hey. Here's Louie!" She jumped up from her seat and ran across the Platinum Room toward a short man wearing a silver warm-up suit. I'd seen him before. He was the mystery man, Blazer's pal from last night, at the Hotel Xanadu. Letting out a delighted squeak, Kristi gave him a hug. My gut twisted. The maître d' hovered in the background. The mystery man kissed Kristi's hand. I turned back to my beer. There was one swallow left. I left it. I never had liked Beck's.

Kristi tugged her friend over to be introduced.

"Louie, I'd like you to meet a dear friend, Matt Murdock. Sir Sherlock, this is Louie."

I got up to shake hands. Louie stood five-seven, maybe five-eight. Ego crackled from his eyes. Macho handshake, oily grin. "Sherlock," he said. "Like in Sherlock Holmes?"

"It's a nickname, Louie." Kristi tugged at his sleeve. "Can you join us?"

"Love to." Louie blinked once at the maître d' as he pulled out a chair and sat. "So," he said. "Did you get my message?"

Kristi touched his hair, the light flashing off a ring on her right hand. "Eleven is great. Ten would be greater."

"Ten it is, kiddo." He turned to me. "Who else but a man's personal hairdresser would work on Christmas Eve, hey?"

Kristi winked at me. "Louie's got a big party coming up."

I nodded. Louie's drink came, brought by the maître d'. It was Perrier, a glass of shaved ice, a twist of lemon. Right behind the maître d' was our waitress, bearing fresh drinks for Kristi and me. Louie nodded, a slow dip of his chin, and turned to me as he poured. "So, how long you guys known each other?"

"Six years," I said.

"Great." He lifted his glass. "Terrific. Any friend of Kristi's is a friend of mine." He drank, carefully, measuring his sips before setting down the glass. His movements were measured. His eyes measured me. "So, what business are you in, Mr. Murdock?"

"Can't you guess, Louie?" Kristi said, giggling. "He's a private dick."

"Hey," Louie said, smiling. "My kid brother Rico wants to be a private eye. How do you get started?"

"There's a state exam. If you pass, you get a license.

It helps to have some experience working law enforcement."

He blinked. His eyes reminded me of photos of a prehistoric lizard. "You carry a gun? All that stuff?"

"Sometimes."

Louie looked admiringly at Kristi. "Kiddo, you know the best people. No, really." He turned back to me. "Quite a coincidence here, Mr. Murdock." He shook his head. "Hey, this is California, right? I'm Louie. How about I call you Matt?"

"Sure." I paused. "Louie."

He glanced at Kristi. "So, speaking of my kid brother, how would it be if you, like, took him under your wing, so to speak. Kind of taught him the ropes, the tricks of the detective trade?"

"We could talk about it."

"Hey, I'm not talking a freebie here. We'd make it worth your while. Whatever your rate is, plus some perks, like. Kristi can tell you. You do something for us. We reciprocate. Right, Kristi?"

"Absolutely."

"I'm on a case right now. But let's discuss it." I paused, longer this time. "Louie."

He nodded, but his frown lines deepened into furrows as he measured out his Perrier. I pictured him sailing through the day, making measured deals. "You don't like that, I got a cousin, Bobby Santini. Bobby's a Beverly Hills lawyer, only lately he's picked up some clients down here. Newport. Costa Mesa. Anaheim Hills. Villa Park. Just the other day we're talking, Bobby and me, and he asks me to recommend someone who can do some work for him down here. How about I pass along your name to my cousin?"

"That's nice of you, Louie."

He held out his hand. "So. Matt. How about a business card."

"I don't carry business cards."

Kristi passed over one of hers. It said *Kristi Flamingo's Hair Emporium, Newport's Only One Chair One Hair Stop.* She handed me a ballpoint. I turned the card over and wrote down the phone number of an answering service I used two years ago. I handed it to Louie, who nodded, then slipped it into a jacket pocket. "You a tennis player, Matt?"

"No."

"Too bad. Got a game coming up." He checked his watch. "And we're looking for a steady fourth. You look steady."

Kristi kicked me underneath the table. "He's just being modest, Louie. He really has played."

"That right? You just being modest?"

"No. But some of my best friends are tennis players."

Louie's face clouded. He crushed it back into a smile. "Yeah, yeah. That's good. That's very good. Well, I see a friend across the room. Maybe he'll fill in for us." Louie stood up. I could feel his eyes probing me from above. He held out a hand and we shook. "Be seeing you, Matt." And he walked off.

Kristi grabbed my arm and squeezed. "Hey. Hey, you, Sherlock?"

"Sorry."

"The door was open, big bucks on the horizon. You slammed it in his face. What's going on, anyway?"

I didn't want to tell her what I'd seen last night, my pal Blazer huddling with Louie at Hotel Xanadu. "Sorry, Kristi. I must be edgier than I thought. Didn't mean to ruin your contact."

Sporting a hurt look, Kristi retreated to the ladies' room. Over at the fun table, Louie and Uncle Jamie were chatting away like two long-lost frat brothers at a twenty-year reunion. Louie punched Uncle Jamie on the arm. Uncle Jamie floated a slow-motion right cross at Louie's blue-shadowed jaw. A guy like Louie would always need a shave, which guaranteed steady business for a professional barber. Kristi came back to the table just as Louie and Uncle Jamie headed out the door to the tennis courts, the blonde between them, like a porcelain doll.

I spent five sweaty minutes trying to smooth Kristi's feathers, but the brave shoulders were in a slump and the wonderful smile had gone away and it was no use. She insisted on signing for the drinks. "My treat," she said. "Your money's no good here."

Her face was drawn as she added a tip and scribbled her name. She folded the carbons carefully before tucking them into her purse.

Outside, the sky was dark over Newport Bay, promising more rain for Christmas. Kristi gave me a brief hug. "You have yourself a Merry," she said.

"What do you know about Louie?" I said.

"He's been nice to me." She held me at arm's length. "What's going on, Sir Sherlock?"

"I'm not sure."

"You know him, don't you?"

"No. I've seen him."

"You're into something that he's into." She gave me a little shake.

"Maybe. What's his last name?"

"Palermo."

I didn't recognize the name. "He's a customer, right?"

"Uh-huh. A very good customer. Tips you would not believe. Presents. Connections. Referrals." Her shoulders sagged as she let me go. "You won't tell me, will you?"

"There's nothing to tell, Kristi."

She shook her head, then turned and hurried away. She waited at the curb for a break in the traffic and then she darted across the highway to her barbershop. I waited until she had climbed the stairs and gone inside, and then I jogged the two blocks to my Ford. As I started the engine, the first raindrops glazed my windshield. Traffic was heavy, so it took me a couple of minutes to get turned and headed back to Le Club. The dashboard clock said 4:15. I parked in a restaurant lot across the street from the entrance to Le Club. The sky was darker now, the rain changing from random cosmic spit to steady drizzle. I reached under the seat and brought out my hunter's binoculars, made in Germany. They'd been a present from a client.

At four thirty-one, a dark Mercedes eased out of the lot, followed by a white Volkswagen Rabbit. Through the glasses I caught the first three letters of the license plate: DUK. Squealing rubber, my hazard lights flashing, I cut across traffic and swung in behind the white rabbit. The Mercedes led us south on the Coast Highway, through Corona Del Mar, past the stalled construction at Duke Harbour, past Jamaica Cove and the light at Main Beach, past the Hotel Laguna and the Place Across the Street and Fahrenheit 451, the bookstore. The light at the top of the hill caught me. I was about to run it when I saw a Laguna Beach police vehicle sitting catty-cornered to my left.

Sweating now, I waited for the light to change, and then I drove at the speed limit up the hill until the cop was out of sight. There was no sign of the Mercedes or the white rabbit.

Cursing, I cruised south for ten blocks. I came back north on Glenneyre, which was fast becoming a secondary main street. At the stop sign on Arroyo, I saw a motel vacancy sign. Nothing to lose, so I made a right and drove up Arroyo to the Edgewater Lagoona Motel. A couple of years ago, I'd met an old army buddy here, a rundown man in a rundown room. The tide would have to rise a hundred feet before the Edgewater would be at the water's edge. This was not Uncle Jamie's sort of place.

I went in anyway. The Mercedes was parked in front of room 29. I beamed it with my five-cell power flash. DUKE VII. The white rabbit was parked two cars down, between a Porsche and a new Chevrolet. I wrote down the numbers of the five rooms nearest the two cars: 27, 28, 29, 30, 31. Uncle Jamie and the white rabbit were three minutes ahead of me, barely time enough to register and get inside. Was Uncle Jamie a planner? Could he think far enough ahead to book the room? Was the porcelain blonde the driver of the white rabbit?

I drove to a 7-Eleven store and dialed 411 and got the number of the Edgewater. A man answered. He sounded half bombed.

"Is this the Edgewater Motel?"

"The Edgewater Lagoona. Yes, sir. How can I help you on this rainy December evening?"

"My name's Deputy Hanks. I'm with the Orange County sheriff and we're coordinating a drug sweep in the area. Am I speaking to the manager here?"

"Yes, sir." The voice trembled. "I certainly hope nothing's wrong at the—"

I cut him off. "We don't want to alarm you, sir, but a combined task force is about to move on the sweep and—"

"What? What's that?"

"Who am I speaking to, please?"

"What's that?"

"Could you give me your name, please?"

"Tallent," he said. "John Tallent."

"Right, Mr. Tallent. This is a pretty good-sized operation going here. We're expecting upwards of a hundred million in illegal contraband. I suppose you've heard about our Citizen's Alert Award?"

"No, I—"

"Yes, sir. Well, it goes like this. Any citizen providing peace officers in effecting an arrest will be considered for an award consisting of a plaque or medal containing that citizen's name and the time and place of assistance to said officer and in addition will receive a cash stipend not to exceed the sum of ten thousand dollars. Now, how does that sound?"

"Ten. Thousand?" He was close to passing out.

"Yes, sir."

"H-how can I help?"

"What I need from you right now, sir, is the registration information on five rooms in your facility."

"Five rooms?"

"That's right."

"Are they part of the . . . the operation?"

"Afraid I can't tell you, sir. That's classified."

He gulped. "All right. What are the rooms?"

I read him the numbers. As he passed me the information dope, I wrote down the names and the makes of cars and the state license plates. Hanzl, room 27, Buick, Kansas. Evans, room 28, Chevrolet, California. Roberts, room 29, Porsche, Arizona. Pomeroy, room 30, Ford, California. Rodriguez, room 31, Cadillac, B.C., Mexico. B.C. meant Baja California. No Uncle Jamie Duke. No Mercedes. But he was there. So he had to be registered. What name was he using?

I thanked John Tallent and said we'd be in touch about his award. The rain was falling harder now. I stared into it, waiting for an idea to happen. I could break down all the doors at the Edgewater. I could stage a fire and ring the alarm.

I bought myself a cup of coffee at the machine inside the 7-Eleven. To use the phone, I had to wait while a kid in white Jalisco pants and a Mexican serape begged his girl friend to let him come back, *querida*. The girl said yes, finally. The kid left, skipping through the puddles to his van. Then I called Wally St. Moritz.

When he answered, I told him what was up and read him the names of the people in the rooms at the Edgewater. "Hmm," he said. "One name rings a bell. Where are you, Matthew?"

"At a 7-Eleven in wonderful Laguna. Which name?"

"Pomeroy. Let me call my professorial friend. Buzz me back in five minutes."

I had to wait another five minutes for the phone. Wally answered on the first ring. "Pomeroy," he said, "was the maiden name of James Duke's mother, Edith Adams Pomeroy. That's where the P comes from."

"Jamie Pomeroy Duke."

"Assuredly."

Pay dirt. The jerk had registered using his middle name. That showed zero imagination.

I drove back to the motel. Pomeroy was in room 30. I sipped the coffee and waited. At six thirty-seven, the white rabbit came out of the lot and drove past me. Fifteen minutes later, the Mercedes followed. I left the pickup parked on the street and jogged through the rain to room 30. Tonight, my timing was on. The lock took fifteen seconds.

Room number 30 was a mess. Rumpled sheets, bedclothes on the floor, a chair tilted over. The air reeked of marijuana and sin. In the bathroom the towels were still draped on the racks. One corner of a washcloth held a single glob of drying blood. I stared at the bed. The white rabbit had left. Then Uncle Jamie in his Mercedes. He hadn't used the fifteen minutes to tidy up. Maybe he'd been on the phone to Louie.

A closer check of the sheets showed a couple more blood streaks. Dim, like blood from a scratch. Or scratches.

I sat on the edge of the bed and swept the room. Something didn't mesh. I walked to the closet, saw what it was. The lock was a brass dead bolt Schlage, professionally installed. This one was tougher. Ninety seconds, hands sweating, listening to the internal mechanisms, losing it, trying again, heart pounding, waiting for that click. At last it opened into an over-size closet, larger than the ones I remembered in my motel experience. Back against the wall was a metal cabinet, office-tan in color and seven feet tall, with a padlock securing the wide double doors. Uncle Jamie's secret cache.

The third lock took me two minutes. Outside, in the parking lot, a car braked, doors slammed. Sweat popped out on my forehead as I paused, feeling my way through the picks into the mystery tumblers inside. Voices at the door, the knob turning. Had I locked the damned thing behind me?

"Hey, Jimmy," a voice said. "You got the wrong room, you spud!"

Laughter then, the voices drifting away, then coming more faintly through the wall from the room next door.

The lock clicked loose. Using my handkerchief on the handle, I swung the door open. The locker was a portable closet unit filled with hanging costumes. Boy costumes on the right, girl costumes on the left. I found a frock coat and black pants and a wide black belt. The frock coat was a size 48, maybe larger. The pants were huge. So was the pirate outfit. So was the space suit.

The girl costumes, on the other hand, were on the petite side. Frilly gowns, a leather jumpsuit, a micro-mini that couldn't have measured more than fourteen inches from hem to waist. All the gowns were see-through. One needed laundering. Several strips of dried blood ran diagonally along the bodice.

At the rear of the wall I found a riding crop, two pairs of handcuffs, and some wicked switches. Birch, I thought. Or maybe weeping willow.

I felt like torching the place.

Instead, I packed Uncle Jamie's toys back into the metal cabinet, relocked the padlock and the closet and the front door, and got out of there.

Back at the 7-Eleven, I bought a beer to steady my nerves and I phoned John Tallent at the Edgewater desk. When he answered I identified myself as Deputy Hanks and asked him about the party in room 30.

"What is it you'd like to know, Deputy?"

"How does he pay?"

"Beg pardon?"

"How does he pay?" I growled. "For the room."

"Oh," he said. "That's Mr. Pomeroy. Always pays cash."

"How long has he had the room?"

"Oh," said John Tallent. "I think he's been with us now for several months. He's a wonderful tenant, pays on time, never any problem of any kind—" He stopped. "I hope you aren't implying with your questions that something about Mr. Pomeroy is amiss, because if you—"

"No. Nothing like that. Give me the same information about the other four."

He gave me the information. I stared into the rain, watching the traffic slosh by on Glenneyre Street in wonderful Laguna.

12

An ambulance droned past me as I swung into the parking lot at El Toro General. A sheriff's vehicle, its roof bar rotating, trailed the ambulance. Behind the sheriff's vehicle was a red truck that said EAST COUNTY PARAMEDIC UNIT.

The south parking lot was full, so I located a slot near the Emergency Room. Two orderlies in white uniforms were wheeling a stretcher inside while a nurse supervised. Inside the automatic door a deputy took down a statement from a teenage girl. Her left arm was in a sling. Her hair was matted down. The left sleeve of her white coat had been ripped away by something sharp and jagged.

A sign directed me to the lobby. I turned right, away from the stringent hospital smells and the face of fear.

The elevator was crowded going up. I got off at Four, with several other folks. They turned right. I turned left. A nurse came out of Heather's room and walked to the nurses' station, where she picked up a phone. As I went past, she was speaking into the phone and I heard her say "out again."

I knocked lightly before sticking my head inside the door to Heather's room. Senator Jane stood at the window, her arms folded, staring out at the freeway and the lighted bulk of Xanadu Mall. She looked like a ruler worrying over a kingdom. She turned, saw it was me, and uttered a soft cry. We met in the center of the room. She gave me a hug. The room smelled of sweat and sterile disinfectant. Heather lay in the bed, her eyes closed. A bandage covered the right side of her face and tubes and wires connected her to three different computerized medical devices. Jane led me outside, where we sat down.

"Thank you for coming."

"How is she?"

Jane looked at me questioningly. "You got my message?"

"No."

She shook her head. "I left one, around four. And again just after five. Heather was awake, twice. The first time she didn't know where she was and she called me Mommy. She hasn't called me that for years. The second time she asked where she was and how long she'd been here. It seemed to take a terrible effort to ask."

"She's had a rough time of it."

"The doctor examined her. Her respiration was better, he said. And her heart seemed stronger, but not much. He's talking about surgery."

"When?"

"Soon. Tomorrow, if she's strong enough. Surgery scares me."

"What about the other hospital?"

Jane nodded. "Newport Beach. We're moving her in the morning."

"Would you like me to be here?"

"Thank you. You're so thoughtful." She squeezed my arm and stood up. "Could you wait a few minutes more, Matt? I had this feeling Heather might—"

"Sure. I'll park right here. It's been quite a day." Jane had started to walk away when I asked her a question. "How many people know Heather was awake?"

"The doctor. A couple of nurses." She paused. "That policeman."

"Hanks?"

"No. Lieutenant Rome. I phoned him at the substation."

"Good old Lieutenant Rome. How was he?"

"He remembered us. They were very busy, he said, because of the holidays, but he promised to stop by the hospital later."

"Has he been here?"

"No."

Jane went back into Heather's room. I borrowed paper from a nurse and sat down in a purple plastic chair. From my pocket I pulled out the bubble diagram I'd made earlier, before my meeting with Wheeler Duke. I studied what I'd done, and then wrote fresh notes:

If Marvin hates California, why does he race out here? Best guess: Cindy's in trouble. After ruffling Duke family feathers, Marvin meets Heather at Xanadu. Did he witness the hit-and-run? Why is Barb Duke edgy about Marvin's visit? Why was there no record of his entry into Carcassonne?

Maybe Swensen would find something out, when he took his trip to Madison.

I stopped writing for a moment and closed my eyes. Lots of connections, but no clear pattern yet. A bell clanged, echoing down the corridor. A voice said something in medical jargon. I opened my eyes and tried another diagram. I wrote *Xanadu* in the lower left corner, drew a line from that to *Carcassonne* in the center of the page. I wrote *Hospital,* connected that to *Xanadu,* added the names of Jane and Heather. I wrote *Le Club* on the far right, and added the names of Uncle Jamie and Louie Palermo.

Louie.

Where did he come from?

Are Louie and Uncle Jamie just tennis pals?

I wrote down *Edgewater Lagoona,* added Uncle Jamie's name, along with the letters *S&M.* I connected the *Edgewater* to *Le Club.* I wrote down *Xanadu Hotel,* and added *Louie Palermo, Blazer, ladies of the evening,* and *Barb Duke.*

So:

Louie Palermo knows Uncle Jamie.

Louie also knows Blazer.

Blazer knows Barb, Uncle Jamie's sister.

Louie, Louie. Who knows him? Who can brief me?

At the nurses' station, I asked about a pay phone. Around the corner, the nurse said, and down the hall near the Coke machine. At the phone, I dialed information for Los Angeles, area code 213, and got the number for Alicia Beringer. A rainy December night, maybe she'd be home, snug. The phone rang five times before she answered. "Yes?"

"It's Matt Murdock, Counselor. Calling from Murdock Country. How are you?"

"Sherlock? Is it really you?"

"Yeah. It's me. I've got a favor."

"Funny you should have called." There was a crackle on the line, and then Alicia's voice. "The office is hiring some extra help. Investigators of known prowess. I turned your name in."

"Thanks, Counselor. They'll put me in the fed

computer. The IRS will audit me, hunt me down with trained attack dogs."

"Your paranoia is showing, Sherlock. This is a grand jury probe, federal, of course, on your turf. Knowing your situation, I thought I'd throw some business your way."

"Thanks. Any idea when this probe will start?"

"Next year. Late spring, maybe early summer. So. What can I do for you?"

I told her what I wanted, anything on Louie Palermo. She recognized the name. The Palermos were big in L.A. crime. She said I could call her back tomorrow, noonish. We said good-bye and hung up. I got back to my purple chair just as Jane came out of Heather's room, blowing her nose with a tissue. Her eyes were puffy from crying. She needed a breath of air, so we headed outside, stood under a canopy on a tight fourth-floor balcony. Jane was beat. She'd been here from early morning, when she left me at the hotel, until one, when Amanda had relieved her. She'd come back around three-thirty to relieve Amanda, who was due back at nine. When I told Jane about Wheeler Duke's spies and the eighty grand, she grabbed my hand.

"Surveillance? Eighty thousand dollars?"

"Yup."

"You don't sound surprised."

"I've had a chance to digest."

"Then he's hiding something."

"Rich people usually are. The question is, can we find it? If we find it, can we use it?"

"I feel violated. How dare he?" Jane crossed her arms and hugged herself. "That dirty old man, setting his spies on people. He should be thrown in jail."

"My fault, for not spotting them last night. Visiting your room got me going. I let down my guard."

She pecked me on the cheek. "I'm cold. Let's go back inside."

I held the door for her and we were back inside with the hospital smells. A nurse passed, looking trim and professional in her hospital whites. Was she spying for Wheeler Duke? An old party rounded the corner in his wheelchair. He had earphones in his ears, a yellow Walkman-type radio in his lap. Was he a spy for Wheeler Duke?

I waited outside the room while Jane checked on Heather. No change, she said, taking my hand. "I feel eyes, everywhere."

"Yeah."

"This is your profession. Spying."

"Detecting," I said.

"Um." She let go my hand. "What about the man from Chicago? The one you hired?"

"A good man. We were in Vietnam together. He can't get up to Madison until tomorrow."

"That was a good idea. Amanda telephoned my connections in Madison. One didn't answer. The other two are out of the city until after the holidays."

We sat there for a while without saying anything. A voice on a loudspeaker announced that visiting hours were over. People came out of rooms and headed for the elevators.

Jane turned to me. "About tonight, Matt. I need to stay here, stay close to Heather. Last night was, well, glorious. There's nothing I'd like better than a repeat performance." A flicker of a smile in her eyes. "Rain check?"

"Done. I'll stay with you."

She nodded. Tears came to her eyes, making her fish in her purse for a Kleenex. She blew her nose. I walked to the men's room and used the facilities.

When I came out, Jane was waiting for me. Her face was pale.

"What's up?"

"A phone call," she said. "For you, at the nurses' station. It's Dr. St. Moritz. Something about your house."

"My house?"

We hurried to the nurses' station.

"Are you Mr. Murdock?" a nurse said.

"Yes."

"Use that one, over there. Your call is on line eight."

I walked to the corner and picked up the phone. I pressed eight and heard a clicking on the line and then Wally's voice: "Matthew? Did you hear?"

"Hear what?"

"A fire," Wally said. "At your abode. They've contained it, fire department on the scene. No one's allowed up yet, but it appears most of your living room's gone."

"Jesus." Sweat broke out on my forehead, under my arms. "What the hell happened?"

"Revelers," Wally said. "Holiday revelers."

I snapped at him. "Speak English, Professor!"

"Right. Sorry. Three drunks were shooting off fireworks near the pier. The fire department people think a rocket pierced your side window, near your stereo wall. Fire broke out. Leo and two employees were first on the scene, with fire extinguishers. The employees contained much of the blaze. The department was called and they responded quickly. Leo took his dog and went in search of the perpetrators."

Good old Leo. "Any luck?"

"It seems that he located one. Chased the poor fellow around, finally ran him out onto the pier, where Leo bashed him."

"Good. Who was it?"

"We won't know until he wakes up, Matthew. He's in the jail ward at the medical center. Leo's blow knocked him off the pier, where he hit his noggin. At the last report, the man was still unconscious."

"Jesus." I was mad now. "Leo's okay?"

"Oh, yes. And bristling with visions of his former pugilistic prowess."

"Anyone else hurt?"

"Two customers were taken away, suffering from smoke inhalation. It could have been worse, Matthew. Much worse."

I was starting to shake. Other people get burned out. You see it on the nightly news, the scorched varnish, the wet ashes, the grief. But it never happens to you. My mind was racing.

"What about your shop? Leo's café?"

"Smoke damage. Leo's quick work saved the property. The insurance people are en route. Since the policy is yours, they'll want to talk to you. What are your plans?"

I was aware of Jane, standing by, sending waves of sympathy my way. God damn the holidays. God damn holiday drunks. I wanted to start rebuilding right away. This instant. The fire, my home burning, drove everything else out of my head: Jane, Heather, Holly, Cindy, Wheeler Duke's money, Uncle Jamie's secret sex hideaway. Murdock's Castle had been damaged. Murdock's friends had been threatened. I wanted to kick the shit out of the geeks that did it. My stomach felt queasy. "I'm leaving now, Prof. Thirty minutes. Meet me at Leo's, okay?"

"I'll be waiting, Matthew."

I hung up and turned to Jane.

"A fire?" she asked.

"Yeah. Assholes with fireworks, took out my living

room, God only knows what else. Goddamn place will stink with smoke."

"Oh, Matt," she said. "I'm so sorry."

I checked my watch again: 8:42. "Look. I need to get over there and meet with the insurance guy. I should be back here by ten, maybe ten-thirty. I hate to leave, but—"

She came into the circle of my arms and I felt her body, warm and solid, against mine. She nodded, and then put her face up for a kiss. "You have to go," she said. "And I only wish I could go with you. Amanda's arriving any minute. We'll be here when you get back."

I wanted to stay. I had to go. I gave her one more hug and then I let her go and headed for the elevator. The last thing I saw before hitting the stairs was Senator Jane standing at Heather's doorway.

Outside the hospital, the rain had stopped and a soft breeze was blowing in from the west. Cars drifted past me, on their way out. Across the freeway, Xanadu glimmered like a Christmas tree from a kid's happy dream. I saw the car as I was starting up, a black BMW in a slot off to the right. The car, a twin to Blazer's German-made honey, was low-slung, gleaming, expensive. The windows were tinted dark, making it tough to see inside. No exhaust plumes. No sign of the driver. I backed up, rammed the Ford into first, spraying water, and barreled out.

Zooming north on the San Diego Freeway, I kept the Ford at eighty, zipping past holiday slowpokes. Screw the highway patrol. Murdock was going home. I turned the radio to KNX, hoping they'd have a report—vandals have been detained in connection with a blaze at the residence of Matthew Murdock, a private investigator based in Newport Beach; arson is suspected—but all I got was a report of the President leaving Camp David for Palm Springs. The needle climbed to eighty-five. I saw brights in the rearview, so I slowed to seventy, sixty-eight, alert for the highway patrol. The car slid past, a sleek black Lincoln. I climbed back to eighty-five and started an inventory of my stuff. What was ruined? What was salvageable? What would I have to replace?

The sofa, gone. I'd need new upholstery, at least. The stereo, gone. Six hundred bucks to replace it, maybe more. Should I move up to a compact disc player? The television, question mark. The miniblinds, probably melted away into glue. The kitchen appli—

Headlights on high beam zinged my eyes in the rearview, cutting into my inventory review. I slowed to sixty-five, sixty-two. The limit was fifty-five. They're supposed to let you go five miles over. The headlights jammed my rearview mirror and a red light came on, shit, and I recognized the unmistakable outlines of a CHP cruiser. We had just passed Lake Forest and were rounding the curve over Interstate 5. A sign said right lane for Irvine Center Drive. The CHP cruiser pulled alongside and waved me over. There were two officers in the car, unusual, because CHP boys travel alone. The officer in the passenger seat waved at me to slow down, which I did. The cruiser eased ahead of me and a voice on a loudspeaker directed me to follow along. My speedometer read fifty, then forty-seven. Bad time for a ticket. Bad time for a hassle.

My road speed was down to forty when I saw a vehicle coming up behind me fast, headlights on high beam. Two cars slid by on the left. I flipped down the bright nightguard shield on my rearview and leaned to the right.

At the Irvine Center off-ramp, the CHP cruiser

slowed to thirty-five and ordered me onto the wet shoulder. Up ahead, I saw a blinking red beacon and then a Cal Trans sign announcing more construction. NO SHOULDER, the sign said. NO STOPPING ANYTIME.

The headlights behind me slowed and swung into the right lane, behind me. That was a surprise. Here Mister High Beams had been barreling along at seventy, seventy-five, coming up fast, and suddenly he slows down and pops into my lane. Checking him out in the rearview, I saw a big square van, blue or maybe black. As he came closer, the headlights went to low beam. Thank you for your courtesy. More cars passed as we approached the blinking red beacon. This was a lousy place to stop. Mud everywhere. Concrete drainage tubes. A nice deep ditch. Bad police work.

The next exit was Laguna Canyon Road and I wondered why the cruiser wasn't pulling me off there. Suddenly, the van was on top of me, headlights on high again, and now the brightness was magnified by a blinding spotlight aimed in my side mirror and another aimed at my inside rearview. The nightguard wasn't much help. I blinked my lights at the CHP cruiser, to let them know the van was crowding me, and then he was around, big flat nose edging up close. Two figures in there, a driver, a passenger to work the second spot.

The CHP cruiser braked, red lights bright against the glare, and the van pulled alongside me. I slammed on my brakes and the window of the van slid down and I knew they hadn't lowered it to ask me directions to Disneyland. It was an ambush and they had me dead. I kicked myself for not spotting it sooner.

Nice trap. I couldn't turn right, into the muddy muck of construction. If I slowed down, I'd lose mo-

mentum, so I cranked the wheel to the left, smacking
the side of the van, feeling my face splashed with
splintering glass as I hunkered down, head between
shoulders to make less of a target, goosing the accelerator, ramming the police cruiser.

I leaned sideways and clawed at the glove box for
my Beretta.

Locked. The special key was on a ring with the
ignition key.

Tires squealing, the van reeled into the next lane,
where it collided with a passenger car, a yellow
Toyota, and slid off the road to the left shoulder. I
kept on shoving the cruiser.

The bumper of my pickup is big and heavy, made
of reinforced steel, so it chewed up the cruiser's rear
end. The cruiser was a recent model, juiced up, but
no match for the four-hundred-plus horses in my
Ford. Go, horses! Whoo-ee. With the accelerator on
the floor, I shoved the cruiser ahead of me maybe a
hundred feet along the shoulder before it got loose,
the driver fishtailing as he tried to pull away from
me, which is the way I caught him the second time, at
an angle, the Ford bumper ramming the rear door on
the driver's side, sending the cruiser off the road and
into a handy ditch filled with construction mud.

I braked about twenty yards up the road from the
cruiser, turned off the engine, yanked out the ignition key, and, with fingers sparking adrenaline,
jammed the key into the lock of the glove box. The
van roared past me on the left, accelerating. I ducked
below the window level and saw muzzle blast as they
fired from the passenger window, the bullets thudding into the body of my truck, pockmarks appearing
in my windshield.

A pain knifed through my shoulder, red, burning.
I grabbed the holster, jerked out the Beretta, and

jacked a shell into the chamber. The van turned right, heading for Laguna Canyon Road. I cranked the starter of the Ford, but the engine wouldn't catch. Behind me, and to the left, the Toyota was stopped, blocking two left lanes on the freeway, and motorists gave me their horns as they cranked on past. The Toyota's hazard lights blinked on-off, on-off, on-off. The Ford started. There was another near miss with a zooming motorist as I ground into first and headed after the van.

Anger flared, a bright, burning blaze behind my eyes. First, my house is torched, pulling me away from the hospital. Second, a setup with a fake CHP team and a killer van. So who wanted Murdock dead? A long list. People I'd hurt. People I'd sent to jail. Relatives of those people. Nuts. Creeps. Geeks. World full of dingdongs. No time to work through the list now.

Had to nail that van.

There were puddles of water on Laguna Canyon Road. Something warm and gooey oozed down my face. My arm hurt like hell, telling me I'd been shot. The death van was ahead of me by thirty seconds. Pros would have a preplanned getaway, a hideout in Laguna Canyon, a helicopter chop-chopping.

The pickup slammed through a puddle and sloshed around on the road. I passed two vehicles, party folks, it looked like, on their way into Laguna Beach for fun and frolic. The speedometer needle raked over to eighty-four, eighty-six. Speed rocked the pickup. Up ahead, the road narrowed and I came within inches of clipping a pair of eyeball headlights that zoomed at me out of the gloom. The pickup shuddered as I swerved and I took out some bushes at the side of the road. If I'd had a cellular phone, I'd have alerted Webby Smith to set up a roadblock.

On the straightaway before the signal at El Toro Road, I caught a glimpse of taillights. I punched the accelerator. The pickup leaped ahead. I came around a curve to see the signal, red, and the van knifing aside a sports car as it bulled on through. The signal was still red when I reached it, but now traffic on El Toro had stacked up behind the sports car, leaving me a narrow slot for passage.

My speedometer clocked eighty-seven as I left the signal behind. I hadn't gained on the van, so he had to be going the same speed. About a half mile beyond the signal, the straightaway loops into Big Bend, a wicked hairpin curve where speeders die. The posted speed limit is thirty.

The van rocketed into the first curve of Big Bend. At the side of the road, a red roof flasher came on, help at last from the local law. The van swerved—you could see the taillights bobbling as the rear of the van knocked the police vehicle sideways—and then, in slow motion, the blue and white rolled over, away from the road, and settled on its left side, throwing mottled red beams from its turning roof light onto the surrounding trees.

Damn.

As I closed on the scene, the death van was stalled across two lanes. A car coming from the other direction cut behind it, into my lane. The police vehicle was on its side, the right front wheel slowly rotating. I swerved to avoid the oncoming car. A horn honked angrily.

I was thirty yards from the van when it backed up and made an awkward turn and headed around the curve. My tires skidded on the wet pavement as I fought for traction, and then I was gaining on the van on the curve, my headlights on bright, pushing up behind the wide black double doors, pushing and pushing, hoping to shove him as far as the sobriety checkpoint down by the Irvine Bowl.

You'd like to kill him but you have blood in your eyes and you're feeling weaker and weaker, strength fading now, and then the right rear door swinging open as we come around the last curve of the hairpin and a figure kneeling in the maw of the van, wearing dark battle dress and a commando skullcap, glint of light on metal as he brings an automatic weapon to bear, muzzle flash as he fires, bing, bing, headlights popping as bullets stripe your pocked windshield, the van lurching ahead, whine of bullets, this is it, pal, this is the moment, you're in his sights and you've got only one good hand because the other one is out of commission, leaving you no time, and so before he has a chance to blow you away you floorboard the Ford, crunching your nose into the van's rear, not feeling much impact, but just enough to send the van zigging off the road and sideways into a great big eucalyptus tree.

Whump.

It slammed into the tree and was still.

13

It took much effort to bring the Ford to a stop. Seven motorists, count 'em, slowed to gawk at the crash, then went on about their business. The eighth motorist stopped.

I found the Arnica bottle, but it took me a hundred years to get the top unscrewed. Arnica is strong stuff, five pellets recommended, maybe six, but by the time I got the top off the pain was pumping through me like a jackhammer so I upended the bottle and took in a bunch, not counting, just wanting the pain to stop long enough so I could climb out from behind the wheel and check to see who those bastards were.

Didn't make it.

The motorist who stopped was an old guy wearing a raincoat. He kept asking questions. What's your name? Where do you live? Fire, I said. Set fire to scatter me over the blacktop. Pricks set me on fire.

I passed out. I came awake hearing voices. Lights hovered over me. My feet were cold. My teeth chattered.

"He's awake, Lieutenant."

"Sherlock?" a voice said. "God damn you, Sherlock. You okay?"

"It hurts," I said.

"Sherlock." Someone shaking me now, rattling my bones. "It's me, the Iron Man. What's your name, pal?"

"Hey, Iron Man." I felt weak, like a baby floating in a diaper ad. Upsy-daisy. Upsy and daisy-doozy. Murdock the human yo-yo. "Tried to herd them down to you but—"

"The sedative's working now," a voice said.

"Where are they taking him?"

But before I could hear the answer, I floated off.

Lights. Hospital smells. A flicker of pain in my arm, getting deeper, meaner, trying to back away as it bloomed larger, shoulder, neck, belly, head, and then the sound of someone moaning.

Me.

My voice.

Voices.

And then tumbling into a dark, troubled sleep.

"Matthew. Here. Take this."

Something in my mouth, a little sweet. Mouth, dry as the Mojave. Pain, still there. I opened one eye. Dim in here, like a man losing his eyesight. It took a major effort to close the eye. I worked up saliva, just a dab, to dissolve the pills under my tongue, tiny time pills, my head trapped in a plastic bubble. Voices outside the bubble, mumbling, not getting through the plastic.

Mumble, mumble.

Mumble.

Speak up, you guys.

"It's working." Wally's voice, on my left, where the pain was.

"We had a lunch date, Sherlock. Friday, remember?" Webby Smith's voice, on my right.

This time I opened both eyes. Webby Smith wore his watch commander's uniform, black, with silver rank markings. Wally St. Moritz wore a tweed jacket, no tie, and a button-down-collar shirt. In his hand was a small brown bottle.

"Did you get 'em?" I croaked.

"You did."

I nodded. "Good. Who were they?"

"Shooters. Pros. No ID. We're running prints through."

I played the tape backward inside my head to the red beacon and the CHP cruiser. I asked about that.

"We found the cruiser in the mud on northbound I-405. It had been lifted earlier in the day from the CHP motor pool in Oceanside. Your Ford crumpled it pretty good. There was blood inside, and some ejected hulls."

Hulls. That meant shell casings. I was alive. "No perps?"

"We've got an APB out. Traffic's still tied up south of there because of the accidents, way past Xanadu Mall. What the hell went down?"

Speaking slowly, I ran them through the scenario of events on the San Diego Freeway. Webby jotted notes. It seemed to take a long time. Telling takes longer than doing. Who was it said that? When I paused, Wally shoved more pellets under my tongue.

"Arnica tonight," he said. "Staphysagria tomorrow."

"Where am I?" I asked.

"El Toro General."

"How's the kid? The Blasingame girl? When I left,

they thought she might wake up and tell us something."

There was a long pause. Wally coughed. Webby put his hand on my arm. "She didn't make it, Matthew."

"Huh?"

"She went under again. Didn't come back out."

"Jesus. What happened? Where's J— where's the Senator?"

"She came apart at the seams, so they gave her a shot."

"A shot? What for?"

"A sedative, to calm her down. She was pretty crazy."

"What happened, guys?"

"She was yelling," Webby said. "Screaming at the nurses. Got in the way of procedure. They were afraid she'd do herself some bodily harm, so they gave her a sedative."

"What was she screaming about?" There was a silence while Webby looked at Wally, while I looked from one to the other. Pals were supposed to level with you. "Come on, you guys."

"Her version was, somebody pulled the plug on the daughter."

"And?"

"And so they gave her a shot."

"Are you checking it out?"

"Not my jurisdiction, Sherlock. You know that."

"Don't tell me. The sheriff."

"Right. We're unincorporated here. It's his baby."

"Who's in charge?" Some lieutenant. Couldn't remember who.

"A lieutenant. Rome, I think his name is. Sharp guy, great dresser. Came from back east somewhere, big-city cop, they say, worked lots of homicides. He says, no way the plug got pulled."

I tried to sit up, but the pain dragged me down again. I wanted to see Jane, talk to her, hold her. My face felt wet and cold. The door opened behind Webby and a doctor came in, followed by a nurse. Webby stepped aside to give the doctor room. He wore a long white coat. His face was dark and accented by a mustache. His name tag said Arfazi.

"I am Dr. Arfazi. Would you gentlemen leave us alone, please?"

Webby and Wally left us alone. The doctor listened to my chest with his stethoscope. He examined my arm. The nurse took my blood pressure and wrote something down. They did not comment on how well I was doing.

"How are you feeling?"

"Tired. Bruised. Angry."

His eyebrows went up and he clucked. "What is your name, please?"

"Santa Claus."

"Hmm." He bent closer, an instrument held up to his eyeball. A strong light slid into my eye. "Please state your name, first name first, then your family name after."

"Santa. That's my first name. Claus, that's my family name."

"Hmm. And where do you reside, please?"

"The North Pole, and I'd like to see Senator Blasingame."

He straightened up. "Who did you say?"

"Senator Blasingame. Weren't you taking care of her daughter? You remember, Doc, the hit-and-run."

"Not possible," he said. "Nurse, take this down." He rattled off some medical gobbledygook and left the room without saying good night. Before she left, the nurse flicked a switch so I could watch television. The President appeared on CNN, saying all was right with the world, and wishing everyone a Merry Christmas.

When Wally and Webby came back in, I asked them to turn the goddamn thing off. The nurse returned with a hypodermic needle, which she jammed into my upper thigh, which allowed her a good long look at the repairs they'd done on my left leg, back after I was shipped home from a battlefield in the last war. She ran a finger along the scar. Then the hypo put me to sleep.

I woke to the smell of coffee. Wally St. Moritz sat in a chair by the window, making notes on a yellow legal pad. I grunted. He looked up. The coffee smell came from a container sitting on my bed table.

"It's not good for you," Wally said.

"Help me get the goddamn top off."

"My, aren't we chipper this morning." He eased the plastic top off and handed me the cup. The smell was wonderful. The taste was only fair.

"What time is it?"

"Eight-twenty."

"When is breakfast?"

He brought out a paper sack that said EL TORO BAKERY. From the sack, he produced three kinds of sweet rolls and two muffins. "Carbohydrates," he said. "For quick energy."

The muffins were wonderful. I felt my strength coming back. Wally gave me more Arnica and said we would start the next remedy at midmorning. You're the doc, Doc, I said. I stumbled to the bathroom. In the mirror, my father's face, bearded, hard lines, weary. Cuts on the left side, dried blood where I'd been showered with broken glass. Where was my Ford? I used the facilities, splashed water on my face with my right hand, had trouble drying off the hand. Man is a two-fisted creature.

"Have you seen the Senator?"

"Briefly."

"And?"

"She's resting. Aside from the depression, she seems to have calmed down."

"You think she's off the rails?"

"It's possible. She works under conditions of constant stress, woman in a man's world. Losing her daughter could have sent her mind reeling."

"They wanted me out of here, so they torched my house. With me gone, they got the kid."

"They?"

"Palermo and company."

Wally nodded. "I trust your instincts, Matthew. The police will require substantially more."

Damn the police. "Phone L.A. Information, Prof. Get the number for Alicia Beringer. See what she's got on Palermo."

"Alicia of the fiery red hair?"

"The same."

"I shall enjoy making that call."

"Now help me get dressed."

"Your personal physician won't like that."

"Up his."

Senator Jane's bed had bars, the chrome-plated kind. The bars were part of a cage that surrounded her bed. The blinds were closed, dimming the room. A breakfast tray sat on the bedside table. The coffee cup was turned over. The food had not been touched. On its wall mount, the television flickered without sound.

The Senator lay propped against pillows, staring at the wall to her left. I pulled up a chair and sat down.

She turned her head slowly. When she saw me, she reached out her hand. A smile ghosted across her face, then vanished. Her hand was cold. "Oh, Matt. Did they tell you? About Heather?"

"Yeah."

"I was devastated." She tightened her grip on my fingers. When she spoke, her voice was a hoarse whisper. "*They* killed her."

I nodded. "They got me out of here. Clear field of fire." I knew it. She knew it. The trouble was proving it, taking it to court, making it stick. "Tell me what happened," I said.

"Could I have some water first?"

"Sure." I handed her the glass and she took a couple of sips. She handed me back the glass and sank deeper into the pillows and told me her story.

"Heather woke up again," Jane said, "right after you left. She was groggy, of course, but she recognized me right away this time. She asked where she was. I told her. She asked how long she'd been here, in the hospital. Three days, I said. Then she asked how Marvin was. You can imagine how I felt. We'd been searching for him, hoping to assume a connection, and now Heather confirms our effort. 'Marvin,' she said. 'He gave me his book. He autographed it and gave it to me as a gift, along with some money. Is he okay?' "

Jane coughed weakly, then went on. "So I said something motherly. I told her she'd been hurt. I said we'd been trying to find Marvin so that he could tell us what happened. I asked her if she remembered anything. She nodded, but then she made me wait a long time before she said anything. She closed her eyes and I thought she'd drifted off. But then she opened them again and said, 'We were walking toward his car. There were lights behind us. I was holding on to the book and the lights came closer and I thought it was Steve and then poor Marvin—' " Jane stopped to blow her nose before going on. "My poor baby. She stopped talking. She reached out to me, and then she closed her eyes and went to sleep. Her breathing seemed very deep, very regular, and I remember thinking back afterward that the whole conversation had seemed to take forever, with me hanging on every word, but that it had actually taken only a minute or so."

"Who's Steve?"

"I asked, but she was already asleep. I sat by her bedside for a few minutes. Then the doctor came in."

"The Egyptian guy? Arfazi?"

"No. His name tag said Dumont. He spoke with a slight accent. Addressed me as Madame."

"How was he dressed?"

"A white lab coat, knee length. He startled me when he came in because he wore a face mask. He mumbled, then put his hand over his mouth, to give me to understand he had a little cold."

"What did he do?"

"The usual routine with the stethoscope. He seemed very interested when I told him that Heather had just been awake. He examined her. He took her pulse. He spent a long time studying her chart. He said, mumbling again, that things were looking very positive and went out of the room, saying he needed to get some special medication. A nurse came to the door to tell me I had a phone call. The phone in Heather's room had been turned off—I hadn't wanted her to be disturbed—so I took it at the nurses' station. The call was from Amanda. She was in Newport Beach at a service station. She'd driven down to make a final check on Heather's new room at South Bay Hospital and our rental car had a flat

tire. It had taken her more than an hour to get someone to help her. They were fixing the flat now, she
said, and she'd be back here at the hospital around
eleven. I checked on Heather. She was still sleeping.
I went to use the rest room down the hall. I wasn't in
there more than a couple of minutes. I splashed my
face with water and put on fresh lipstick.

"There was no one at the nurses' station when I
walked past. I walked to the end of the corridor,
swinging my arms. I stood out on the little balcony,
breathing in the air. I was slightly chilled when I
came back inside. I saw the doctor coming out of
Heather's room. I called to him. He looked at me
quickly and then went on his way. When I got back to
the room, Heather wasn't breathing. I was horrified!
I panicked. I pressed the call button. I ran to the door
and called for help. There was still no one at the
nurses' station. I ran to the phone and phoned the
Emergency Room. They said someone would be up
immediately. I ran back inside and tried to do CPR. It
was then I noticed that the screen above Heather's
bed—the green monitor—was blank. Someone had
to have turned it off. That doctor? But why? Why?
Why? I was listening for her heartbeat, my head on
her chest, when help arrived. I was hysterical. They
pulled me away from her. I screamed at everyone. I
called the doctor a murderer. They have procedures
here for people who lose control. The procedures are
like machinery. They gave me a shot and put me in a
room, in a bed with bars, caged, like some kind of—"

"Easy," I said. "Easy."

"It was awful, Matt. Awful."

"Remember anything else about the doctor?"

"How many times have I answered that question?
Sorry. He was about your height, only much more

slender. My impression was gray hair and piercing
eyes. I'd put his age at mid-fifties."

"You think the accent was French?"

"It sounded foreign. He mumbled. A hospital ad-
ministrator assured me there's no one on the staff
named Dumont. Even Dupont. I'm very confused
now, everything slipping away."

"Did the doctor say anything else? Move a certain
way?"

"Just what I've told you."

"And when you called from down the hall, he just
kept going?"

"He glanced at me, a sideways click of the eyes.
Nothing more."

"Was he hurrying, walking fast?"

"I don't know. I just don't know."

"Are they doing an autopsy?"

"I've demanded one, of course. God only knows
when it will occur."

I patted her arm. "You've had a tough time, lady. A
real tough time."

"Yes. And they've succeeded in wearing me out."
She shook her head and I noticed tears running down
her cheeks, catching the light from the silent television. "I'm tired, Matt. I'm weary and battle-scarred
and I'm going to take my baby girl and go back
home."

"Don't give up yet, Senator."

She gave me a long look. She snuffled. She reached
for the Kleenex box, knocked it on the floor, and said,
"No. It's over." I handed the box to her. She pulled
out a tissue and blew her nose.

"It's over, Matt. Thank you for trying. And damn
the Dukes—their whole clan—forever."

We sat there awhile, not saying anything. When I
left the room, Senator Jane was crying.

Out in the corridor, I heard my name called and turned to see Amanda True hurrying toward me. Tears had reddened her eyes. She gave me a brief hug that made me stiffen from the pain, but when she tried to speak the words stuck in her throat. She stepped away from me to blow her nose.

"Write to her, Mr. Murdock. Give her a call. She needs people now, more than ever."

I nodded and took the elevator down.

14

The blaze from the illegal holiday fireworks had gutted my living room. The guts of the stereo had melted. The television was a box of charcoal. The sofa was a mess of wetted ashes. Half the roof was gone, but the other half, over the kitchen area, was untouched. The electricity was off. The phone didn't work. Vandals had stripped my fridge, but a kid who works as a fry-cook for Leo Castelli had run them off before they'd taken the fridge too.

The gun case was intact. I was pleased that the fire had not reached my ammo store. In the liquor stash underneath the cabinet I found eight beers, a half bottle of gin, and an unopened bottle of cheap brandy.

The heavy smoke smell still lingered in the bedroom. I was trying to pack a suitcase when Wally came up the stairs to hand me five hundred dollars in cash. I wanted to go to a motel. He insisted I bunk with him, out on the Peninsula. He packed the suitcase while I tossed clothes into a laundry bag. When you've been burned out, the first thing you want is to get rid of the sick smoke smell. The second thing you want is revenge.

"Any word on the perps?"

"They're working on it. How are you feeling?"

"The occasional twitch. And I get woozy if I stand too long."

"How about lunch?"

"I could use a cold beer and a long nap."

"How was your chat with the Senator?"

"She's saddling up and heading home, back to Texas."

"Beautiful woman," Wally said. "A Thoroughbred with lots of backbone. She'll come out of it. These clothes do reek. It's off to Wally's Laundromat."

Wind whistled at us from off the Pacific. "Did you ever get in touch with Alicia Beringer?"

"Yes. She should have something by early afternoon. I told her you'd be at my place."

"Thanks."

"Can you drive?"

"Automatic only. Leo loaned me his Mazda."

Wally nodded, started down the stairs, then stopped, looking thoughtful. With my laundry sack over his shoulder, my suitcase in his left hand, Wally looked like Santa in mufti.

He went around back. I heard his Saab start up. I found the clothes with the least amount of smoke smell and changed. The rain had let up, but now a cold wind knifed through my house. I walked downstairs to use Leo's phone to check with my insurance guy, who said a check would be in the mail today. Then I called Zeke Torres, over in Santa Ana. He promised to have the place boarded up by nightfall. The banks were closed. He said he could wait until next week for his money.

I had just gotten back upstairs when a voice hailed

me from down below. Looking over the railing, I saw
Blazer, all spiffy in his leather jacket and drill pants.

"Ahoy, Foxy. Permission to come aboard?"

"Sure. Come on up."

He came up the stairs without making any noise,
then stood on what was left of my deck, assessing the
damage. "Damn shame, Foxy. Do they know what
happened?"

"Fireworks," I said. "I think it was arson. Planned."

"Who?"

I started to say Palermo. Then I changed my mind.
"I'm making a list. Want a drink?"

"Gin," he said. "On ice."

"No ice."

"Okay." He grinned and moved around the room.

I poured us both a shot of gin and handed him his
glass. His body was loose and angular beneath the
well-fitted clothes. His face was tight with whatever
he wanted to say. He raised his glass. "To the old
days. To fighting men and the women they left behind. To honor in battle and comrades who save your
ass." We toasted without clinking glasses, then drank.
"Know what I miss, Foxy? More than anything?"

"What's that?"

"Heat. Sweat. Lush women. Lush tropical growth.
The lilting tinkle of foreign tongues."

"Not me. I like California."

"Too much grime here, beneath the glitz and
gloss."

"Yeah, but I'm used to it."

"When I was a kid, growing up in Charleston, I
read Jack London and Melville and Conrad. I'd go
down to the harbor and watch the ships easing out
and wonder if I'd ever get out of there. More than
anything, I reckon, I wanted to be Lord Jim. Sail to

Java, speak twenty languages, romance a sloe-eyed princess."

"The South Seas. That where you're headed?"

"Who said I was going anywhere?"

"You've got that look in your eye, Blazer. The far-away gaze. You came to say good-bye."

"I never could fool you, Foxy. Tomorrow, early, I fly to Singapore." He sipped his gin.

"What about the business? CEO Security?"

"I'm being bought out. Tidy little sum."

"Quick sale. Who's buying?"

"Investors." He set the gin glass down on the stove top and stood there, hands hanging loose, feet spread in the shooter's stance.

"I saw you with Louie Palermo."

A vein twitched in his right temple and he rubbed the back of his neck. "I had a feeling, Foxy. Where?"

"Hotel Xanadu. A couple of hours after you bashed the college boys."

"How much do you know?"

"It's mostly a hunch. I saw you and Louie and two of Louie's goons. Then I saw Louie and Jamie Duke. The old man, Wheeler Duke, offered me eighty grand to leave town. Louie offered me a job. Five hours after I turned it down, a team of hitters tries to take me out on the interstate. That takes planning, Blazer. And now you show up, my old army pal, talking smarmy about princesses and shipping out for Singapore."

He took a step toward me, hands clenching. Then he stopped. "God damn you, Foxy. God damn your meddling."

"How deep are you in, Blazer?"

His shoulders sagged. He averted his eyes. "Remember that scene in *Warlock* where Widmark and Fonda have their final face-off?"

"No. I don't remember."

"Okay. Here it is. Widmark's the new klutz deputy who has to go out and face Hank Fonda, the ace gunfighter. In the scene, Fonda makes a monkey of Widmark with his twin pistols, then tosses both guns into the dust and walks away."

"Where'd he go? Singapore?"

Thin smile from Blazer. "It's the end of an era, Foxy. It's the place we all come to, all us gunfighters, sooner or later."

"Cut the hero stories, Blazer. What's going down on my turf?"

He shook his head, like a prizefighter who couldn't take any more punches. "You know why I'm here in la-la land?"

"Same reason as everybody. Sun, surf, sin, lots of money. It's the edge of America, the last frontier."

Blazer's smile was bleak. "They passed me over, Foxy. I was about to be Brigadier Blaisdell and the bastards passed me over. It happened three years ago, when I was just back from Christmas in Charleston. My kid sister stayed drunk, the whole bloody holiday. My brother Bobby had just gone begging to the bankruptcy court, so he kept whining after Mama for money. I carved the bird on Christmas Day, but my daddy's old gray ghost presided over my shoulder at the table."

He heaved a sigh. "So I was spooked at the family manse, things falling apart, old Horace Cooper dead —he was my childhood friend—and then I get back to the Pentagon where people are looking at me sideways, to find out my generalship has not gone through. No one would say why, precisely. But I knew. It was because I was operational, a black-bag boy, a covert type. I was the guy who did the dirty jobs, who cleaned up the arena after some CIA asshole had screwed things up. The bastards had even inflated the kills in my file. Forty-seven, they said. Forty goddamn seven. When the true goddamn number was thirty-eight." Blazer's eyes narrowed. "Didn't they understand? Didn't they know I'd remember every face, every photograph, every stinking VC profile? Jesus, Foxy, I'm out there in the bush, trying to stay ahead of Charley and the rats and the bugs, and those deskbound turkeys at GHQ can't even count right! Jesus!"

He finished his gin. He walked awkwardly to the bottle and poured more, sloshing it over the rim of the glass. He gulped half of it down. "Okay. So before they can wear me down, before they can grind me up in their fucking bureaucracy, I resign. Since soldiering's all I know, all that keeps me from going crazy, I try some things. Africa. South America. Then one day I'm reading *The Wall Street Journal*, a piece about executive vulnerability and the high price of protection, and I get this idea. I can make money. I can get my revenge. So I huddle with some backers and we launch CEO Security. Next thing you know, I've set up headquarters in sunny California. Things go fine. Money rolls in. I meet a lady who turns me on. I connect with heavy hitters. But you know what?"

"What?"

"I'm still operational. Still Doug Blaisdell, the janitor who mops up the mess. Still the black-bagger, the spy, the cloak-and-dagger guy. You know what else?"

"What?"

"I envy you, Foxy."

"Why?"

"I read about it in the paper. The chase down Laguna Canyon Road. The way you hung in there, shot to hell, until you rammed those punks into a tree."

"Louie Palermo's one of your backers, isn't he?"

His grin was weary as he unzipped the leather jacket and stuck his right hand inside. Alarm bells rang inside my head, and I thought of the people he'd killed—with plastique, with a garotte, with guns and knives, with his bare hands—but then he brought out a sealed envelope that he tossed onto the countertop. "I've lost it, Foxy. But you haven't."

"Lost what, Blazer?"

"Whatever it is that keeps a man upright. Honor. Strength. Willpower. Duty. Bravery. Sense of self. Whatever ingenuous dumbfuck abstraction you want to call it." He wiped his eyes with the back of his hand, as if to push away a film. "I used to think words were the thing, Foxy. Say the right word, get the incantation just right, and you could reshape the world. That's what happens when you grow up reading books. They said my reports were works of art, Foxy, artifacts of the venerable art of record keeping. Then when they turned me down, when I realized I would not be a brigadier, I . . . all those years, Foxy. All those years in the Corps—" He stopped. He realized he was whining. And in Blazer's code of behavior, whining was not allowed. "Shit, I feel like Doug MacArthur saying good-bye at the Point." He indicated the envelope. "There's mad money in there, Foxy. I quit trusting the banks when Reagan bloated up the deficit. Something happens to me out there, it's yours."

His hands clenched once more. He shrugged to relax his shoulders. His neck twitched. He could kill me where I stood, wounded, my arm in a sling. He was a killing machine who had been passed over by the Corps, and now he knew things I needed for my case, things he wasn't telling me. I understood. Oh, yeah. I surely understood the not-telling. Because Blazer and I were alike, peas in a pod, trained soldiers, blood brothers from the jungle wars. And now in my burned-out living room on the edge of America in Orange County, California, we stood on opposite sides of an invisible DMZ, Blazer and me. He knew things I wanted to know. If he stuck around, we'd kill each other in a shootout. That's why he was leaving. One reason, anyway. Because when you're a killer, you learn to keep things to yourself. You kill. You keep your own counsel. You do the job. You move on, alone, the gunfighter in the dark. Brothers, the knowing brunette had said back at the Côte d'Azur. You boys are like the flip side of an old LP. And then Blazer had said: Foxy, my dark side of the moon.

I knew one thing: Blazer was the dark side.

He did not shake hands. He strode out through the charred house like a knight in tarnished armor heading for a battle that only he could fight. I tucked the envelope into my jacket pocket. It was lumpy, sealed with heavy packing tape.

From my charred deck, I watched Blazer climb into a late-model Ford, dark green. A $40,000 drop from the fancy black BMW at the Côte d'Azur. On his way to Singapore, Blazer was shucking gear, dropping it on the trail. Travel light, travel fast. The door closed. The engine fired. Blue exhaust puffed from the tailpipe onto the December air. And with a single toot of his horn Blazer drove away.

I was still standing there wondering why Blazer had switched cars when Leo hollered up. Webby Smith wanted me to meet him at an address in Laguna. One hitter from last night had been identified.

* * *

When he had been alive, security guard Lance Woolford had lived above his means in a contemporary condo on a hill overlooking the Pacific. His street was Bella Vista. The monthly rent on the condo was $3,600. Working as a security guard at Jamaica Cove, Lance had pulled down $1,700 a month.

I knew the cop on the door, a young guy named Horvath. He shook hands with me, whispered, "Nice work last night, with those perps," and waved me inside Lance's condo. The entry was parquet. The carpet was red plush. The entertainment center was rosewood. The CD, a top of the line Sony, was wired into speakers strung throughout the house. The television was hooked to seven cable services.

Webby Smith met me in the master bedroom. Light from the domed skylight caught his lieutenant's bars. "How you feeling, Tonto?"

"Wobbly. But I'll make it to Christmas."

"The ID on your shooter from last night came through a couple hours ago. Took us this long to get a warrant. He lived here." Webby read from his notebook. "Woolford, Ronald R. Nicknamed 'Lance.' I like that. Served three years in the U.S. Navy. Applied for SEAL training, refused. Reapplied. Refused. Discharged in 1983. Flunked out of a police academy in Pennsylvania. Turns up in Georgia at a school for mercs. Ever hear of this? Pickett's Charge?"

"No. Where is it?"

"It's not anywhere now. It used to be in the woods outside Macon. There's a certificate of completion hanging in the other bedroom. Our boy used that as a command post and staging area. And some photos you can look at in a minute."

"Okay."

"Our guess is Lance spent some time—six months or so—fighting for a mercenary outfit in Africa. That was after his graduation from Pickett's Charge. He turns up in California two years ago. First in L.A., where he does some stunt work for the movies. Then he shows up here in Orange County. Before the job at Jamaica Cove, he worked at two other gated communities. One in Long Beach. The other in Huntington Beach. He had the reputation of being a lover boy whose zipper fly the ladies could not leave be. My lab guys found hairs not belonging to Lance in the sheets. They are certain other evidence will surface and I have saved the best for last."

He led me down a short hallway to a second bedroom with a view overlooking the hills and the Pacific. A citizen's band radio sat on the desk. The telephone was a three-line job. On a table next to the desk was a powerful shortwave, made in Japan.

Webby flicked a switch on the shortwave and we heard the end of a report of fighting in Lebanon. The voice had a British accent. In the background you could hear the crackle of gunfire. Immediately following the news was an announcement of interviews for possible employment. Wanted: action-oriented men with three or more years of military training. Contracts: six months to eighteen months. Stipend: to be negotiated. Interested parties were to report at zero eight hundred hours at an address in San Francisco. East Coast interviews would be held in three days at an address in Savannah, Georgia.

The single bookshelf in the room held magazines. The bottom shelf contained *Oui* and *Hustler,* men's magazines. The other shelves contained *Soldier of Fortune.*

"The issues go back six years," Webby said. "How could he haul around this kind of crap?"

The closet contained seven uniforms. Three were from Jamaica Cove. The other four were from a paramilitary organization called Rigdon's Raiders. Behind the uniforms in the closet was a box containing thirteen hand grenades. Next to the grenades was a rifle. On the shelf were three handguns.

Webby flipped through his notebook. "Nothing so far on our second shooter. We've queried Washington and they're supposed to query Interpol. A vehicle was registered to Lance, but is not on the premises. It's a late-model Ford Bronco, California license. We're checking on it. According to his co-workers at Jamaica Cove, Lance seems to have had lady friends, but no close men friends." Webby grinned at me. "Since the last thing we want to do is disturb the peace and tranquillity of Jamaica Cove, we're treading lightly, waiting for some socially conscious matron to step forward and tell us all."

Someone called to Webby. He left me in the room. On the wall behind the desk were two certificates and some photos. The certificate on the left was the military discharge from the U.S. Navy. The certificate on the right announced that R. R. "Lance" Woolford had completed the course of instruction at Pickett's Charge with highest honors. It was signed with a scrawled signature I could not read.

There were seven photos on the wall. In five of them Lance stood alone, armed, wearing battle dress, ammo belt, backpack. In two of them he posed with his action pals, who were dressed for battle. There were five soldiers in the last photo on the right. Lance stood in the center of the crowd, his arms around the shoulders of his buddies. The man at the far left caught my attention, the way he stood, his slender build. He wore a fatigue cap and smiled into the camera. The smile was weary, as if he'd seen too many battles, too many soldiers die, too many generals get fat and red-faced from drinking.

I'd seen that same smile this morning, at my place. It belonged to Blazer Blaisdell.

15

I phoned the Hotel Xanadu from Lance's place, but they said Blazer had checked out. I phoned Barb Duke at Carcassonne, but the line was busy. I had a connection, Lance to Blazer and maybe to Palermo, but what did it mean? I hauled Webby Smith away from his cops to show him the photo.

"I'll run it through," he said.

"How long will that take?"

He gave me a look. "On Christmas Eve, who knows."

"What about an APB, right now?"

"On what charge, posing for a photo that was taken five years ago? The D.A. would chew my leg off."

"Okay. So I'm reaching. But I knew this guy in Vietnam. He's good. Whatever he's into, it's big."

Webby nodded wearily. "With you, Sherlock, it's always big. Go home. Get some rest. You smell like Smokey the Bear. And you look like the ghost of Christmas past."

"I'll be at Wally's place if something breaks."

"How about I bring along a lady for you tomorrow?"

"Don't you ever give up?"

"Love," he said. "It makes the world go round."

Since my Ford had been impounded, I was driving Leo's Mazda 626. The Plymouth was in the shop with a $1,900 repair bill. The little Mazda hummed along. Damn you, Blazer. Damn you.

I arrived at Wally's place on the Peninsula to find him busy with the wash. One load of my clothes was dry. There were three more piles. Two for the washer, one for the dry cleaner. He helped me out of the shoulder rig and I took a shower to wash away the smoke smell. I came out to find clean clothes stacked neatly on the lavatory. Getting dressed, I felt almost human.

I phoned Alicia Beringer, the assistant U.S. attorney in Los Angeles. "Anything?"

"Like turning over a rock, Sherlock. You find worms writhing in the light. How deep are you into this?"

"Bits and pieces, Counselor. What can you tell me about Palermo and Family?"

"General stuff. I get too specific, I lose my job."

"Whatever you've got, Counselor."

"Okay, here goes. They own Le Club of Newport Beach. I've been to dinner there. *Très* ritzy. They also have interests in two trucking firms, in three stockbrokerage houses, in an ice-cream plant in Fullerton, in a real estate corporation in Irvine, in a major shipping company, and in a boat-building concern."

"The Mob comes to Orange County."

Alicia kept going. "They're from Perugia originally. That's a hill town in central Italy. The first Palermo landed on Ellis Island around 1894. His name was Nicolo. He was a watchmaker by trade and he settled in Little Italy, where he was valuable to the criminal element because he knew jewels and their value. Nicolo had three sons, Ricco, Paulo, and Fabiano. Ricco died during Prohibition. Paulo was killed in Las Vegas in the fifties. And Fabiano, that's Papa Palermo, died last year. He had three sons. Fabiano Junior, Sergio, and Louie. Louie's the baby."

"Some baby. When did they come to California?"

"In the late fifties. Smart money says they made oodles peddling dope to the Woodstock Generation. I hate it, thinking I once got jazzed on Palermo grass."

"The flesh is weak, Counselor."

"To finish up the scenario, mob money is going legal all over the country. They find a legit business with cash-flow troubles. They buy in, just like venture capitalists. If your business was in trouble, wouldn't you welcome a cash infusion?"

"Depends on the cost. Remember Duke Construction?"

"Of course."

"Anything cooking between the Palermos and the Dukes?"

"If there is, we haven't heard about it. Damn you, Sherlock. You've got something. I can hear it in your question."

"Nothing solid, Counselor. Anything I find, it's yours."

"You're a rascal, Sherlock. Who's your client on this?"

"A fourteen-year-old kid," I said. "She's hired me to find her father."

"Who was her father?"

I told her about the missing Marvin Holly. Alicia, the Grand Inquisitor, questioned me for a couple of minutes, trying to make a connection. In no mood for interrogation, I sidestepped her. She pressed. I dodged. She accused me of flying blind. I should plan more, she said. I refrained from boxing her ears about the law profession. Talking to her always wore me out. I thanked her for the scoop on the Palermos and we hung up.

Lunch was beef stew, French bread, a green salad, and beer. I drank the first beer in three swallows and began to feel better immediately. I was a hell of a detective. Heather was dead. Jane was headed home. Marvin still wasn't found. I had zip on the Palermos. Had no idea what was bugging Cindy. By the end of lunch, during which time I raved about lawlessness and greed and how the rich get richer, I remembered drinking a mere four beers, but there were six cans stacked in front of my plate. Couldn't solve crimes. Couldn't even monitor my beer intake. I kept telling Wally about the case. Jane and Heather. Marvin and Cindy. Marvin and Roald Swensen. Wheeler and Barb Duke and Uncle Jamie. Blazer and Palermo. Blazer and Barb. Blazer and Murdock. Wally stopped me a couple of times to ask clarifying questions. Whole world, coming on like the Grand Inquisitor. Why? Why? Why? I was lost. My head swirling in suds, I babbled.

Wally was smiling at me like a monk from a cave in the Gobi Desert. His Thinking Look.

My bedroom was ready. I was ready for my bedroom. He said he'd wake me in time for my appointment with Professor Roth. Let Roth wait. No need for him now, not ever. I was tired, a battery with no juice. Yeah, tired.

The last thing I saw before drifting away into dreamland was Wally's face smiling above me. In the dream, I rode a sleigh through the snow, cracking a bullwhip and shouting, "On, you huskies!" and behind me there was a man on a gray snowmobile, a grim gray gunfighter with pale eyes, the machine gaining fast, the white snow spraying up behind him as he aimed a high-powered rifle at me, and then squeezing the trigger, knocking off my dogs, my beautiful huskies, one at a time and smiling a weary gray smile and calling me—

"Matthew. It's time."

"Screw it, Professor. I'm beat."

"I'll come with you. This could be important."

"Go away."

He hauled me up to a sitting position. Surprising strength in those tennis muscles. From the other room, I heard his printer printing. "What's the beef, Prof? I'm whacked out. The case is over."

"Not until the fat lady sings."

"Christ." I sat up and swung my legs over the edge of the bed. The pain in my arm made me grunt. Wally gave me a remedy. The pain eased enough so I could use the facilities. Since people wanted to kill me, I decided to go armed. Wally helped me into the shoulder harness. The cops had my Beretta. Evidence, they said. I packed the Colt Diamondback.

We climbed into Wally's Saab. I was still groggy from the beer and my unfinished nap. As we passed my place on the pier, I looked to the left and saw two guys on my deck and one on the roof. They wore carpenters' belts and they were boarding up my place with sheets of plywood. Good old Zeke.

The campus at UC-Irvine was deserted and the rain was into a drizzle as Wally parked in a lot that slanted darkly up toward the pale peach-colored building that housed the School of Social Ecology. I waited while Wally locked his Saab and then we walked up the hill. The glass entry was locked, so Wally pressed a button on the adjacent wall. A man came hurrying down a flight of stairs and across the lobby. He was a chunky guy, mid-thirties, spiffily dressed in a three-piece suit and Italian loafers. He was clean-shaven and starting to bald on top. The uniform was more IBM corporate than rumpled tweedy professorial. He opened the door and gave Wally's hand a quick shake.

"Professor," Wally said with formality, "this is Mr. Murdock."

I held out my hand, but the professor only flicked his eyes at my arm in its sling before leading us upstairs to his office. Like the man, the place was fussy and neat. Orderly bookshelves, fine British Burberry hanging on an antique coat tree. Except for an IBM personal computer and a manila folder, the desk was bare. I looked around, spotted a copy of *Jungles Burning*. Roth hemmed and hawed for a moment, stalling, before picking up the folder and leading us down the hall to a conference room. It had a table and eight chairs.

Roth rapped the folder with a knuckle. "It's my only copy. Do be careful." He flipped open the title page. "This is the chapter on the Duke family. Number seven. That's manuscript pages four-eleven to four-eighty-five. My bibliography is at the back, manuscript pages eight-oh-one to eight-oh-two. You requested a chronology. There's a handwritten one. I trust you can decipher my scribbling." Roth shucked back his cuff and took too long checking the time. "I just queried the airline. They want us at boarding twenty minutes earlier, so I'm afraid that leaves you a half hour at best." He pursed his mouth, the hotdog teacher giving the rube students last-minute scare tactics before the all-or-nothing exam, and left us alone.

The door closed.

"Nice guy, your pal. Reminds me why I dropped out."

"He's not a pal."

"Then how come he lets us look at this?"

"We traded favors."

"The old scholarly deal?"

"Hmm. Read, Matthew. Read."

Wally divided the manuscript. Front half for me. Back half for him. The title for Chapter Seven was "Newport Dynasty: The Dukes of Duke Castle."

I began skimming. The manuscript was crisply written and accompanied by several sets of photos held together with rubber bands.

The scion of the family was Elroy Duke, Alaskan gold miner and western adventurer. He hit Orange County in the eighties, a century ago. Made a ton of money in land and cattle, oranges, avocados, oil, real estate sales, and then real estate development. Once he was rich, the old man had backed some of the area's first film-making, hoping to gain entrance to the hopeful hearts of beautiful starlets. Roth credited Elroy Duke for whisking the movie industry from New York to California. Half as rich as Howard Hughes, but still a bona fide tycoon.

Elroy's wife, and Wheeler Duke's grandmother, had been a half-breed Indian, part French, part Iroquois. Her name was Anastasia and Elroy had shot a man over her in a hotel in Santa Ana. Violence lurked in the Duke genes. A batch of photos chronicled the building of Duke Castle, a project that had taken a dozen years, from 1899 to 1911. In one of the photo captions, Professor Roth called Elroy Duke a "small-time William Randolph Hearst."

Ephram P. Duke, Elroy's son and Wheeler Duke's father, had sold Duke Island in 1930, to pay debts. In the late sixties, Wheeler Duke bought the island back and rebuilt Duke Castle. The rebuilding took five years and carried an estimated cost of four million dollars. Where had the money come from?

"Here's something."

Wally handed me a second batch of photos showing two kids, a boy and girl, playing in the sand while above them on the rugged seacliffs Carcassonne was being built. Both kids were dark from the sun. Both had dark hair. There were five photos of Barb Duke in her late teens. Her hair was a mess. She wore squaw dresses and tie-dyes and did her best to look earthy and poor. It didn't work. She still looked like a rich kid who was into slumming.

One photo had her carrying an antiwar placard that said SPLIT THE SCENE, AMERICA. OUT OF HERE! Only you weren't sure where HERE was. Another showed the family assembled in front of a huge Christmas tree. Barb Duke, at twelve or thirteen, looked a lot like her daughter Cindy. Jamie Duke, a couple of years younger, looked like a brat. In his photos, Wheeler Duke looked important, powerful, the ultimate Big Daddy.

There were photos of wives—pretty women dressed in the draped, lacework finery that only money can buy—but they were overshadowed by their husbands. A final photo was of Edith Adams Pomeroy Duke, the mother of Barb and Jamie. Her eyes were sunken, her face steeped in sadness. She looked like a very sick woman.

There was no mention of Marvin Holly.

"Here's the chronology." Wally passed me a single sheet on yellow legal-size paper. It was a chronology of Wheeler Duke, dates and events printed in a tidy scholarly script. It began with Wheeler Duke's birth, November 9, 1918, in Santa Ana, California, and then continued on:

1931	delivery boy, corner grocery store
1937	construction gang
1939	radio station, announcer
1941	radio station, manager
1941–43	U.S. Signal Corps, codebreaker
1943	OSS, Burma, India
1946–48	Washington, New Delhi, CIA
1949	Yale, classics major
1949	buys radio station in Santa Ana
1950	Korea, State Department, observer, guerrilla warfare
1954	Stanford, MBA
1955	buys more radio stations
1960	moves to Newport Beach
1962	resides in Mexico
1965	trades radio station empire for construction company
1966	builds tract houses
1968	Duke Construction founded
1969	buys back Duke Island; rebuilds Duke Castle
1981	James Duke becomes Vice-President of Community Relations

At the end of the chronology there was a disclaimer stating that there was no connection between the Newport Dukes and the Duke family of North Carolina.

Footsteps outside the door. It opened and Professor Roth came in briskly, rubbing his schoolmaster's chalky hands, man in a hurry. "Well. All finished? I'm afraid I really must scoot."

"Couple of quick questions, Professor. Marvin Holly and James P. Duke."

Roth gathered his papers up, racked them in a neat

stack like a Vegas dealer working his playing cards. "They'll have to wait, Mr. . . . ah . . ."

"We could drop you," Wally offered.

He blinked, gave me a power smile. This guy relished control. He was starting to piss me off. "Sorry. No can do. My car's outside." Roth marched out, clutching his manuscript.

"Whipsaw," I said.

"I thought you'd never ask." Wally patted his jacket pocket.

We followed Roth back to his office, where he was putting on his Burberry. With a flourish, he plucked his umbrella off the coat tree and walked briskly to the door. He was annoyed we were still there. "Did you remember to bring that note, Doctor?" He opened the door, held it open like a doorman. That turkey-turd smirk again.

Wally reached into his jacket pocket and brought out an envelope. He handed it to me. *Charles Tuchmann*, it said. *Chair.*

The name did not ring a bell with me, but I now knew why Roth had let us see the manuscript. He and Wally had cut a deal deep in the groves of academe. I made a small tear in the envelope, bringing a yelp from Roth.

"Wait! You can't—"

I gave him my best Clint Eastwood grin. "Here's the deal, Professor. I ride to the airport with you. You answer questions. This is life and death. It takes precedence over your Christmas vacation. If I like your answers, you get on the plane with the letter. Otherwise—" I made the motion of tearing.

Roth swung around to confront Wally. "This is an outrage, Doctor! I held up my end of the bargain and now you think—"

Time was short, so I took a handful of Burberry and

spun the good professor around, throwing him off balance. When he was facing me, I pulled open the left side of my rain parka so he could see the butt of the Diamondback.

"If I were you, Roth," Wally said, "I'd do what he says. Someone shot him last night. He's going on grit and painkiller. He'd like nothing better than an excuse to deliver some pain."

The color left Roth's face. He gulped, man coming to a decision. He nodded. "All right. All right. But please hurry."

I took his briefcase, handed it to Wally. "How come Holly's not in the book?"

"That was, ah, part of my bargain."

"What bargain?"

He looked pained. "If you must know, I made a . . . trade with the Duke family. They would turn over certain documents—most of them were photographs—if I would submit drafts for their perusal."

"Who read it?"

"A Ms. Andrea Devereaux."

"Who's she?"

"Secretary to Mr. Duke."

"Jamie Duke?"

"No. Wheeler. The elder statesman."

The old censorship game. We walked him between us to the parking lot. He was talking now, bumping his words together. To pay the rent, Marvin Holly wrote westerns and mysteries. His best work was a detective series starring a lady investigator named Beverly Warmbold. For the titles, he punned on the color blue. *Lady in Blue, Blue Dreamer, Crime le Bleu.* Instead of writing under his own name, Holly used the *nom de plume*—in English, that means "pen-name"—of Derek Melville. Roth had not heard from Marvin in over a year.

We reached his car, a late model Audi. He unlocked all four doors with one turn of the key, upscale vehicle here. Carrying the briefcase, Wally jogged to his Saab. Tires squishing on the wet pavement, Roth drove out of the lot onto Campus Drive, with Wally two car-lengths behind.

"Jamie Duke. What about him?"

"There's not much. He's ego-centered, childish, a brat, a bully."

"I need something from his childhood, maybe. Or when he was a teen. Something in high school or college. How did he handle military service? Was he in trouble with the law?"

"Mmm," Roth said. "I'm beginning to see. Yes, well. No military service. The ostensible reason was a heart murmur. Actually, his father brought influence to bear. He was at four colleges. Stanford. San Francisco State. Amherst. And the University of Georgia. He received no degree."

"They threw him out?"

"In a word, yes."

"Why?"

"Fraternity pranks, mostly."

"What kind of pranks?"

"He was heavyhanded with pledges. A bruise here, a bloody nose there. A pledge was hospitalized at Georgia. Again, paterfamilias bought off the lawsuit."

We arrived at the airport. The professor maneuvered into line for the long-term parking. Behind us, Wally blinked his lights. Roth took his ticket to lift the traffic bar and parked the Audi. Wally found a space two lanes over.

I repeated my question. "Jamie Duke, has he got a record?"

Wally opened the rear door and climbed in back, tilting the car with his weight.

Sweat beads dotted Roth's brow. He knew, all right. "There's not much and I did not follow it up because, as I pointed out, it was irrelevant and unusable, but something did surface concerning James Duke and an . . . incident."

My pulse thrummed. "Where?"

"Somewhere in Los Angeles. One of the outlying suburbs. The incident involved two women, a mother and daughter, I think. There was some sort of trouble—I assumed it was of a sexual nature—and James Duke was charged with a crime. I do not know what sort of crime. Again, as in the various fracases at school, money crossed palms in the usual pattern. Charges were dropped. The two women, whoever they were, left town."

"Where did they go?"

"Back east. Not being an investigative reporter, I deigned not to probe further."

"What year was this?"

"Ten years ago. Perhaps eleven." He looked at his watch, squirmed in his seat.

"What else?"

"Nothing."

"Give, Professor!" I shook him. "Give!"

"All right. Wheeler Duke had a boating accident. Getting help fell on the shoulders of young James, sixteen at the time. He took a very long time going for help and the old man came close to dying. There was bad blood between them. A Freudian psychologist, which I am not, would see an Oedipal fixation rearing its ugly head."

"Oedipal what?"

Roth looked at me like I was dirt. "Oedipus. A Greek tragedy in which the son does away with the father in order to possess, in a sexual sense, the mother. Freud's currently out of fashion, but I—"

I cut him off. "Sounds like the Dukes. What else?"

"This family drama has its own twist, turned up by one of my researchers who interviewed Duke domestics." Roth paused, a sly smile on his lips. "The brother, *l'homme en colère,* as the French would say, was sexually entangled with the sister. Once, according to the source, his intense ardor caused him to smash through her bedroom door to get at her. The mother was quite ill at the time and—"

"The sister was a mother substitute?" Wally said.

"So it would seem. This information was not followed up. Now may I please go?"

"Did Jamie marry?" Wally asked.

"Yes. The wife's name was Millicent. She was three years older, quite matronly. In some photos, Millicent resembled the dead mother. The couple was incompatible. After a few months, Millicent sued for divorce on grounds of infidelity, receiving a handsome settlement."

I had more questions, but Wally put an end to the session by climbing out of the Audi. He opened the door and handed Roth the briefcase. I climbed out. Wally hauled Roth's suitcase out of the trunk. It had wheels and a cute fold-out handle. Roth held out his hand. I handed over the letter. He folded it, stuck it into his pocket, then hurried off toward the terminal.

"What was in the letter, Professor?"

Wally grinned at me. "He's dying to leave California. To do that, he needs a position back east. A job opened up at Harvard, associate professor, with prestige and perks. I know the chairman there, Chuck Tuchmann, and a stray Dean or two. I wrote Roth a letter."

"So you could see his manuscript?"

"So we could see it, Matthew."

I bopped Wally on the arm. I had a ton of scoop on

the Dukes, but zip on the whereabouts of Marvin Holly. "Let me call my guy in Chicago, then I'll buy you a drink. We'll toast academic blackmail."

Wally turned to eyeball the line of cars waiting to leave the parking lot. "You make the call. I'll pay the duty. Perhaps we can escape before Roth brings down the might of the law."

Wally hurried to the car. I jogged through the misting rain to the pay phones. It was nearing twilight. In the west, out over the Pacific, dark clouds were building. I was third in line for a phone. The minutes ticked by. When my turn came, I crammed in some quarters and called Roald Swensen in Chicago. Three rings before he answered. He had something.

"Holly wasn't there," Roald said. "But someone else had been."

"What do you mean?"

"A real mess, like done by a search team. Furniture ripped. Books torn apart. Pots and pans all over. And feathers. Why are there always feathers?"

"No trace of Holly?"

"No bloodstains. No hint of foul play."

"Did you try the neighbors?"

"Nothing there. He lives in a trailer park by a lake, keeps to himself. Works all morning, sleeps all afternoon, teaches at night. Comes home and works some more. The two nearest neighbors could go a month and only see him once."

"What about colleagues? Students?"

"Ah," Swensen said. "A little Viking luck."

"What? Tell me."

"As I was leaving the trailer park a girl showed up. Very blond, very apple-cheeked. Her name was— wait, I wrote it down—Sue Crandall. She lives and works in Janesville, secretary in a farm equipment plant. Drives up to Madison on Tuesdays to take Holly's class. She said they've been intimate since October. She's been trying to reach him by phone all week, but he doesn't answer. Then yesterday she receives a package from Holly, so she drives up to Madison to see what's what."

"Package? Where from?"

"Postmarked Laguna Hills, California. Mailed last Tuesday."

"Jesus. What was in it?"

"She gave me the package, for safekeeping. There are three computer disks and a manuscript of a book he was working on. It's about our little war, yours and mine. The title is *Nam, Nam, Nam.* The manuscript and the disks arrived in an envelope labeled 'Backup Number Thirty-seven.' Seems when Holly goes away he mails copies of what he's working on to someone, in case there's a fire in his trailer."

"Can you read the disks? Maybe there's something on them."

"I've got a friend coming over tomorrow who'll do that. Meanwhile, there's one other thing from Holly's package. It's a copy of a letter from his daughter, I suppose. She refers to our big November snowstorm. Sue Crandall didn't want to let me have it, but I was very persuasive."

"You have it there?"

"That's affirmative."

"Well, read it, man. Read it!"

I heard the rustling of paper. There was a crackle in the telephone line. A man in back of me asked was I about through. Then Roald said, "Here it is," and read me the letter:

"Dear Daddy. I saw on TV it snowed in Madison. It's very hot here for November, so Phyl and I are like hitching to Xanadu. Yesterday I rode Mingo. He needs a new saddle. Mom's p . . . . . (that's cen-

sored) at me again. She owes me three weeks of back
allowance. Lucky I have that money from Uncle Jamie. He's at our house all the time. His breath really
stinks up close and I don't like him much. Mom and I
had a fight today when she called me a Mall Rat. It's
okay for Phyl or some of the kids, calling you a Mall
Rat, but it's different coming from your mother,
right? Please write and tell me how the work is going.
How is your love life? Love, Cyn."

16

Blood thudded inside my head.

"Did you get that?" Swensen said.

"Yeah," I said. "I got it."

"You about through, mister?" the man behind me said. "I got a call to make."

"I'll talk to you, Roald. Send me a bill, okay?"

"Affirmative. Sounds like a kid in trouble."

I depressed the disconnect. The man behind me, a big hefty guy with a big beer gut, put a hand on my shoulder. I turned around and opened my parka enough to show him the butt of my gun.

"Drug enforcement, pal. I'm on special assignment. Mess with me once more and you'll be in jail for obstructing an officer."

"Hey!" He backed away. "I didn't know! No problem. No problem."

My hand was shaking as I dialed the number for Carcassonne. The maid answered. Ceendy, the maid said, she no *está*. I asked for Barb Duke. There was a long wait until she came on. Behind me, Beer Gut was keeping people in line. "That's a federal officer,"

I heard him say, in a stage whisper. "He's calling the fucking Pentagon!"

"Hello. Hello. Barb Duke speaking. Who is this, please?"

"Matt Murdock, Mrs. Duke. I think Cindy's in trouble. I was hoping you knew where she was."

"Who did you say?"

"Matt Murdock. I was—"

She broke in, slurring her words. "You've been warned, Mr. Murdock. You'd better stay away, if you know what's good for—"

"Do you know where Cindy is?"

"That's none of your . . . affair." Her voice sounded drunk, or stoned, or both.

"And your brother? You know where he is?"

There was a long pause. Mutters behind me, a choked silence while Barb Duke did some heavy thinking. "What are you saying?"

"Just tell me where Cindy is. Okay?"

"It's Christmas Eve," she intoned. "Every Christmas Eve, the Dukes gather at mighty Duke Castle. Cynthia-gal went over early, to help decorate for the party. Everyone dances. Dear Daddy pays the piper. Now, are you satisfied?"

"When did she leave?"

"Midafternoon."

"How did she travel?"

Another pause. "If you must know, she went with my brother."

"Uncle Jamie?"

She sighed heavily. "I have only one brother."

"Did he come to the house?"

"No. He was to pick her up at the mall."

"Xanadu?"

"Um. Where she hangs out with the other Mall Rats."

"When did you speak to her last?"

"Really, Mr. Murdock, I assure you—"

I broke in. "Phone her at the castle, Mrs. Duke. Ask to speak to Cindy."

"This is . . . ab . . . surd." But the certainty had gone from her voice.

A small crowd had bunched up behind me and I felt like a man in one of those television ads, yuppies in pure white tennis clothes leaning close, ears cocked, to listen to the secret investment scoop from a stockbroker whose name I could never remember.

"Mrs. Duke. Listen to me. Call the castle. Ask for Cindy. If she's there, tell her to go to her grandfather. Stay with him until you get there. Do you understand?"

"What are you saying, Mr. Murdock? What . . . are you trying to tell me?"

"If she's not there, wait by the phone. I'll call you back."

"This is alarmist and I—"

"Do it."

"I don't like you, Mr. Murdock. Things were fine until you stormed—"

I repeated my instructions. She said, "All right," but her words dragged. I hung up, wiped the sweat off my cold forehead. I felt dizzy. Behind me, a man asked what was going on. Beer Gut tapped me on the shoulder. "I got 'em lined up. Okay?"

"Okay."

"You want I should alert security?"

"Not yet."

There were three phones hanging off this wall near the exit to the terminal. I was at the phone on the far left. On the middle phone, a woman argued with someone in rapid Spanish. To her right, a marine in uniform hung up, shaking his head, and his place was

taken by a teenage punker with purple hair. The
airport loudspeaker played "Winter Wonderland."
My watch told me a minute had ticked by. It seemed
like a hundred years. I phoned Carcassonne. The line
was busy. Behind me, a woman's shrill voice called
out for me to use it or leave it.

Sweat on my chest now, wetting my shirt. Sweat
pockets underneath my arms. I fumbled the quarter.
It fell on the floor and rolled away. Beer Gut held up
two dimes and a nickel. "You owe me," he said. I
dialed Carcassonne again. I had the number memo-
rized, proof I was still hanging in there, Murdock the
Tenacious. A woman had called me that once, after
some memorable loving on a warm weekend in
April. It was winter now, the phone ringing and ringing again on the darkest night of the year, and I
wondered if I'd ever see another spring.

Barb Duke answered, her voice dulled. I asked
about Cindy. She was not at the castle, Barb Duke
said. She was with Jamie. Where are they? I asked.
"With Jamie," Barb Duke said. "He picked her up at
Xanadu and they're probably driving around
some—"

I cut her off. "They're not driving around, Mrs.
Duke."

"He's my brother," she mumbled. "He's her uncle.
What are you—?"

We'd run out of time. In a harsh voice, I told Barb
Duke to meet me at the Edgewater Motel in Laguna.

"Where?" she asked, dully.

"The Edgewater Lagoona. It's four blocks off the
Coast Highway."

"Edgewater," she said, slowly, reaching for the
word. "Is that still there? I remember that dump
from high school when the kids used to . . ."

I heard no more. People behind me were pressing

forward like an edgy herd of cattle about to stampede. I heard mutterings, curses. Beer Gut had done his best.

I handed him the phone and pushed my way through the throng. Barb Duke's voice faded. Would she ever stop talking and act? Someone grabbed my left arm, sending pain up the shoulder. "Hope you're happy, pal!"

I shook him off. Tears came to my eyes. I passed a couple arguing about what to give Mom for Christmas. At the edge of the crowd a security guard tried to separate two college joes and three kids with punker haircuts. I made it through the door and out into the softly falling rain. Good night for a party. I jogged to the parking lot, where Wally waited for me in his Saab. His FM radio was tuned to the classical station.

"Laguna," I grunted. "A motel called the Edgewater."

"What for?"

"Checking the prof's theory." I hauled out the Diamondback and made sure it was loaded.

Wally backed out, cranking the wheel, and headed for the airport exit. "What theory is that?"

"Freud," I said. "Oedipus. How fast will this tub go?"

We came into Laguna past the sobriety checkpoint and Wally headed up the back streets like a Zulu guide in the African bush. He asked about calling the cops. I said let's wait. At the Edgewater Lagoona, a vacancy sign flashed in the window. On, pause, off. On, pause, off. Like a heart missing a beat, then trudging on. All the windows were lit in all the rooms. I spotted a four-door Mercedes as we drove in. There was no sign of Barb Duke's vehicle.

Wally grabbed the last empty parking slot, way down at the far end of the lot. My hands were shaking so bad he had to help me unlock the seat belt. When I climbed out of the car, a wave of dizziness hit me and for a moment there I thought I might black out.

"Matthew?" Wally's voice, at my side. His strong hand steadying me. "Are you all right?"

"Sure." My voice sounded funny. "Let's go."

But as we passed the door of room 29 the whirlies hit me again and I had to slump against the wall to keep from falling. The pain in my head was almost as bad as the pain in my shoulder. From a door across the way came a blare of raucous music. The door opened wide and a voice called into the night, "Merry Christmas, motherfuckers!" The door slammed shut, but the thud of music still pounded our ears. I sucked in a deep breath.

"Listen!" Wally said.

From behind the door of room 30 came a voice, high-pitched, like a woman suppressing a screech, letting it out in angry cadenced bursts. It was a demonic chant. "Bad. Girl. Bad. Girl. Bad. Girl."

I wiped my face and nodded at Wally. "Out of gas, partner."

"My pleasure," he said, and rammed his shoulder against the door.

There was a splintering sound. He backed off, gave it another try, and this time the door came loose from itself, the cheap wallboard coming unglued from the support struts along the edges, catching Wally off guard with its flimsiness as he roared like a green recruit in basic and slammed his head into the door frame and sank slowly down.

Red light bathed the room, and now the chanting had stopped. I stepped inside, the gun trained on the bed, my eyes blinking against the fierce glow. Someone moaned. A weight like a falling tree slammed into my right arm. The Diamondback left my fingers. A man cursed as the red lights went out, leaving the room in darkness.

I went to my hands and knees, searching for the pistol. Something slammed into my shoulders, driving me to the floor. I rolled away, kicking out. My heel connected with bone. A small slit of light came from the side of the window, where the heavy curtain did not meet the frame.

"God damn you," Uncle Jamie said, from a few feet away.

My hand moved in a circle, but did not make contact with the Diamondback. I heard rustlings from the bed, a gasp. In the slender shaft of light, I saw pale movement flickering.

"God damn you!" Uncle Jamie growled again. Scuttering of feet on thin motel carpet and then he was on me, a big man, thick with fat and good living, strong hands, his breath heavy with marijuana. He had two good arms. My left arm was still in a sling. He pounded at my face. I rammed my knee into his rib cage, driving him off. He came at me again, letting go with an animal growl. I rolled aside, aiming a kick just below the growl. My toe connected with soft belly flesh. He grunted and backed into the light and then through it. Going for a weapon, I thought. Uncle Jamie was not a fighter. He wanted something to tilt the balance.

There was no sound from Wally. I figured he was still out. My ears were hot from doing battle, but the adrenaline would not keep me in much longer. Feeling frantic now, I scrabbled around on the floor for the Diamondback, but couldn't find it.

I felt him and heard him at the same time. Cursing, he thumped me with something hard that fell

sharply on my right shoulder. Once. Twice. Again.
Pain lanced at me from where I was taking the hits. I
rolled aside. Thump on the hip. Thump on the back.
Pain can wear you down and I was about to that place
when the lights came on and I saw Wally against the
door, his head bleeding where he'd conked himself,
and Uncle Jamie standing over me with a king-size
bullwhip, and on the other side of the bed, hunkering
down behind it, Cindy Duke, with only her forehead
and eyes above the line of the bed. Her hands and
arms were out of sight. You could not see what she
was wearing.

The light, a bleak yellow glow, came from a lamp
screwed into the wall above the rumpled bed. There
were bloodstains on the sheets, along with a scatter-
ing of twenty-dollar bills.

Uncle Jamie was holding the bullwhip by the
wrong end. He'd been pounding me with the handle,
leather wrapped around a pipe. He stopped now,
blinking against the sudden glare, and looked over at
Cindy.

"You whore!" he said.

And that's when she brought my pistol up and shot
him.

The sound slapped through the motel room. Uncle
Jamie's eyes got wide. The force of the slug slammed
him backward, into the wall. The bullwhip fell out of
his hand. He cried out and clawed at his right shoulder. He reached out to her. A second shot rang out,
but this one missed Jamie and blew out the window.
He called her a whore again and crashed through the
window into the night.

Heavy rock music pumped through the broken
window. From the room next door, a television
blared through the wall. The music was a jazzed up

rendition of "White Christmas." Welcome to peaceful Laguna.

From his place near the door, Wally moaned, then opened one eye. "Matthew. What?"

My solar plexus felt crushed. I was having trouble breathing. "Cindy?" I said. "You okay?"

"Did I kill him?" Her voice was not quavery.

"He's gone, kid. Are you okay?"

Her eyes were blank. "I want to see Gramps."

I got to my feet. Things to do. Take care of Cindy. Take care of Wally. Call the cops. Have them catch Uncle Jamie. Take Arnica. Keep from fainting, somehow.

Still holding the Diamondback, Cindy stood up slowly. She wore a white gown, a garment from an earlier century, fluffy around the neck and shoulders, with three or four petticoats. She was pale, and my guess was she'd fainted to get away from the pain.

She dropped the pistol on the bed, turned, and headed for the bathroom. The petticoats and outer skirt had been pinned up around her waist, leaving her buttocks and upper thighs bare for the master's switch. Tiny red stripes, a dozen of them, crisscrossed her soft flesh.

The door to the bathroom closed. I moved to Wally. He had a large lump on his head. The blood was clotting. He sent me out to his Saab for his homeopathic remedy kit. Outside, music trumpeted from half a dozen rooms. Where the Mercedes had been parked was an empty slot. A marine recruit with a short haircut opened the door of room 21 to ask where were the fireworks. On the beach, I said. He wished me a Merry Christmas, then went back inside, closing the door behind him.

I found the remedy kit in Wally's trunk and headed back. In the room, Cindy had changed into Levi jeans and high-tops and her blue jacket and was squatting beside Wally, pressing a cold washcloth to his wound. The money was no longer scattered on the bed.

Wally prescribed Arnica.

Cindy popped the pills into her mouth, then asked again to see her grandfather. Her cheeks were streaked with black mascara.

"Hospital first," I said.

"All right." Her hands were shaking. Her face was pale from shock.

"Home," Wally ordered. "I'm feeling better."

"God damn it, Prof. You need an X ray."

"A pox on X rays. Get me home. I'll be fine."

We climbed into Wally's Saab and headed out. Cindy was watching out the window. "Look," she said. "The police."

A cruiser was pulling into the parking lot at the Edgewater.

"One thing we don't need," Wally said, "is the police."

On the way to Wally's place on the Peninsula, Cindy broke down and cried. She wouldn't tell us what had happened. She kept asking if she'd killed Uncle Jamie. And she wanted to see her Gramps, bad.

By the time we reached the Wedge out on the end of the Peninsula, Cindy had stopped crying and Wally said his head had cleared. The headache was better and he could stand without reeling. He wanted a drink and a second remedy and a warm bath. I could taxi Cindy to the safety of Duke Castle and then return shortly. The crisis was over. The child was safe. Even Cindy seemed to be breathing easier.

We walked with him inside his house, where Cindy

used the bathroom again. Her face was pale when she came out. Wally seemed steady as a rock. Maybe we should trade places. He could take the kid home. I could stay here and get drunk on his booze. He shook hands with Cindy and said she should visit him at the surf shop after Christmas. She gave him a half smile and called him "Saint." He squeezed my arm.

Walking back to the Saab, I stumbled on a wet spot and Cindy grabbed my arm to steady me. "I can drive, Mr. Murdock."

"You sure?"

"Um. It'll be like old times. Okay?"

I stared at her. "I better drive."

"I feel okay, Mr. Murdock. Really. Must be those pills the Saint gave me."

I didn't believe her, but I was too beat to argue. I held out the keys. She reached out, her hands clutching the air in my direction, grabbed the keys, and then dropped them. She let out a strangled cry and came into my arms and buried her face in my shirt and cried some more. She felt frail and thin, like a wounded bird. I felt helpless. We stayed that way for a while, and then, when the crying had subsided, she let me go and picked up the keys and opened the driver's door. I climbed in beside her.

"Old times," she said, starting the Saab.

"Seat belt," I said.

"Oh. Thanks." As she buckled her belt, her eyes caught mine.

They were cold, like stone from a gray quarry.

We headed north, toward Duke Castle.

17

Cindy kept the needle at fifty-five. She seemed twitchy. When we passed Fashion Island, she said: "I still feel funny, Mr. Murdock. A little sick, I guess."

I nodded. "Turn right. We'll head to the hospital."

"No. I want to see Gramps." She glanced over at me. "It's those pills, I think."

"Which pills?"

"The ones he gave me. Uncle Jamie. When he picked me up. He made me swallow them and things got very fuzzy. I really hate him."

"Yeah."

"I thought I'd killed him. Not like on television. But really."

"He got away, kid."

"I'm sorry." After a couple of minutes she said: "Damn! Damn! Damn!"

A cry of frustration.

We were over the Lido Bridge before she mentioned Marvin Holly. "Have you found him yet, Mr. Murdock? Have you found my daddy?"

"Not yet."

"I'm worried now."

"He'll turn up, Cindy."

"I hope so."

Balboa Island is a fat sausage of overpriced real estate that rests sedately in Newport Bay between the curving mainland and the Balboa Peninsula, home of the Fun Zone. Balboa Island is connected to the southern shore by a two-lane bridge. Duke Island, a pie-shaped wedge, is connected to the western tip of Balboa Island by a footbridge. The only structure on Duke Island is Duke Castle.

Parking on Balboa on normal days is tough. You can get ticketed, towed, or jailed for parking in the wrong spot. On party days, parking does not exist. To handle the cars for the Christmas Eve party, Wheeler Duke takes out permanent leases on the parking lots within a half-mile radius, and then the castle provides ground transportation to carry guests to and fro. The police try to control traffic with sawhorses.

We saw the first electric tram as we swung off Jamboree. It was decorated with red and green Christmas lights. A sign said: PARTY, THE CASTLE. PLEASE SHOW INVITATION.

A cop in a yellow raincoat saw Cindy at the wheel, moved a sawhorse, and waved us past. Cindy drove through congested streets, past happy costumed partygoers. Santas and punkers mingled with belly dancers and fops from Shakespeare's time. On one loaded tram, Dracula was kissing a woman in a long white gown while Frankenstein's monster poured champagne. Fun time at Duke Castle.

Cops with red-tipped flashlights kept waving us right, then left, then left again, until we reached a parking area that said FAMILY AND FRIENDS. Cindy saw it before I did.

"He's here!" she said.

"Who?"

And then the headlights caught the big Mercedes and the DUKE VII license plate. Cindy slammed to a stop, with the Saab angled awkwardly across three spaces, and made a grab for my shoulder holster. Her eyes were crazy. She still wanted revenge. I clutched her wrist. She wrestled with me for a moment, then collapsed in a frail heap against the door. One hand was in her pocket. She held up a fistful of money. "He paid me!" she wailed. "He called me names!"

Before I could answer, a surfcat hurried up, a young guy with a face full of teeth and a cutaway tux. The light fell on Cindy, then on me. A horn tooted behind us. I was sweaty and weak. I knew she wanted to go in. If she went in, I'd have to follow her. Could I make it to the door?

The decision was made for me as the surfcat opened Cindy's door. "I'll take it from here, okay? Just leave the keys . . ."

And then Cindy slipped under his arm, goddamn, heading like an arrow for the castle. Uncle Jamie was there. She wanted her pound of flesh.

I hesitated for a couple of seconds. Too tired. Couldn't think straight, Murdock the Weary, not in a partying mood. Headlights stacked up behind us. Cindy was hell-bent on revenge, and for a long moment I thought about letting her fight it alone. It was, after all, a family matter. She could tell her Gramps. He could handle Uncle Jamie.

Then with a groan I heaved myself out of the Saab and trotted breathily after her, the Diamondback slapping against my battered ribs.

Syrupy Christmas music slurped from outdoor

speakers. Tum te *tum* te *tum* te yatta ta *tum*, the little drummer boy. To my left, the walkway was packed with happy-go-lucky merrymakers. A fat Santa trundled by on a three-wheeled bike, chortling "Ho-ho-ho" from behind his fake beard. At the drop-off point for the party tram, I saw Louie Palermo and some hired muscle. Palermo was dressed like Cortés, the conquistador. Tight leggings, pointed-toe shoes, puffy shorts, a grape-colored jacket, and a tin hat. His goons were dressed as faithful retainers. Palermo carried a sword.

A flurry of movement up ahead and to the right. I picked up speed, the pain jolting through my shoulder, and ran all the way to a high wall separating the island from the mainland.

"Pssst!" from the shadows.

I coughed, then jogged that way. Cindy stood in the shadows of a stone overhang. Behind her, a chunk of gray stone wall stood open.

"I knew you'd come," she said. Beyond her shoulder, I saw a narrow tunnel that turned left after twenty steps.

"What's this?"

"Gramps's secret passage," she said. "He showed it to me when I was a kid."

"Where does it end up?"

"The kitchen. We can take the service elevator and find Gramps. He'll fix Uncle Jamie. Come on."

I followed her inside, stopping to close the door. She led me to the end of a corridor, turning left. The floor was smooth gray stone. It led to a stout wooden door that opened onto a library. We heard distant music, distant hilarity.

"Andrea's office," Cindy said.

The office was functional—a narrow desk, a computer terminal, a space-age phone system, desk

chair, two chairs for visitors, shelves, filing cabinets.
Cindy opened the door to the main house and the
music got louder. "The kitchen's that way." This hallway was carpeted. As we drew near the kitchen, you
could smell meat cooking, herbs and spices, the tang
of sugar glaze. A double door here. Cindy opened it.
Inside, a gang of sweating cooks prepared the Christmas feast. I counted twelve of them, all dressed the
same—white smocks, tall white chef's hats. An old
guy with a mustache waved his butcher knife and
called hello to Miss Cindy. She waved back. We kept
going, past the five Kitchenaid dishwashers, past the
industrial-gauge pot scrubber, past gas ranges with
burner surfaces the size of king beds. We crossed the
kitchen and went through another door, where we
found two tuxedoed waiters waiting for the elevator.
They were speaking in French, talking about which
guests were big tippers.

"Miss Cindy?" said a voice from behind us.

We turned to see a thin-faced cook beckoning with
his left hand. His right hand was out of sight. I did not
like his face.

"What?" Cindy asked.

"Your *nonno*, signorina. Your grandfather, he wish
to see you."

"Gramps? Where is he?"

"I will take you to him. Please?" With a cute little
bow, the man stepped aside, making room for Cindy,
who tugged my sleeve and started toward the man.

The elevator came and the two waiters got on. As
soon as the doors closed, the cook's right hand came
into view. It was holding a small automatic.

"Mr. Murdock!" Cindy said.

The cook motioned me forward. "The hardware,
Jack."

I stepped in between him and Cindy. As he

reached inside to disarm me, I slumped against him, carrying him down and backward, and said, "Go, kid!" I felt a sharp blow on the back of my neck. As I went to my knees, I saw Cindy racing down the hall. She disappeared around a corner. Good kid.

The man jerked me to my feet. His hands smelled like garlic and grease, his breath stank of party wine. The elevator came and he shoved me onto it. I watched the buttons light up. Two. Three. There were blood spots on the floor of the elevator.

We stopped moving and the door opened onto a gallery decorated with a line of family portraits. Number one was a man in a frock coat and a frilly shirt, standing next to a handsome horse. Next was a man in a business suit watching the building of Duke Castle. Then Wheeler Duke himself at a construction site, wearing a hard hat and his down vest. And last in line, our own Uncle Jamie, fat and smug behind a big desk in an office high above the rest of us.

There was one portrait of a woman. Dark hair and a dark face and wonderful Indian cheekbones. She wore a floor-length white dress with a choker at the throat. I guessed she was Anastasia, Cindy's great-great-grandmother.

Wine Breath muscled me down the hallway past the Duke portraits and into a room where Louie Palermo sat in a swivel chair talking on a black phone.

Louie saw me and smiled.

18

The walls of the room were covered with maps and charts. An ancient Underwood typewriter sat on a typing table with wheels. The desk was an old rolltop and Louie had his heels on it, like a family member making himself right at home. The sword lay on the desk. On the floor was a trail of blood spots that led from the door where we stood to a narrow bed against the far wall. A man lay on the bed, moaning like a little kid. The man was Uncle Jamie Duke. There was a blood-soaked bandage over the wound where Cindy had shot him. He drank from a bottle of whiskey and handed it to one of Louie's retainers, a fat-hipped man in a jerkin and Renaissance tights.

Louie Palermo finished up his conversation and hung up the phone and spoke to Uncle Jamie. "Hang tough, bubby. Help is on the way."

"God damn you, Louie. It better come quick."

Louie turned away from Uncle Jamie to speak to Wine Breath in rapid Italian. Wine Breath answered. I heard my name but didn't catch anything else. Louie gave an order. Wine Breath handed the gun to the man in tights and walked out. Louie turned to me.

"So, Mister Private Eye, you changed your mind."

"About what?"

"About working for me and my friends. A job here. A job there. Lots of money. A grab bag of benefits."

I said nothing. If I could stall long enough, Cindy would get help. Maybe. My neck hurt from being clobbered by the skinny cook. Pains sang through my wounded shoulder. My eyes kept wanting to close. Pinch yourself and wake up and it would be Christmas Day and all would be right with the world.

"Waste him," said Jamie from the bed.

"Hear that?" Louie said. "We got a guy here wants blood. We got the son of the richest cat in southern California, a guy who's such a puss he can't get it up without some heavy special effects, who's been shot by a little girl one-third his size, and boy is he thirsty for blood."

"I hope you get yours, Louie. Jeez."

Louie picked up the phone again and pressed zero. "Hello, operator? Get me the Lakeview Rest Home in Roxbury, Vermont. Attagirl." He covered the phone and spoke to Jamie. "It's ringing, Puss. It's ringing. Hello, Lakeview. Would you connect me with—hang on a minute—what's her name again, Puss?"

"Fuck you, Louie."

Louie grinned at me and turned back to the phone. "Get me Miss Linda Dallas, please." He covered the mouthpiece with his hand and described her. "Lemme see, these days, Linda's maybe forty, forty-two, black hair, great tan, nice set of tits, if you'll pardon my French. In the real world, she was named Linda Trevino, a Chicana lady, but when we shipped her off back east in a straitjacket, we changed her name to—"

From the bed, Uncle Jamie threw a shoe at Louie, barely missing his head. The shoe hit the far wall with a feeble clunk. Louie grinned at me, then held out the phone toward Jamie.

"Puss," he said. "Don't you want to wish your sweetie a Merry?"

"God damn you, Louie. I'm bleeding to death and you keep screwing around with—"

Louie winked at me as he covered the phone with his palm. "Hey, Puss. No fair. I take care of you, clean up your vomit, your special effects. I find girls for you, twinks, teenyboppers—some of them so young, I wonder if they got quiffs—and what thanks do I get?"

"You'd sell your mother, Louie."

Louie appealed to me. "How's this, Mister Private Eye. This Trevino kid, she was one big bruise, purple turning green, like bruises will. Her neck was snapped like this, see, so she looked like one of them angels from a wall of a cathedral. Like so." He allowed his head to flop over to one shoulder. He stuck out his tongue. "The mother, she had to have a new lip, new set of teeth, new identity. She freaked out, needed treatments for the nerves, like, the screaming meemies. We got just the place." He spoke to the phone. "Hello, hello?"

Uncle Jamie tried to push himself off the bed so he could get at Louie, but he didn't have the strength, so he sagged back down, cursing. The Dukes were having a bad night. Louie hung up, then pressed some buttons to make another call. You could tell he was a guy who loved the telephone.

"Hey, Gianni. Any sign of General MacArthur? Yeah. Yeah. We got a shipment on the way out." He grinned at me. "A special delivery." He hung up and took some time arranging his heels just right on the desk. "So. When my cousin Rocco was in stir and a guy was on death row, they gave him a last wish and a good meal. Since you ain't got no time for a good meal . . . how's about a last wish?" His acid smile would have cut through metal.

"Where's Marvin Holly?"

"Who?"

"Marvin Holly. He was the Duke girl's dad."

"Hey, that would make him the brother-in-law to—"

"Up yours, Louie. Up yours!"

Louie shrugged. "Check with the General, okay? He's our guy in charge of disposals. Since I can't fix your wish, you get another try."

"What did Uncle Jamie do to Linda Trevino?"

"Hey. You're fast. This is a story I love. This puss liked getting it on with mother-and-daughter teams. So one night he's up in Cahuenga, putting the blocks to some kid—she's maybe all of twelve—and when she don't perform the way he likes he slaps her around. The kid fights back, yells for her old lady, Linda, who also fights back. Puss here hits the kid too hard. Her neck breaks. She dies. Someone calls the Cahuenga cops, of whom the captain in charge is a cousin of a friend who owes me. For some considerable cash, we are able to purchase said records—a confession tape, a transcript of the tape, photos of the crime scene—and we got a lock on old Puss. And on his daddy."

"When was this?"

"Hey, ten years back. Maybe eleven. I lose track. Puss there, he was maybe twenty-seven. Should have sent him off to Roxbury, instead of sending Linda baby."

"You used Jamie as a wedge to get into the corporation?"

Louie picked a piece of lint off his tights. "Good thinking, Mister Private Eye. I knew when I heard about you, we'd have ourselves a confrontation. You got a very long nose." He studied the lint, then dropped it to the floor. "This Duke company, now, it's been a great little Laundromat."

"What about the old man?"

"Would you believe how fast those tapes and photos brought him around?"

"Where are they?"

"Safe."

My head ached. My shoulder burned from the shot, from tussling with Uncle Jamie. My stomach was in knots. Here I was at the end of the case, and the only reason Louie Palermo was telling me anything was because he knew I was a dead man.

"Why Orange County? Why bring your dirt here?"

Louie laughed. He was enjoying himself. "We'd had our eye on the area for a time, since the sixties, when we did some jobs for the old guy, Signor Nonno Duke. We made some offers, some overtures, but he kept putting us off. Papa was alive then. He loved the orange groves, the way the moon hung over Laguna Beach. So we kept after it until we found the weak link. This is it." He gestured at Uncle Jamie. "Couldn't find a weaker link if you prayed for it. Puss gets hurt, he crawls to me for help."

"You're telling me that's why Holly died? Because Papa Palermo loved orange groves?"

Louie stood up and slapped me, showing surprising strength for a desk-bound hoodlum. I tasted blood in my mouth. Uncle Jamie laughed. Louie sat back down, making a tent of his fingers, and stared past me at the wall. "Psycho Dad was all your fault, Puss."

"Up yours, Louie."

Louie leaned back in his chair. "Picture this. In one afternoon, Psycho Dad breaks into the Cove in Laguna. He bangs up a vehicle owned by a security guard. He terrorizes Puss here inside his own parking building, the heart of Duke territory. Wish I'd seen him lay into that Mercedes."

"Eat it, Louie."

"Here's this guy, a bantam-weight alcoholic. Here's Puss, two hundred and eighty-three pounds of meat, fists like Muhammad Ali. You think, who's the winner here? Puss, right? All he's gotta do is pick him up and shake the fucker's brains out. But no."

"He had a goddamn baseball bat."

"Wonder weapon, right?" Louie went on, shaking his head. "We know Puss doesn't have the stones for anything but kids and their mothers, so we've hired us a frigging war hero to watch over him, only he can't stop this guy either."

"War hero?"

Before he could say any more there was a knock on the door and Blazer Blaisdell entered the room. He wore a tuxedo, tailored to perfection. Around his neck was a white silk scarf. Behind Blazer was a man wearing a business suit with wide lapels and a hat from a thirties gangster movie. The man was Goon Two, Louie's man from the Hotel Xanadu.

"Hey, General. You're just in time to answer a question."

Blazer's gray eyes looked at me, then at Uncle Jamie. He took in the blood, the wounded man, the gun in the hand of Louie's Renaissance retainer, the sword on the table, and finally Louie. "Reporting as ordered, sir," he said.

Goon Two stood to one side, eyeing the scene.

"The screw-up, General," Louie said. "This guy Holly getting killed. And the kid, what's her name, from Texas, making it all the way to the hospital. Your pal here's curious about how that happened."

"A mix-up in the orders, sir."

"Hey," Louie said. "We owe this guy. I mean, you and him were pals in the jungle, right?"

"Excessive force was employed," Blazer said. "This command accepts full responsibility."

"Ain't he a kick." Louie's grin was fading now. "We send in our enforcer. Shake him up, is the order. Rattle Psycho Dad's cage. See he gets out of town. But does he follow? No. He bunts the guy with a truck, sideswipes some kid in the process. Our disposals people are slow that night. While they're loading Psycho Dad, the kid crawls off. While they hunt for her, some citizen drives by. Doesn't stop, but spooks our moron enforcer anyway. Then the paramedics arrive. The General was on the scene. That about it, General?"

"You were advised, sir."

"Woolford," I breathed. "He killed Marvin?"

"A loose cannon, sir." Blazer was tight-lipped now. "A history of resorting to excessive force. You were advised. You were cautioned."

Louie kept going. "So now we're mopping up, General. Cleaning up after you." He waved a hand at me. "Your old jungle pal here's the last detail. Cover him up, we're clean. So how about a firing squad, General? Stand him up against a wall, execution style. Wasn't that your trademark, General, back in the good old days? Bang, bang, like?"

Blazer's eyes were steely. "Affirmative, sir."

"Then we need a—what do you call it—a burial detail. Think you can handle it for us?"

Blazer did not look my way. "Affirmative, sir."

"Bury him deep, with Psycho Dad."

"Yes, sir."

"See?" Louie turned to me. "Take a soldier. Give him an order. The guy follows the order. Right, General?"

"That's affirmative, sir."

"So let's get cracking."

"Right away, sir."

Louie spoke to Goon Two. "Aldo, you stay here."

Blazer, his smile like a razor, reached inside his tux and brought out a silver Beretta. Louie's eyes narrowed. Aldo dug under his suitcoat. Louie's man in the tights brought the muzzle of the small automatic to bear on Blazer. There was a long moment of silence. My heart slammed in my ears. I was sweating. Blazer wasn't. My legs were weak as I got set to dive for Louie's sword. Then Blazer's eyes wavered, man in trouble, and he motioned me out without a word.

A cold draft blew on my neck as we walked back down the corridor past the family portraits to the elevator. "Detour on your voyage to Singapore?"

"God damn you, Foxy." His voice was a harsh whisper. "Why didn't you take the old man's money? Why didn't you stay the hell out of this and leave me room to maneuver?"

"You were there, weren't you? When Holly broke the windshield?"

He nodded. "A foul-up."

"Why Woolford?"

"Jamie was afraid Holly would blow the whistle. He went to Louie. To show me up, Louie sent Woolford in." Blazer shook his head. "A hopeless troop, Foxy. A real cowboy. Middle name was excessive force."

The elevator doors opened and we stepped on.

Blazer pushed the button for One and the doors closed. "I told them you were trouble. I warned them. That's why they tried to take you out."

"Who flew to O'Hare in place of Holly? Woolford?"

"No. One of Palermo's geeks."

"He tossed Holly's place?"

"Yes."

"Where's Holly?"

"Buried. Construction site."

"Does the old man know?"

Blazer blinked as the car passed the second floor. "No."

"They torched my house to pull me away from the hospital?"

"Yes. Sorry about that."

"How did they know the girl was awake?"

"Palermo's mole network. At least ten cops on the payroll, with more on the way. A guy named Rome relayed the message."

"Who did it, Blazer? Who killed Heather Blasingame?"

Blazer stared at me, but said nothing. The elevator was almost to the ground floor. He shifted gears, all business now, the CO in the field, surrounded by enemy emplacements. "Okay, Foxy. Listen up. First we get clear of the castle. Second, we get through the perimeter. That's a toughie. You're wounded. They've got the fire—"

The door opened. We had reached the first floor. Two men in business suits blocked our way. New faces to me.

"Hey, Gianni," Blazer said.

"Hey, General. Mr. Palermo, he wants me and Nick here to tag along."

Blazer didn't bat an eye. You could almost see him recomputing his battle plan to fit the new increase in enemy strength. Once a soldier, always a soldier. The only question was, whose side was he really on?

"Fine."

We started into the kitchen. Blazer and I walked in front. Gianni and Nick walked behind.

"Hey, General?" Gianni said.

"What?"

"We get to the car, you're the pilot, okay?"

"Fine."

"Where we're going, it's that building site, on the Coast Highway."

"Fine."

"We're gonna bury your pal here under another ton of concrete slab."

"Fine."

Gianni chuckled. "It'll be like old times in Nam, hey, General?"

We were halfway across the kitchen. Two cooks stopped what they were doing to watch us, but the party was in full swing—Christmas carols and the sound of a brass band pounding from the great hall— and the food had to keep on rolling. I did not see Wine Breath. Without looking at me, Blazer stopped in the middle of the kitchen. A brass skillet, full of sizzling grease, was two feet from my right hand. Blazer turned to face Louie's goons.

"Don't call it Nam," he said.

"Hey, General. No offense." Gianni's eyes looked edgy, like he didn't know what he'd gotten into.

"You weren't there. You don't have the right."

"Hey, Nick," Gianni said to his pal. "Get that. I don't have the right."

Blazer's right arm shot through the air and at the same time he twisted his hips and shoulders to get that extra little pivot into his thrust. The heel of his hand caught Gianni under the nose, driving it up into the man's skull as he clawed the air, trying to push the pain away.

I took a quick step to the skillet. The handle was hot, but I wasn't going to hang on to it for very long. I flipped the hot grease onto Nick, letting go of the skillet. He screamed.

At the far end of the kitchen a door opened and Wheeler Duke stood there, holding a pump shotgun. "No one moves!" the old man roared. "No one!"

Cooks scattered, shouting in a gaggle of languages. I ducked down, hunting for a weapon. Then someone opened up from a door behind us, over by the elevator, and at the same time someone fired from behind a butcher-block island to our right. One of the slugs took Blazer along the neck and shoulder. He staggered, dropped his pistol, and slumped to the floor.

"Blazer!" I said. "Goddamn!"

The old man's shotgun roared, shattering glass or crockery or both. A voice cried out. I picked up Blazer's Beretta and was in time to see Wine Breath trying to slide between the butcher-block island and a Kitchenaid dishwasher. The gun wobbled as I brought it up. To shoot straight, you need two hands, but one of mine was trussed up in a sling, so I snapped a shot at him and missed, the slug ricocheting off the metal dishwasher. Men were shouting now, but I couldn't understand the words. I tucked the gun in my shoulder holster and scooted over to check on Blazer. "Blazer!" I yelled. "Blazer?"

"To your right, Foxy!"

Wine Breath came around the corner, his pistol aimed at me. No time to drag the gun out before he shot me, so I scooped a meat mallet from off the floor and flung it at him. Dodging the flying mallet threw his aim off. His shot went wide, but I felt the bullet

cut the air. By then my gun was out and as he started
to fire again I squeezed off a round that opened a hole
in the white T-shirt, the force of the bullet driving
him backward and out of sight.

The shotgun fired again, this time from a position
closer to us. From behind the doors, the band played
"Jingle Bells."

"Murdock?" the old man called. "You okay? Murdock?"

Before I could answer, someone opened up on me
from the elevator with an automatic weapon. Slugs
ripped out the butcher block above my head. I tried
to remember how many rounds I'd fired from Blazer's Beretta, but my mind would not compute. When
the firing stopped, I wormed my way around a table,
across a pair of lifeless legs in pale blue trousers, and
peeked out. Two figures huddled behind an overturned table near the elevator. One of them was
Palermo. The other was Aldo. They were whispering. Outside the doors, excited voices drowned out
the sound of music.

"Psst!" came from behind me.

I turned to see Wheeler Duke crawling my way on
his belly, an expensive pump shotgun cradled across
his elbows. He was grinning. A lock of gray hair had
fallen across his broad forehead. He was dressed as a
cowboy.

"How many are there?"

"Two. Palermo and a goon."

"Where are they?"

"By the elevator. They're using a table for cover."

He hefted the shotgun. "How about I open up on
the table, drive them out, and you shoot their asses."

I grinned. "When will you fire?"

"On my signal, count to ten. We go together."

"Yo."

He touched my arm with two fingers and crawled away. When he got settled behind the line of dishwashers, he signaled and I started counting. Thousand-one, thousand-two, thousand-three.

As I reached thousand-seven, there was flurried movement behind the overturned table. Aldo rose up, head and one shoulder above the rim, to fire at me again. At the same time, Palermo in his conquistador costume made a dash for the elevator, where he stopped to cover Aldo with an evil-looking Uzi. *Splat*, went his little gun. *Splaaaat*.

Then Wheeler Duke's shotgun boomed, the charge splintering the table and spooking Aldo, who leaped up to make a dash for the elevator, where Palermo was frantically jamming the buttons. My first shot was wide. I nailed Aldo with my second shot, just before he reached the elevator. The doors were closing. With a war cry, Wheeler Duke charged Palermo, the shotgun held at hip level. "He's mine, Murdock!"

There was a click as his hammer fell on an empty chamber. Wheeler Duke swore and kept on going. Palermo took aim at the old man. Steadying my arm on the tabletop, I put a bullet next to Palermo's ear, giving the old man time to ram the butt end of his shotgun between the closing doors. His face was red. The doors slid open. With a loud whoop, Wheeler Duke moved on Palermo, pounding him with the shotgun. "Take that. Damn your eyes. Take that!"

Then the doors leading to the other parts of the castle were flung open and costumed guests stood there openmouthed.

People reached the elevator in time to keep Wheeler Duke from killing Louie Palermo.

I crawled back to Blazer.

His eyes fluttered open when I reached him. Blood

pumped from a nasty hole in his neck and the color was fast draining from his face. Artery, I thought, finding it with my finger and pressing to slow down the flow. A goddamn artery.

"It's down to the wire, Foxy. You can always tell it's down to the wire when we make war on civilians again."

"Hang on, Blazer."

"I'm finished, Foxy. Singapore's out for this troop. I've lost it and it's gone."

"Medic on the way, buddy. Don't talk."

"Failure of nerve, old son. The old gunfighter went yellow." A cough rippled through him, jostling my finger off the artery. The blood pumped faster until I tamped it down again. "Hate that, worse than anything, losing my nerve. Felt like shit warmed over. Should have drilled him when I had the chance. Couldn't."

"Drilled Holly, you mean?" I asked.

Blazer sighed and closed his eyes and I recalled how he'd gone through eight years of intense jungle fighting and never been wounded. "Yeah. Barb Duke's ex, old Marvin sad-eye. Should have. She'd have loved it, the irony of it, the boyfriend wasting the ex. Saw his eyes, Foxy. Saw the fear dancing up. Had the piece out, but couldn't pull the trigger. Would have kept the shit away from the fan. My fault. Whole show went to hell after that. Woolford, Palermo. My fault. Everything."

"God damn you, Blazer. Don't you die on me now."

He grinned, his face ashy and waxen. His lips were pale as death. "They bought my ass, Foxy. Bought my soul. Enter Blazer Faust, minus his balls, to Mephisto Palermo. Bought me for thirty pieces of silver. I knew it. Didn't try to stop them. Thought maybe I'd find them again, my balls, I mean, find them working for the devil. One thing, pal. Get Palermo for me."

"He's cooked, Blazer. The old man got him. Help's on the way. So you hang on."

"I like that old man," he said. "But they got him too."

"Well, you both wiped it clean. Tonight."

He grinned at me weakly and gave a tiny shake of his head. "Not clean, Foxy. So dirty now, it could never get clean."

"We'll fix it, Blazer. Come on. I got friends in high places."

He said something I couldn't hear. His strength was pumping away through a hole in his neck and there was nothing I could do to stop it. Behind me, voices, questions, the huddling herd gulping for air because they weren't lying there on the floor, dying. I bent my ear close to his mouth, heard him say: "All the juice in the . . . world . . . can't . . . fix . . . the . . . girl."

My head was hammering in time with Blazer's pulse. "Medic!" I yelled. "Medic!"

He shook his head slowly. "Line of command breaking down, troops out of control, all my fault, for not drilling old Marvin in the back. My fault, shit hitting the fan, feathers all over. Mixed metaphor, Foxy, too bad. Palermo knew about me losing my balls, so he gave me a job, one he figured I could do. General MacArthur, he said. This is your job, cleaning up the mess, so muzzle that little girl in the hospital. I said no. I'd killed my share of Charleys, executing them in the name of the Company, the U.S. Army, and the President of the United States. But God damn it, killing children is not a hero's bag. Okay, he said, you don't like the chick, so kill Murdock the dick." Blazer stopped to cough, his blood dark against my hand. I thought of the hospital parking lot, the black BMW. My stomach felt sick as he sighed, then went on. "So that was it. Knew I couldn't take you, Foxy. Once, maybe, before I lost my balls, but not now. Gave you to Woolford. Went for the girl in the hospital bed. A total innocent, Jesus. It's the worst thing I've ever done, Foxy, pulling that plug. Made me sick. Told me everything was finished. The end of Blazer Blaisdell. Had to wipe it out, so decided to nail Palermo. They come after you when you take out one of theirs. They run your ass to earth. Too late for me." He coughed, a hollow sound. "Hated it like a son of a bitch when they called me General. A man has to earn the right to do that." He was about to go on when there was an interruption behind us, a muted buzz from the crowd. Blazer stared over my shoulder, his eyes crinkling into his final laugh, as a woman's voice cried:

"Douglas! Douglas!"

And Barb Duke crashed through the circle of onlookers to muscle me out of the way at Blazer's side.

Her face was hysterical, thick tears, mascara glopped on her eyelashes, rough smear of lipstick across her mouth. In honor of the Christmas season, she wore a dress of slick red leather. Miniskirt, deep cleavage, her nut-brown arms gleaming through artful slashes in the sleeves. A flashbulb popped behind her as she leaned over, breathing in Blazer's face, crooning his name. "Douglas? Oh, Douglas!" But Blazer, a soldier to the end, reached for me, his battlefield buddy. No strength left in his grip now.

More flashbulbs popped, brightening the dark stain on Blazer's white tuxedo shirt. Out of the corner of my eye I saw costumed guests with cameras pressed to their cheeks. Snap. Click. Clickety. Recording the last Christmas party at Duke Castle.

"Foxy, you dumb fuck. Why didn't you take my job offer? Why didn't you butt out? Why didn't you take the money from the old—" And then his eyes opened wide and the last breath fluttered out of him and he sighed and was gone.

And Barb Duke, her eyes glittering with the madness of drugs, took a wicked swipe at me with her red fingernails while her twisted mouth let loose a horrible scream at the insistently clicking cameras.

19

We were nine for Christmas dinner at Wally's house on the Peninsula. As host and supreme carver of the bird, Wally sat at the head of the table with Dorene Wilson on his right. Dorene looked pretty in a red dress. On Dorene's right was Webby Smith. Next to Webby was Guillermina Gonzales, Zeke's girl, and then Leo Castelli, who ran Leo's Café, where they served the best breakfast between Los Angeles and San Diego. I sat across the table from Leo. On my right was Julie Treadway, Webby's smiling girl-jock from UCI. Zeke sat next to Julie, on her right. Mary Castelli, Leo's wife, sat between Zeke and Wally.

Everyone except Murdock had someone.

I missed Senator Jane.

The turkey was smoked to perfection. The mashed potatoes were perfect, the gravy not too greasy. The cranberry sauce, made from fresh berries by Mary Castelli from a recipe inherited from her maternal grandmother back in Skaneateles, New York, was tart instead of sweet, to make your mouth pucker at just the right moment. The dressing was moist, but not too. The English peas were the exact shade of holiday green.

From where I sat I could see the stack of newspapers in Wally's living room. The Duke Castle fracas had made news in New York and Paris and London and Tokyo. Reporters from every major paper in the world had converged on Orange County to sniff out the dirt and hold it up to the world as ultimate truth. There was a front-page photo of Uncle Jamie being hauled away on an ambulance gurney. Because of his wounded shoulder, he was being held at the jail ward at the UCI Medical Center in Orange. The charge, so far, was molestation of a minor.

Louie Palermo was on the critical list, put there by many blows from Wheeler Duke's shotgun butt. Gianni was dead, killed by the heel of Blazer's hand. Nick, Gianni's pal, was in the hospital with grease burns and a concussion. Wine Breath—his real name was Vicente Tomasino—was dead from a bullet from Blazer's gun fired by me but attributed, so far, to Blazer. Aldo was wounded, shot in the ass by me with the final slug from Blazer's Beretta.

Police in Huntington Beach had caught another member of the arson gang who had torched my place the night before Christmas Eve. He admitted being paid two hundred dollars to fire half a dozen rockets at my house. His description of the man who hired him—medium height, medium thick, middle-aged, squinty eyes, losing his hair, big nose—could have fit half of the goons who worked for Louie Palermo.

There was no trace of Deputy Hanks, who had failed to return from his vacation. Lieutenant Rome was on the duty roster for Christmas Day, but had not reported in for work yet. His home phone did not answer. Inquiries would be forthcoming, said a spokesman for the sheriff's department.

Barb Duke was in St. Boniface Hospital, suffering from shock and a drug overdose. Cindy was staying with Phyl, her fellow Mall Rat. I'd called her earlier to wish her a Merry Christmas and she'd sounded subdued and distant. I'd thanked her for warning her grandfather I was in trouble and she said it's okay, she owed me one. The grown-up talk hadn't fooled me: brave Cindy was finally allowing herself to understand what had happened to her. In a whisper, Phyl told me Cindy hadn't eaten anything. "She just stares at the wall, Mr. Murdock. Or at the rain outside her window. And she won't let go of that book her dad wrote."

Marvin Holly's body had been found buried under one corner of a building at the Duke Harbour construction site.

The papers blossomed with photos. Duke Castle. Carcassonne. Duke Harbour. The Duke headquarters in Newport Beach. There were mug shots of the Duke Family: Wheeler, Jamie, Barb, Cindy, Elroy, and Anastasia. There were diagrams of the action in the Duke kitchen, with little arrows showing who shot whom. Blazer was identified as the president of CEO Security, Inc., a firm retained by Duke Construction. Out of five major papers, only one linked the Palermos to the Mob.

There was no trace of Wheeler Duke, who had vanished last night after walloping Palermo with the shotgun butt. Federal charges were being brought, said the U.S. attorney, against Wheeler Duke and Duke Construction. The charge was money laundering.

None of the newspaper stories had tied in Heather or Senator Jane to Marvin's murder.

Good.

This wasn't in the papers, but Webby Smith had

told me the Costa Mesa police had turned up traces
of a Ford Bronco registered to Lance Woolford. The
traces were in a chop shop a block off the Coast
Highway and preliminary lab reports had identified
the Bronco as the vehicle that had struck down
Heather Blasingame and writer Marvin Holly.

In private, Webby had shown me a computer
printout about a Stephen Two Trees, a suspect in
custody in Escondido. Stephen was a Navajo, twenty-
four years old, with a record of arrests starting eight
years back when he'd been charged with boosting
car stereos in Gallup. Stephen, who'd been caught
trying to buy a six-pack with someone else's credit
card, had named Heather Blasingame as a member
of the so-called San Diego Kids.

He'd last seen her, he said, when she walked away
from his car in the parking lot at Denny's in San
Clemente last Tuesday morning. He denied following her, denied being at Xanadu at the time of the
hit-and-run, but Webby said there was a chance this
kid had called the switchboard to alert the sheriff and
the paramedics. According to Stephen Two Trees, he
and Heather and an accomplice named Roy Umbarger had been operating a lonesome-traveler scam in
the Phoenix area since September. It had been Roy
Umbarger's idea to head for California, where he
knew some guys who were running a similar scam on
lonesome travelers. Better pickings on the road, he
said. An APB was out for Roy.

Two unnamed witnesses had come forward,
Webby said, who claimed credit for alerting Xanadu
security about the hit-and-run. Both witnesses had
refused to give out their names unless a reward was
involved. Webby dismissed their stories on grounds
of greed. "They've read the papers," Webby said.
"They've smelled Duke money and Mob involve-

ment and they'll be crawling out of the woodwork with their palms turned up."

"A very Merry Christmas," I said.

It was my turf, my slice of what was left of the dream that was southern California, but I was sick of it. A friend had died. A little girl had been molested, maybe crippled for life. A lady had gone away, leaving me alone again. So I drank too much wine before the turkey was served, and then during dinner I drank a lot more, and so during dessert, when I got loud, Leo and Webby led me off like a sad little kid to bed, and there I plunged into a wine-dark sleep.

In the dream, I was pedaling uphill on a bicycle, breathing hard, lungs working at full bore. I came to a dark dwelling where a man stood guard outside, his arms folded. He wore a doctor's white coat and a mask over his face. He called me Foxy and said I couldn't go in. I shoved him aside. He bumpity-bumped down the hill. One arm came off. Then the other arm. He was not a man. He was a doll, what the French call a *poupée*, and his head was under my arm. It had come off during our tussle. "Foxy," the head said. "You are my dark side of the moon."

"Why, Blazer?" I asked, shaking the head. "Why? Why? Why?"

"Foxy," he said. "I owe you, old son. I've got *dinero*. Let's get laid. One dolly evens us up, hey?"

Then the mask came off and I saw it was not Blazer's head I was holding, but my own. We were crying, both of us, big soggy tears. "Shit," I said. "Soldiers don't cry." I set the head down on top of a potted plant and shoved the door open. I was in a bedroom, a big square room with a big bed. Wheeler Duke stared down on the room from a portrait on the wall. A man lay under the covers. It was Uncle Jamie, big as a walrus, with huge white arms and a teenager's acid-eyed smirk. "Send her in," he said. "I'm ready. Send in the little bitch."

Barb Duke stepped into the room, holding Cindy by the hand. Barb wore her workout togs, skintight pants of silver Lurex, a hot-pink halter top. Cindy wore a filmy white dress that you could see right through. Her face looked garish. Dark red lips, purple eyeshadow, orange rouge. She was barefoot and forever vulnerable. Her eyes were stoned with dope.

"Go on!" Barb Duke whispered, shoving her daughter toward the bed. "Go to Jamie. Go. Go. Go."

"No!" I grabbed Cindy's hand. Cold as ice.

Uncle Jamie swung at me with a Ninja stick. Barb Duke clawed at my eyes. I fought them, brother and sister. My arm was in a sling. Cindy, zonked on drugs, was no help. The Dukes were too much for me. Blows rained down, the power of the Dukes. They wanted me out of town. I felt myself falling and falling and—

And then I woke up sweating. Webby Smith was shaking me gently. "Sherlock," he said. "You got a phone call."

Jane, I thought. It's Senator Jane.

But the caller was not the Senator. It was Wheeler Duke. He had some business and he wanted a meeting. Time: fifteen minutes. Place: the Newport Pier.

I was happy to borrow Wally's Saab. It's an automatic and for another couple of weeks, I'd be a one-armed man. I wore my shoulder holster and in it a Colt Python. The Newport Beach police had confiscated my Diamondback when they took it off Uncle Jamie, who had snatched it off Louie Palermo's desk at Duke Castle.

Wheeler Duke was waiting for me in a white, mud-smudged Range Rover that was parked in the quad that looks across to the pier, the beach, and the ocean. The license plate read GWR1999. Like the vehicle, it was smudged with mud.

I parked behind him and climbed out. He saw me coming and leaned over to open the passenger door. The Range Rover was loaded for an overland trip. Luggage and boxes of food and liquor and a couple of rifles in gun cases. Tucked into one box was a black license plate, a custom job that had been removed from the vehicle. I could read only the first three letters—DUK—but I could guess the whole plate would read DUKE I.

Wheeler Duke wore a down vest over a heavy cable-knit sweater, khakis, hunting boots, and a safari hat with a feather in the brim. He shook my hand. "Thanks for coming."

"Thanks for saving my skin last night."

His grin was the expression of a strong man with a lot of kills. "Bagged a couple of bad guys." He indicated the heavily loaded Range Rover. "They'll be after me now. You shoot one slicker, the pack hunts you down. That's why I called."

"I owe you, Mr. Duke, and I'd like to help." I tapped my left arm. "Until the arm comes back, we'd better bring on some extra help."

The grin stayed. "Hell, son. Thanks for the offer, but no thanks. I travel alone. Always have. Always will. No, it's Cindy-gal I want you to look after. My family's come apart at the seams. If she needs someone, it'll be you."

"I spoke to her today. The shock has finally taken hold."

The old man's voice was gravelly. "Think she'll come out of it?"

"Sure. She's tough."

There was a moment of silence. Wheeler Duke's

eyes were moist, probably as close as he ever got to crying. "Let's walk."

We climbed out of the Range Rover and I waited for him to lock up, and then we hiked across the quad to the pier. The sky was iron gray and there was a stiff breeze blowing off the ocean.

"Sorry about what happened to your house."

"It's fixable."

"You got insurance?"

"Enough."

We were on the pier now, heading into the wind. A family of fisher folk—mom, dad, three kids—dropped lines into the water. Wheeler Duke spoke to them in Spanish and the father answered back.

"How did you find me at Wally's?" I asked.

"Dossier," he said. "We ran one on you back in the seventies. Then we updated it when you showed up at Xanadu."

"How complete is it?"

"Semi," he said. "It's got that cop down in Laguna, and Dr. St. Moritz, and Leo the café owner." He looked over at me and smiled. "I admire your taste in females."

"You kept dossiers on me, on the Senator, on God only knows who else. Why not a dossier on your boy?"

He grunted. "Don't get moralistic on me, son. My boy's a sick puppy. I know that. Have known it for years. What I didn't know was just how sick. You know where I was headed when I shot Louie Palermo?"

"Where?"

"I was hunting for my son. My plan was to blow his balls off, one at a time. Cindy-gal routed me through the kitchen, held me by the hand. She's real high on you, like I said. She's the one you should thank."

"I will."

We were halfway out to the end of the pier. Colder out here. I had to ask Wheeler Duke to help me zip the parka up. He ran the zipper up to my beard and we kept on walking.

"Where are you headed?" I asked.

"Mexico," he said. "A two-bit town south of Ensenada called Maneadero. Got a ranch there, some people who work for me. There's some reports I want to write, and when I get them done I'll mail them to you and you can make sure they get to the right people."

"Okay."

"You don't want to know what kind of reports?"

"I can guess."

He licked his lips. "Okay. Guess."

We stopped at the end of the pier and leaned on the railing and stared out at the whitecaps.

"You got rich twice, Mr. Duke. The first time was in 1962, when you built Carcassonne. The second time was in 1969. That's the year you bought your island back and also the year you founded Duke Construction."

"Smart of you, following the cash."

"The money came from marijuana," I said. "You ran it up from Mexico and Central America on a private vessel. You probably started sometime in the late fifties. The market grew in the sixties, because of hippies and the war and free love. That's how you built Carcassonne. And then, for the really big money, you found a distributor."

"Fucking Palermos," he breathed. "How long have you known all this, Murdock?"

"A day or so."

"Jesus, I hated it, getting into bed with them. They were snakes. They wormed in. They had cash. I was paying twenty-two percent to meet payroll and pay off suppliers. I used them for a while, then sent them back to Los Angeles. They kept after me. Wanted a silent partnership, they said. They'd pass me the cash. I'd run it through my business. Didn't like their smell, so I wouldn't budge. A couple of years later, they came across that police report on my boy. Called him a mad-dog killer. Offered to blow the whistle on him, spread the mud all across the headlines. I should have shown them the door, but you know how it is, you start moving boulders and one boulder bangs into the next boulder and pretty soon you've moved a mountain and people are kissing your ass and you get used to them doing it and—" He stopped. "What would you have done?"

"I don't know."

He dug into his watch pocket and brought a handsome gold timepiece. "Time to get moving," he said.

We started back. He talked about his daughter and Blazer. He'd known they were courting. He'd liked Blazer and had hoped it would come to something. He was always looking for a man who could handle his daughter. I said nothing.

Just before we reached land, he said: "Orange groves into gold, Murdock. Those were the good old days."

"The California dream," I said.

"There were five of us back then, comers, guys on the go. Harry Mechum, he ran for governor six years back, almost made it. And there was Norm Gutenberg, he was Harry's lawyer cousin who became a partner in Williams, Gutenberg, Stern. Then there was Ben Trane Junior, the local philanthropist, and Walt Cuzack. Walt was mayor of Newport two times running. We formed a secret corporation to transport the stuff up here. We had cash when the pinko liberal Demo-Rats were handing the country back to the Reds. The world was going to hell in a handbasket, so the feeling was, why the hell not?" He grabbed me by the shoulder. "I ask you. Why the hell not?"

His eyes were silver blue, his face alive with energy. He had inherited Indian cheekbones from Anastasia, his maternal grandmother, then passed them on to his daughter and son. But on an aging king, cheekbones only deepen the look of lingering gauntness angled toward the grave.

He was still holding on, still talking. "I wanted something lasting, something that would be here after I was gone, so I settled on Xanadu. Got the horse laugh from my friends. Xanadu, they said, it'll drive the people off. A name like that, no one will spend a nickel. I didn't go along with that. Give the public a chance, I said. Give them credit for having some brains. So we chiseled those lines from Coleridge up above the entrance and the name caught on and the place coined money from the day we opened our doors."

The old guy knew how to hang in there.

"Damn. One way to know you're an old fool is when you run off at the mouth."

He let me go and we walked back to the Range Rover. Before getting behind the wheel, he said: "My granddaddy built this country. My daddy threw it away. I got some of it back. Jamie, well, he's like my daddy. Both of them, they pissed away their chance. Maybe the good stuff skips every other generation. Anyway, all we Dukes got left is my Cindy-gal."

His hand was on the door. "You probably won't believe this, but I didn't find out about what they'd done to old Marvin until last night at the party when that guinea Palermo threw the news in my face. I was sorting things through with the help of the brandy bottle when Cindy came running to get me. I don't condone murder."

"I believe you, Mr. Duke."

There was a pause. "Thanks, Murdock. You look after my Cindy-gal, hear?"

I nodded. He closed the door with an expensive click and started the Range Rover. I stood in the quad, the Blue Beet Café on my right, the burned ruin of my home on the left, and watched him turn the corner and disappear.

As I was driving back to Wally's house, the sun came out, an orange wafer on the horizon, heralding the end of another happy Christmas and the start of a fresh new year.

20

That first week in January, I huddled with Webby Smith and Assistant D.A. Harriet Trueblood. I gave Harriet the name and whereabouts of Linda Dallas, aka Linda Trevino. "She's at Lakeview Rest Home," I said. "In Roxbury, Vermont. Uncle Jamie Duke murdered her daughter, up in Cahuenga. Ten, eleven years ago."

Harriet, the oldest daughter of a blue-collar family, liked the idea of nailing some Dukes to the wall. Since she couldn't get at Wheeler or Barb, she settled for Uncle Jamie.

"Child molestation creates a big flap in the press," Harriet said. "Horrifies us, seeing innocence dirtied and reviled. But it's tricky, building a good case. We'll have to put Cindy on the stand." She blew a trail of cigarette smoke toward her office window. "It would really make my day to nail Uncle Jamie on a count of murder two." She crossed her legs and smiled. "Boy, do I hate fat cats."

The problems with the murder two charge started right away. In Cahuenga, where the crime had been committed, the watch commander from a decade ago had died of a heart attack. A fire had destroyed a wing of the old police station, so no records could be found. The state's case against Uncle Jamie now depended on the testimony of Linda Trevino.

I was in the courtroom when they led Linda in. The papers said her age was forty-three. She looked seventy. She was bent, withered, dazed by being thrust back into the world. A woman in pain, battered by fists, pounded by circumstance.

Linda stared at Uncle Jamie, her mouth working. Then she stared at the floor. When they tried to administer the oath, she said, "I do. I do. I do. I do. I doooo—" A long, low wailing sound. The judge pointed a finger. A matron in a green uniform hustled Linda out.

Harriet Trueblood squared her shoulders and asked for a recess. It was Friday afternoon. You could feel the weekend coming up. The judge scowled. "Monday morning, counsel. Ten A.M., sharp. And I'm admonishing you, be prepared."

So much for the majesty of the law.

Around four o'clock that afternoon I followed Harriet's BMW east across a gray wasteland of California concrete to the UCI Medical Center. My arm, though still tender, was out of the sling. I was driving Wally's Saab. My mission: keep Cindy off the witness stand.

In the jail ward, Harriet introduced me to the man in charge, a soft-faced marshal named Sanchez. He gave me a form to sign and checked me for weapons. Harriet handed me a sheet of paper with a place at the bottom for a signature. Sanchez blinked when I showed him the mini cassette-recorder strapped to my right ankle.

"Right this way," Sanchez said, leading me down an echoing corridor. "His Highness is receiving."

I took a cue from Sanchez's tone. "How's Uncle Jamie holding up?"

"A real fat cat," Sanchez said. "Fat and sassy. Some days he sinks ninety-nine out of a hundred of them putts. What's the recorder for?"

"Mood music," I said.

"You get too close, he could take off your nose with that putter."

"Maybe you better loan me your piece."

Sanchez grinned and unlocked Uncle Jamie's door.

Uncle Jamie had a room with a view that looked eastward, out across the ribboned freeways to the hills of Orange County. It was late winter in California. From here, he could study the snow patterns on the distant Sierras. The room boasted a television, a recliner to watch it from, a desk, a swivel chair, a shortwave radio with a police band, and a telephone with three lines to the outside world. The bed was neatly made, maid service, no doubt. A black plastic shelf held his collection of videotapes, a hundred or more, so he wouldn't get bored. I had expected silk pajamas and a dressing gown, but Uncle Jamie was dressed for a day on the links, white slacks and a red Arnold Palmer golf shirt. In the courtroom, he'd been wearing his sling. There was no sign of it here.

He was putting golf balls toward a little plastic target cup across the room. The cup was red. It gobbled up the balls with a gulp and stored them in a leather pocket behind the cup.

"Well, well." Uncle Jamie brandished the putting iron. "What's up, Mur-Dock?" He sank the putt, giving it extra body English and snapping his fingers, yeah, as the cup snatched the ball. Big smile.

I took Blazer's envelope out of my pocket. It contained a dozen photos. The first photo showed the body of a dead girl. Her age when she died was eleven. Her name was Costanza Luisa Trevino. Her nickname was Connie. I dropped the photo at his feet. "Pinup for your wall, Jimbo."

"Whuuh?" Uncle Jamie's pig eyes narrowed. He poked the photo with his putter. "Where did you get that?"

I dropped a second photo. This one showed Connie's mother, Linda, two teeth broken, her face battered and blue. Uncle Jamie backed up, gripping the putter in both hands, and sliced down at me. I dodged, feeling the steel whistle by. I grabbed him by the golf shirt and, using his momentum, hauled him past me. He bounced off the end of the bed, knocking over a plastic chair, then crashed his shoulder into the wall. He took a second swing with the putter, just missing my nose. I chopped down on his forearm with the edge of my hand, making him drop the putter. His big left fist caught me on the ear. We traded punches. His were like sledgehammers. I wanted to kill him, ram his nose bone up into his slimeball brain. Instead, I sank a fist into his solar plexus, taking the wind out of him. He buckled and fell to the floor, gripping his belly, huffing for breath. Hoo-ha, he said. Hoo-hoo-ha.

Squatting, breathing hard, I showed him the photos. One at a time. Watched his face twist as he felt the evidence mounting. "This is Connie," I said. "You remember? Connie Trevino? You can tell it's her by the angle of her head, means the neck broke when you slugged her. Here's Connie again, with the blood caked on her thighs. And here's Linda, Connie's mom. See that eye? Six months after you slapped her around, Linda developed a cataract in that eye. Had to be operated on before she went blind. Here's the handcuffs you used on Connie. Didn't want her to get loose, I guess. Here's some familiar toys. A whip, a riding crop, and a quirt. Oh, yeah. And here's—"

We went through the photos a second time before he spoke: "Where did you get them?"

"From Doug Blaisdell."

Jamie's eyelids fluttered like lemons in a Vegas slot machine as he processed that information. "But"— his whine was wire-tight—"Douglas worked for me."

"You and Louie," I said.

"Louie promised. He—" A sickly greenish smile from Uncle Jamie. "So. The old mobster double cross. Douglas gets them from Louie. But why deliver them to you?"

"Doug was leaving town. Wanted to make sure you got your day in court." I smelled fear now, and the tang of cologne.

Sweat streaked his fat face. "My experience with the military is that they always screw up. Sissy liked that part, of course. Had a special yen for soldiers. First Marvin. Then that Air Force clod. Then Douglas." Jamie leered at me. "For the first time in her life, she had to give it away. Around our Douglas, Sissy melted, became your perfect bitch in heat."

I remembered Cindy's fat bankroll. "What about your ladies—Connie and Linda and Cindy?"

"What do you mean?"

"Did they give it away? Or did they charge through the nose?"

Uncle Jamie coughed, a hacking sound, and then rested the back of his head against the wall. "We live in a capitalistic system. What I cultivated were buyer-seller relationships, contracts. They—the perfect little bitches—controlled a commodity. I was the buyer. I controlled price, distribution, rendering of service. Lesson in economics, pal." His big hands clenched. "Control. Control. Control."

I stood up, giving him my back, hoping he'd try me, but he stayed where he was. I sat down in his plastic chair. "Is that why you killed Connie Trevino?"

"What?"

"Connie Trevino. She got out of control. You killed her."

He looked sideways at me, his eyes narrowed like a rattler's. "If you're so smart, Murdock, why is your net worth zilch?"

"I'm just trying to understand you, Jimbo. You and the money and the little girls."

He cocked his head, gave me his weasel smile. "They're not so little, those 'little' girls."

"They look pretty little to me."

"Pretty!" he grunted. "They think they're so perfect. Perfect hair. Perfect skin. Perfect little bodies. Little skirts so perfectly short you'd have to be dead not to sneak a peek. Perfect little virgins they're not. You know what?"

"What?"

"This country could take a lesson from the Middle Ages. Back then, the bitches would be wives at twelve, mothers at thirteen. Little breeders, doing their bit for society."

"You could always emigrate to the Middle East. Try your whips and chains stuff there. Probably get a medal."

"Don't think it hasn't crossed my mind." He turned his head toward me. It was like watching a gun turret swiveling on a tank. "What do you think causes gridlock? Kids. What's driving up car insurance? Kids. Who's the target customer for cheap foreign cars? Same answer, pal. Kids. Kids. Kids. Kids. Kids." His eyes glittering with an idea, Uncle Jamie got to his feet. He made a wide arc around me so he could pick up a yellow legal pad off the floor. "Got a pencil? Something to write with?"

I had Harriet's ballpoint. "Sorry."

He got down on his knees under the bed. Came back up with a gold-capped fountain pen. Tongue sticking out, he sat on the edge of his bed and scratched some notes. "Thanks, pal."

"For what?"

"For giving me the key to my defense."

"The Middle Ages?" I asked. "Or Iraq?"

"I was planning on killing you when I got out of here." He tapped the yellow pad with his gold-tipped pen. "Now I think I'll just whip your weary ass."

I wanted him to try. "What's wrong with right now?"

His smile as he wrote was a terrible thing. Money did that. And size. Together, they gave him the power to wound and hurt and maim. "The key concept here, pal, is discipline. The Trevino bitch cried out for discipline. Kids need it. Must have it, or the whole country goes. Discipline leads to control."

"You tried to spank her, she gave you a fight. You killed her."

"Don't get righteous on me, Murdock. You'd give a year's pay to do what I did. To have one-tenth of my experiences."

"Kill a helpless kid, you mean?"

"Subdue. That's a better word. Yes. I subdued a wild-eyed bitch." He jotted fiercely on his pad. "Subdued a wildcat. Yes. That's perfect. To subdue is to initiate first-stage control." Executive at work, Uncle Jamie kept his eyes on the yellow pad. Our scuffling was over. Too bad.

I buzzed for Sanchez.

The shrinks say sociopaths are different from you and me. The scientific terminology, according to

Wally St. Moritz, is "cortically underaroused." Socio-paths have no guilt. They wouldn't know remorse if it split their upper lip. They're clever, wily, shrewd. They do know right from wrong.

My ribs ached. As I waited for Sanchez to open the door, I gathered the photos of Linda and Connie Trevino.

So long, sociopath.

Outside the jail ward, I stood for a moment, suck-ing in gulps of fresh air. All that sickness, back inside. Ugh. I handed over the mini-recorder to Harriet Trueblood. She played it for a moment, nodding. "Where's the release form?"

I gave it to her.

"It's not signed."

"Uncle Jamie refused."

"Without a release form, this is inadmissible."

"Sorry."

"We had a deal. You—" Harriet frowned at me. "What happened to your ear?"

I fingered my ear. Caked blood. Ouch.

"You roughed him up, didn't you? Rousted the prisoner?"

"Self-defense, Counselor. Came at me with a golf club."

"Dammit." Her eyebrows bristled as she shook the recorder in my face. "Everyone's entitled to rights under the Constitution. Even rich-boy perverts."

My aim was to keep Cindy off the witness stand, so I reached into my pocket and brought out Blazer's envelope, which I handed to Harriet. She opened the envelope to find the photos. "Where did you get these?"

I said nothing as she scanned the photos.

Harriet shook them under my nose. "You had them all the time, didn't you?"

I nodded yes.

Her eyes narrowed, legal eagle primed for inquisition. "You used me, Murdock. Used me to get to the defendant. I can have your ticket pulled, mister. I can see you never work in this state again."

I reached into my pocket a second time, came out with a police report. From a cop in Cahuenga to Louie Palermo. From Louie to Blazer. From Blazer to me. From me to Harriet. I handed over the report.

Harriet skimmed it fiercely, flipped the page. "Where did you get these?"

"Legacy," I said. "From a friend."

Her eyes blazed at me. She stared at the police report, at the photos. Maybe now she could build a case. "Oh, all right. Get out of here. And never never never try this on me again."

I left Harriet Trueblood, Assistant District Attorney, holding the evidence in the parking lot at the med center. Let the lawyers and the philosophers turn smaller and smaller circles on the head of their particular pin. Marvin Holly, writer and father, had been avenged. Cindy would not have to take the stand. And me—I had a house to rebuild.

Wheeler Duke's papers arrived in mid-February. Zeke and I were finishing up the last section of roof. Down below on the deck, Cindy Duke worked the circular saw, cutting two-by-fours, while Tony Torres, Zeke's nephew, tried to keep his mind off Cindy. Tony was seventeen and smitten.

It was a perfect California Saturday. The sun was out, the temperature in the low seventies, and I was ready for a lunch break and a cold beer. Zeke and I wore shorts and boots and knee pads. We were both shirtless and the sun felt terrific. Tony wore jeans and a baby blue tank shirt. Cindy wore Levi shorts and a sleeveless blouse with ST. LUKE'S ACADEMY, DANA POINT stenciled on the back. At St. Luke's, Cindy's grades were up and she'd made new friends. Since January, she'd changed shrinks only once. The dark circles had vanished from under her eyes. She was an inch taller and four pounds heavier. She was staying at Phyl's house, but chose to spend her Saturdays—and sometimes her Sundays—with me. Once a week, she spoke to her mother on the phone. Barb Duke was a patient at the Clarendon Clinic, a drug therapy facility in Menlo Park. Uncle Jamie's trial was under way and it looked like the murder two charge might stick. Cindy was not being called to testify.

Cindy looked good. Her legs above the six-inch work boots were lean and tanned. Her hair was pulled back in a ponytail. Twice since we'd started at eight o'clock this morning we'd been forced to stop work to doctor Tony's left thumb, whacked with his own framing hammer because he was ogling Cindy.

Humming at her work, Cindy did not seem to mind being ogled.

We had just started lunch when the mail arrived. Wheeler Duke's papers were in a fat envelope mailed from Acapulco. The envelope was addressed to me, but inside was a note for Cindy. When she came out carrying a platter of sandwiches, I handed her the note. Her face flushed red and she excused herself and hurried back into the house.

With a beer in one hand, I riffled through the papers. There were two copies. One was in longhand on yellow paper. The other was typed. His subject was a detailed history, including a single-spaced chronology of five pages, of the connections between the Palermo family and Duke Construction. In a second envelope was a short note to me and a letter of credit on a Newport Beach bank. The amount was for $100,000.

I read the note from Wheeler Duke:

> *"Murdock. Here's the stuff on the Palermos.
> Put a copy in a strongbox and give the other one
> to some legal eagle who can run with it. These
> days, you may have to scratch awhile to find an
> honest prosecutor. Some pricks hired by the
> Palermos shot up my place in Maneadero. Killed
> some chickens and a pig. Wounded my foreman.
> I nailed one, wounded two more. Had to leave
> that place. Will keep moving now. Hear you're
> doing great things for my Cindy-gal. I'd give an
> arm to see her. The money's for her. More's on
> the way. Just now, I'm strapped. I'm naming you
> executor. You get ten percent. Buy yourself a new
> television and when you watch the Mets, think
> of me."*

It was signed, "Wheeler Duke."

Cindy joined us. Her face was blotchy with tears. Seeing her, Tony's eyes started watering too. I went for more beer. When I came back out, Cindy and Tony were standing at the railing, holding hands but not saying anything. The letter from her beloved Gramps was in her other hand. I handed Zeke a beer and we sat there in the February sun and talked about who would win the World Series next fall.

Senator Jane phoned at three o'clock that afternoon, from John Wayne Airport. She'd taken a couple of days off from her senatorial chores in the Lone Star state and would love to buy me a drink or something. I told her how to find my house.

"Bring work clothes," I said. "We're having a barn raising."

So that afternoon, Jane met my friends. She wore Wranglers with a knife-edge crease and a khaki shirt of Egyptian cotton. Her Adidas sneaks looked new. We hugged and she held on for that extra beat. Her smile was warm. Sadness lurked in her eyes. Memory of pain.

"Welcome to California."

"Oh," she said. "Oh." And then, squeezing my arm: "Introduce me to your friends. We've got a house to build."

I moved Tony up to the roof with Zeke. I assigned Jane as gofer for Cindy, who was trying not to take out the pencil line as she cut two-by-sixes to framing length.

Wally arrived just in time for beer and evening cleanup. A couple of times I noticed Jane and Wally locked in close conversation. She was asking questions. He was giving answers. The sun was dropping as Zeke drove away, taking a moony-eyed Tony with him in the pickup.

The wind was colder as the four of us—Jane, Cindy, Wally, Murdock—pulled on sweaters and walked downstairs to sample Leo's spaghetti and meatballs, a recipe, he swore, from Mama Castelli's Italian kitchen, back in Pennsylvania. Jane sat next to Cindy. They talked about girl stuff. Clothes. Hunk movie stars. Teen magazines. Riding. Jane, with her Texas childhood, had grown up with horses. Cindy was wowed. They made a date to go riding tomorrow.

"Hey," I said. "What about my house?"

"We'll build first. Then we'll ride."

"Great answer, Jane." Cindy toasted Jane with her Pepsi. "He's a slave driver on the job."

Jane patted my hand and smiled. I drank a long swallow of beer. I was happy. I was not happy. Murdock, on the edge.

After dinner, Jane borrowed a down vest from me and she and Cindy walked out onto the pier. They were gone a long time. It was chilly, standing on the deck in the stiff ocean breeze, but Wally and I stood there anyway, leaning against the new railing, drinking Mondavi red, with *Aida* in the background. My record collection had melted in the fire. Wally had helped me select a compact disc player, a sexy Japanese unit, with spaceball features that made me realize I was getting old, stodgy, set in my ways. Too many buttons, lights, dials, readouts, and fail-safe mechanisms. On the new system, Callas's *Aida* was stupendous.

Wally was talking about the Hollywood producer who had bought the film rights to *Jungles Burning.* I cut into his monologue about credits, film styles, the *auteur* school of filmmaking, whatever that was, and said: "What were you and Jane huddling about this afternoon?"

"She was inquiring about Miss Cindy."

"Her health, or what?"

"Among other things, yes. Are you jealous, Matthew?"

"Huh," I grunted. "Why should I be jealous?"

Wally gestured toward the pier. "Your women, getting together. Plotting."

"My women? You're crazy, Prof."

"A toast." Wally raised his glass. "To horsewomen. To warrior queens. To the female spirit in all its majesty."

We toasted the pier. "They've been out there a while. Freeze their buns."

"She came back to see Cindy, you know."

"Why? She doesn't even know Cindy."

"That's why she came back."

"Make sense, Professor."

"Restoring the balance, Matthew. Jane lost a child. Cindy lost a father. They're both yearning. Couldn't you feel the pull of that? The inexorable pull? Something invisible but palpable, between them?"

"Crap. Don't tell me Jane wants to adopt Cindy?"

"No. Nothing so overt, so official. Just touch. Connect. Commune. Heal. Restore the balance."

I grunted. "You're seeing things, Prof. You read too much. Live too much in your head."

"And you, Matthew, are an incurable romantic."

"A romantic? Me? You're crazy."

Wally chuckled and patted me on the shoulder. I took a sip of wine. What a laugh. Murdock the Romantic.

And then I heard them down below, Senator Jane and Cindy. They were coming this way, arms locked, their laughter lilting on the night, coming toward me, coming out of the dark into the light, walking east away from the pier toward my house on the beach, the last lip of America, California, the continent's edge.

They stopped down below. They looked up, the light from Leo's Café on their faces. I waved. They waved back. They giggled, a girl-joke shared between them, a female mystery, a secret not available to us guys. And just then, staring down at the two surviving women, holding on to each other, I felt things click into place, and I knew that life would be okay, not forever, but for a while.

FREE FROM DELL

with purchase plus postage and handling

Congratulations! You have just purchased one or more titles featured in Dell's Mystery 1990 Promotion. Our goal is to provide you with quality reading and entertainment, so we are pleased to extend to you a limited offer to receive a selected Dell mystery title(s) *free* (plus $1.00 postage and handling per title) for each mystery title purchased. Please read and follow all instructions carefully to avoid delays in your order.

1) Fill in your name and address on the coupon printed below. No facsimiles or copies of the coupon allowed.

2) The Dell Mystery books are the only books featured in Dell's Mystery 1990 Promotion. No other Dell titles are eligible for this offer.

3) Enclose your original cash register receipt with the price of the book(s) circled plus $1.00 **per book** for postage and handling, payable in check or money order to: Dell Mystery 1990 Offer. Please do not send cash in the mail.
   Canadian customers: Enclose your original cash register receipt with the price of the book(s) circled plus $1.00 **per book** for postage and handling in U.S. funds.

4) This offer is only in effect until April 29, 1991. Free Dell Mystery requests postmarked after April 22, 1991 will not be honored, but your check for postage and handling will be returned.

5) Please allow 6-8 weeks for processing. Void where taxed or prohibited.

Mail to: Dell Mystery 1990 Offer
P.O. Box 2081
Young America, MN 55399-2081

NAME_____

ADDRESS_____

CITY_____STATE_____ZIP_____

BOOKS PURCHASED AT_____

AGE_____

(Continued)